Bad Case of Lovin' You

Brooke & Zack
The Adlers

Anita Louise

Anita Louise
The Adler Family Series

Just the Way You Are
Aaron & Jane

A House is Not a Home
Michael & Analese

Should I Stay or Should I Go
Connor & Gina

You Light Up My Life
Olivia & Tyler

Candlelite Publishing, LLC

Cover Art by Angie Crawford
www.mapsbyangie.etsy.com
www.signsbyangie.etsy.com

Library of Congress Control Number: 2015959489

ISBN-13: 978-0692594384
ISBN-10: 0692594388

Dedication

To my sister Nancy without whom
The Adler Family Series
would not have been possible.

I love you, Sis.

The Adler family.

What do you get when you combine sexy and smart with kind and considerate?
~ The Adlers.

John and Juliette Adler have done a wonderful job of raising their nine children. Now those children are adults, and Juliette would like to be a grandmother. Besides, she and her husband want their children to experience what it's like to fall head-over-heels like they did over forty years ago. Enjoy the journey as each of the Adler's finds their one true love.

Dear Reader,

Twins are special siblings—especially when they're identical! There is a closeness and connection that is uncommon. Often the two are so much alike in appearance that people sometimes tend to expect them to also be alike in terms of personality traits. However, this is often *not* the case. Brooke Adler and her identical twin, Gabriella are mirror images, but are quite different in many other ways.

When Brooke falls for the handsome Dr. Zack Carter, she also makes herself vulnerable to disappointment and hurt. Brooke and Zack's journey requires both of them to learn how to trust and believe there really *is* such a thing as true love.

I hope you enjoy this romantic story that also contains lots of *sizzle.* Hopefully, you'll fall in love with not only Brooke and Zack, but with Shelly and her daughter, Mary Beth, who play significant roles in this story.

Happy reading!

Anita

P.S. I'd love to hear from you. Please give me your feedback, by writing your review on Amazon, Goodreads, Barnes & Noble, KOBO, iTunes and/or your blog. Also, feel free to contact me on my website.

http://www.AnitaLouiseRomance.com

Thanks!

Chapter One

Brooke Adler wandered through the stores along Pearl Street. It was a historic area and popular destination for both tourists and local residents in downtown Boulder, Colorado. She was on her way to Tom's Tavern/SALT to check out the menu. She'd suggested the restaurant for her brother Aaron and soon-to-be sister-in-law Jane's engagement party. But her mind wasn't on menus, restaurants or engagement parties. Instead, she was, once again, preoccupied with one particular person ... Dr. Zackary Carter.

He's one fine looking specimen of a man, she thought with a sigh. His face was that of a Greek god, with sharply defined cheekbones and an aquiline nose. He wore his dark hair in trendy but not too tall spikes above his incredibly dark eyes. If not for the white lab coat of a doctor, he could've passed for a man who used his muscles to make a living. There was no softness to his frame, just the look of solid granite.

The first time Brooke had seen him, it felt like her entire body was quivering like a leaf on a windy day. She'd

Anita Louise

been sitting in the hospital cafeteria with her brother Aaron and his significant other Jane Barloc when Dr. Carter walked in. The three of them had just left the room of Juliette Adler, mother of the nine Adler siblings. She'd been hospitalized after a totally unexpected heart attack.

Sitting next to Jane, Brooke had stiffened and her mouth fell open.

"What's up with you?" Jane had asked. "You look like a teenager drooling over your favorite rock star."

"Who *is* that?" asked Brooke.

"That's Dr. Carter. He was the physician on duty when I ended up in the emergency room after my car accident. You know, the one I had after I left your parents' anniversary party last month. Dr. Carter actually played a significant role in Aaron's and my engagement."

Brooke wasn't able to take her eyes off the good doctor, but had managed to ask, "How so?"

"Aaron spent so much time with me after I was admitted, Dr. Carter just assumed we were a couple." Jane had then waved the gorgeous physician over. "Brooke, this is Dr. Zackary Carter. Dr. Carter, this is *Miss* Brooke Adler. She's one of Aaron's sisters."

Brooke had almost lost the ability to speak. "Dr. Carter." She'd nodded stiffly. When he'd walked into the cafeteria, they'd been seated at a table, and it was a good thing, because she would've needed to hang onto it to support her wobbly legs.

When the man Brooke immediately dubbed Dr. McDreamy spoke, the sound of his voice had Brooke tingling from head to toe ... especially in the more private places in between.

She remembered him saying, "Please, call me Zackary."

In a voice barely above a whisper, she'd replied, "And you can call me Brooke."

After he walked away, it felt as if something vital to her very existence had left the room. Brooke was totally smitten.

Only a short time later they'd seen each other again. Brooke was waiting to take the elevator up to her mother's room. They'd shared a few very enjoyable moments flirting with one another, but it didn't last long. He'd rushed away in response to an emergency when his name was called over the hospital's loud speakers.

Since then, the handsome physician played the starring role in way too many of Brooke Adler's totally unexpected erotic dreams, dreams from which she awoke to find her skin sensitive and overheated. And other more intimate places were moist and wanting.

Now Brooke was on her way to meet Jane in the private room at Tom's Tavern/SALT, to get some ideas for decorating and menu choices. It was a popular restaurant in the Pearl Street Mall, and Brooke was the one who suggested it for Aaron and Jane's engagement party. She'd been there for another event only a few weeks before their engagement was announced. The private room, called the SALT Cellar, was cozy and unique, plus the food had been fabulous.

Brooke sighed contentedly as she looked at her surroundings. It was a beautiful afternoon in Boulder. The sky stretched above her like a vast blue sea, clear and calm. The delicious smells, sounds and bright colors coming from the multitude of thriving businesses in the area put a spring in her step. The Pearl Street Mall was also one of the best places to indulge in one of her other favorite pastimes ... people watching. Downtown Boulder was an interesting and eclectic place, filled with a multitude of individuals of all ages from around the globe. Brooke was smiling broadly, enjoying the sights and sounds when her cell phone rang.

"Hi, Brooke. It's Jane. I'm really sorry, but one of my clients just called, and according to her, she's 'desperate' to see me right away. Can we reschedule our visit to SALT, or would you mind terribly just checking it out on your own? Anything you decide will be fine with me."

"No problem, Jane. It's an absolutely gorgeous day, and this was an excellent excuse to take a day off from teaching in the middle of the week. Sounds like you've got enough on your plate. It'll be my pleasure to handle a few of the details for you and Aaron."

"Thanks a bunch. You have no idea how much this helps me. You're a gem."

Brooke could hear the sigh of relief in her soon-to-be sister-in-law's voice. "Happy to help. You take care of your 'desperate' client, and I'll take care of the food and décor for the party."

Just as Brooke was ready to disconnect, she heard Jane's voice. "Oh! I almost forgot."

"Almost forgot what?"

"Guess who I got a call from this morning."

Not all that interested, Brooke said, "I give up. Who?"

"Dr. Carter! And guess what he wanted."

Suddenly, Brooke's interest level spiked, and her heart started beating double time. "C'mon, Jane. Enough of the guessing games already. Why did he call you? What did he want?"

"He wanted *your phone number.*"

"He did? Did you give it to him?"

"Of course, I did!" Silent a moment, Jane continued. "That was all right, wasn't it?"

"Yes! Yes. Of course, it was all right. When did you say you gave it to him? I haven't heard from him yet."

"It was only an hour or so ago. You'll hear from him, and I bet it'll be pretty soon too. He said something about having a rare day off."

After a quick good-bye, the two friends disconnected.

Dr. Zackary Carter had been thinking about Brooke Adler way too much ever since he'd first met her at the hospital. Of course, where else *would* he meet anyone since he spent the vast majority of his time in the emergency room of Foothills Hospital in Boulder, Colorado. The way he looked at it, he didn't have much choice. It'd taken him four years of undergraduate training, four years of medical school, and three years of residency to get to where he was today. Consequently, he had over two hundred thousand dollars in student loans to pay back for his education. At some point he might go into private practice, but for now he spent most of his time in the emergency room. Until his humongous school debt was paid off, he had many years of long hours to look forward to. And up until the lovely Miss Adler entered his life, his practically celibate lifestyle had been just fine with him.

Anita Louise

Brooke was the first woman in several years to tempt him away from his dedication to his career. He was in his first year of medical school when he walked into the apartment he'd shared with his then fiancée Miranda, and found her in bed with another guy. Since that time he'd focused his mind on medicine and was able to pretty much ignore his sexual urges. No time, no money, no girlfriend ... no problem.

There was just *something* about the statuesque school teacher. An innate sensuality seemed to be smoldering just beneath the surface, and she'd been haunting his dreams. He wasn't entirely sure he liked that. Nor did he like the fact he found himself looking for her every time he entered the hospital cafeteria where they'd first met.

The first time he'd seen her, she'd practically taken his breath away. Her hair was long and so dark it was almost black, and it moved in shiny waves when she'd looked toward him. Her face was so stunning she could have been a model, except there were no layers of makeup ... only long, dark lashes over big brown eyes and slightly flushed cheeks above full, completely kissable lips. She was taller than average and slender as a reed. Right along with the confidence he saw in her, he also sensed an air of innocence. It made him wonder if there might be another side to her ... a side that he could persuade her to explore and see how good it could feel to be a "bad girl" every once in a while.

Today was one of his almost nonexistent days off, and he'd finally decided to do something about his unexplainable and somewhat unwanted obsession with Brooke Adler. He'd called Jane Barloc and asked for

Bad Case of Lovin' You

Brooke's number. He needed to see if he could figure out what that *something* he felt for the lovely Miss Adler was.

Now he stood in the middle of the living room of his condo in Shanahan Ridge. The stunning view of the steeply sloping and iconic Flatirons had been one of the main reasons for his decision to purchase his home, but he hardly noticed the spectacular vista. Looking at the cell phone in his hand, he thought, *What are you waiting for? Dial the phone, why don't you?*

How was it possible for a man of almost thirty-five years of age to suddenly feel like he was back in high school ... nervous to call the girl he wanted to ask to the prom? What was up with that?

Taking a deep breath, he typed "B-R-O-O-K-E_ A-D-L-E-R" into his phone. Since he'd already programmed her number in, it popped up. He hit the little phone receiver icon and held his breath as he listened ... brrrring, brrrring ... brrrring, brrrring.

This is ridiculous. There's absolutely no reason for me to be acting like a teenager who's never been on a date before. She's probably in her classroom right now anyway. What was I thinking calling in the middle of the week? ... brrrring, brrrring ... brrrring, brrrring. *Should I leave a message? Maybe I'll just hang up and call back later.*

"Hello?"

Oh, shit. "Hi. Brooke?"

"Yes, this is Brooke. Who's this?

"It's Zack. Zackary Carter." *Oh, my gosh, now I* **sound** *like a teenager with a crush. What the hell's wrong with me?*

"Hi, Zackary. It's so nice to hear from you. What's up?"

"You're not in your classroom right now, are you?"

"No, I'm not. I took the day off. It sounds like you're not at the hospital today either, right?"

"Right. I'm at home. Where are you?" Zack asked.

"Pearl Street. Want to meet me for coffee or a drink or something?"

To him, her invitation sounded unplanned, but sincere. "Sure. That sounds good. I don't live too far from there. Where do you want to meet?" Silence. "You there?"

"Yes," Brooke replied. "I'm here. I was just looking around to see what's close by. How about the West Flanders Brewing Company? I'm practically standing in front of it right now."

"I'll find it. See you in a few."

"Great. I'll save you a seat."

No wonder I like her. She makes it so easy ... even when I'm acting like a total spaz.

Zackary practically flew out to his car and drove the short distance from his place to the downtown area. He smiled happily as he looked up at the brilliant blue sky. He'd spent four years living with cloudy skies and seemingly ever present drizzle while finishing his medical degree at the University of Washington - School of Medicine in Seattle. His choice to move back to Boulder had been a relatively easy one. He was more than ready for the three hundred plus days of sunshine found in Colorado. Today was as close to perfect as you could get, and the idea of spending the afternoon with Brooke Adler made it just that much better

The Pearl Street Mall was a four block pedestrian area known for its unique shops and restaurants. He'd found a parking spot fairly close, so it was a relatively short walk to the pub where he'd agreed to meet Brooke. His long strides carried him quickly through the people and vendors who were enjoying another day filled with sunshine.

The West Flanders Brewing Company was one of dozens of microbreweries in a city sometimes called "the Napa Valley for Craft Brewing." This particular one was known for its Belgian style beers. As he approached, he saw her sitting at a small table out front, and once again felt the pull of attraction he'd experienced at their first meeting. Even from a distance, she stood out from the crowd. He watched as she pushed her silky, long hair away from her face. Her glossy locks were the color of spilled ink, so dark it glinted in the bright sun. As he watched, he felt a flame of desire shoot through him.

What is it about this woman? I'd better get my act together before I make a complete fool of myself. Squaring his shoulders, he walked over to where she sat. There was a glass of water with a slice of lemon floating in it in front of her.

"Good afternoon, Miss Adler. I hope I haven't kept you waiting too long." When she looked into his eyes and smiled he felt his heart quicken in his chest.

"Well, hello, Dr. Carter. Actually, I just sat down a few minutes ago. Since I knew it would take you a little while to get here, I decided to walk for a bit and enjoy this beautiful day. Please join me, won't you?" She motioned to the seat across from her.

He did as she requested and suddenly found himself at a loss for words. *Sheesh! Here I go again, acting like a teenager with a crush on his first date.* He picked up the menu in front of him. Even though he wasn't a big drinker, the interesting beer selections available would at least give him something to talk about. "Have you selected anything yet?"

"Not yet. I did look at the menu while I was waiting, and I have some ideas. However, this is my second glass of water, and I didn't want to miss you. So first, I need to use the restroom."

"No problem. It'll give me a chance to look things over."

When Brooke politely excused herself, it gave Zackary the chance to look over more than the menu. It gave him the opportunity to enjoy the sway of her hips as she walked away. He liked that she was taller than average, since he was almost six foot five. Naturally, he'd been recruited to play basketball in high school. Then in college, the basketball scholarship he'd received had helped to at least pay for his undergraduate studies. However, it was medicine and not sports that really got his juices flowing. *Brooke Adler is getting my juices flowing in a whole different way,* he thought. He knew she was a school teacher, but she didn't talk down to him like he was one of her students.

Zackary heard some horror stories from his buddy Jack who had dated a kindergarten teacher for close to a year. According to Jack, having an argument with her made him want to jump off a bridge. Instead of having a good old fashioned shouting match, the trained educator would respond to him calmly with questions like, "Do you really think that was a good choice?" and "Let me know when you're ready to take responsibility for your actions, and we can discuss it." In Jack's words, "If you want passion, stay away from teachers."

Is there a passionate woman in that beautiful body, Brooke? I sure would like to find out. He must've been totally lost in his thoughts as he didn't even notice her walking back up to the table.

"Penny for your thoughts."

The slightly husky timbre of her voice immediately got his attention, and the sound seemed to stir his desire for her even more. Since he couldn't tell her about his thoughts regarding what he'd like to do with her sumptuous curves, he replied, "There are a couple of craft beers that sound interesting. Would you care to try one with me?"

"Hmmm, I don't tend to drink that much. But there are so many cool microbreweries in the area, I *have* started to indulge from time to time." Looking at her watch, she tilted her head thoughtfully. "It *is* getting later in the day, and their happy hour started a little while ago. Why not? Let's go for it!"

Her statement included a fist pump, and he couldn't help but smile in appreciation of her enthusiasm. Once she was seated across from him again, they looked over the beer menu together and discussed the various offerings. By the time the waiter made his way to their table, they'd selected the Canniption Pale Ale for him and the Hoffmeister Pilsner for her.

There was a lull in their conversation as they both watched their waiter walk away. Just then, a soft breeze ruffled her long, dark hair and several strands flew across her face. Almost instinctively he reached to push the stray locks behind her ear. Her hair felt like silk and when the breeze also brought her scent to him, he was hit with an unexpected surge of desire.

She must've felt it too because she swallowed hard and licked her lips. As his eyes followed the path of her tongue, the surge turned into an almost uncontrollable tidal wave. His brain kept telling him, *You've only known her a short time, and besides that, she's a school teacher.* But his body had other ideas ... ideas that included a naked school teacher in his bed.

Somehow he managed to get his libido under control by telling himself, *It's just been waaay too long since I've been with a beautiful woman. That's all it is.* He was certain that once or twice between the sheets with the pretty teacher would be all that was necessary to get him back on track. Of course, he didn't want to hurt her, so he'd be sure they were on the same page before things even got started. For now, he knew he needed to change the direction of his thoughts by starting a totally unrelated conversation.

"So when and where is the big engagement celebration?" Zack asked. "They're a nice couple. I really like Jane and Aaron."

"It's less than two weeks away, and I've *got* to get the menu set and the invitations sent out. We're having it in the private room at Tom's Tavern/SALT which is really a great place. Ever been there?"

"No, but I've heard good things about it. Guess I'll have to give it a try one of these days."

Brooke seemed a little surprised. "You *are* coming to the party, aren't you?"

"Quite honestly, I wasn't sure I was invited."

"Of course, you're invited. In fact, if you'd like, you can even be my date."

The look on her face and the blush creeping up her neck and onto her face told him her words had popped out before she'd thought about what she was saying. He felt strangely protective and wanted to assure her there was no need for embarrassment.

"Brooke Adler, I think that's an *excellent* idea. It would be my honor and privilege to accompany you. Just let me know the place and time. I'll pick you up."

"You don't have to do that." She hesitated a moment before continuing. "I don't know what came over me. Maybe it's from being around teens and pre-teens so much of the time. Sometimes I just say things before I even think."

"Really, Brooke, having you by my side at Aaron and Jane's special event will make it a lot more fun for me. Please, let me take you to the party."

Seeming to regain her natural composure, she looked at him with a twinkle in her eye. "Why Dr. Carter, I'd love to have you as an escort. Thank you for asking."

Somehow she'd made it sound as if she were doing him a favor.

A few moments later the waiter returned and two chilled glasses filled with golden brew were placed in front of them.

"Cheers," she said as she raised her glass.

Thankfully, he was able to catch himself before replying with the old Groucho Marx toast, "A man is only as old as the woman he feels." Instead, his toast was, "Here's to the heart that fills as the glass empties."

"How nice. Are you a poet at heart, Dr. Carter?"

"Me? Heck no, but I do like to have a decent toast available for special occasions like this."

"Is this a special occasion?"

"I'd like to think of this as the beginning of a great friendship." He hesitated. "And perhaps more." When their eyes met, he felt a stirring in his loins. He had an almost irresistible urge to lean in and kiss those delicious looking full lips.

Their glasses clinked, and he watched her mouth caress the edge of what he considered to be a very lucky piece of glassware. She must've noticed his stare because she ran her tongue around her mouth and then touched her napkin to the corners.

Somewhat self-consciously she asked, "Am I wearing my beer?"

"Not at all. I'm just enjoying the view."

"There you go again ... getting me all flustered. You're quite the flirt, Dr. Carter."

"Not usually, but I can't seem to help myself when I'm around you. You bring those qualities out in me." He reached across the table and took her hand in his. "You don't mind, do you?"

"No, I don't mind. I don't mind at all. It's just I'm not really used to it."

He squeezed her hand and held her gaze. "You've got to be kidding me. A gorgeous woman like you must have men hitting on her all the time."

"Not really. You must be thinking of my twin Gabriella."

"I didn't realize you had a twin? Identical?"

"Yep. Sure do. Want me to introduce you to her?"

There was a distinct change in Brooke's demeanor and tone of voice. He got the definite impression that the experiences she'd had with her twin sister and men might have been less than positive. She tried to draw her hand away. Zack not only continued to hold it, but added his other hand to halt her retreat.

"Of course, I'd like to meet your sister one day. It's surprising I didn't meet her, or even realize you had a twin sister when your family was spending so much time at the hospital. To tell the truth, I'm looking forward to seeing your whole family again and getting to know them *all* a little better. From what I saw in the cafeteria of the hospital, it looks like there're plenty of them." He grinned for a moment, but then quickly turned serious again. "Brooke, I hope you know, as far as I'm concerned, there's much more to you than just your looks. You and your sister may be identical twins, but she's not *you.*"

"Thank you for saying that Zackary, but you haven't met my sister. Don't get me wrong. I love her dearly, and we're best of friends, but men seem to be attracted to her like bees to honey. Me? Not so much. It is what it is."

He couldn't seem to help himself and gave into the irresistible urge he'd been trying to resist ever since he'd first met her. Lifting his hand, he ran his knuckles gently down her cheek. Then he leaned forward, cupped her head and pulled her gently to him. It was like a scene in slow motion. Their lips met. At first it was sweet and gentle, but when he heard the catch in her breath, a spark seemed to ignite and warmth turned to heat. Her lips parted slightly, and he felt her hand move to grip his arm, her fingers digging in.

She tasted good. Innately sweet with just a hint of the pilsner she'd sipped. He detected an underlying passion her normally cool demeanor couldn't possibly hide.

The disappointment of his previous relationship suddenly seemed to fade, along with their surroundings. His tongue touched hers,` and the flicker of desire grew into a flame. Deepening the kiss felt only natural, yet as soon as he did, she pulled away.

"Oh, my gosh. I can't believe I just did that, and in a public place of all things." The flush on her face might have been passion or embarrassment.

"I'm sorry, Brooke." He stopped and looked around to see the smiles and amused looks on the faces of the other patrons. Shaking his head, he continued. "No, I'm not. I'm not sorry at all. In fact, I'm ready for a repeat performance as soon as possible."

He was more than surprised ... shocked would be a better description, when she stood.

"I'm sorry, Zackary. I can't. I just can't do this." Leaving her mostly untouched beverage on the table, she walked away.

Chapter Two

I'm such an idiot! Brooke berated herself. *Things were going so well, and then I totally **blew it!***

Brooke had gotten back to her car as quickly as she could. She hadn't even taken the time to stop at Tom's Tavern/SALT, which was the main reason she'd gone to Pearl Street to begin with. Fortunately, her naturally optimistic nature kicked in and she thought, *Oh well, I'll just reschedule a time to go there with Jane. That'll be more fun anyway.*

If only she could be as positive about what just happened with Zackary Carter. He was the first guy who'd captured her interest in a very long time. Unfortunately, she'd let feelings left over from things that'd happened years ago sabotage a potentially good relationship before it even had a chance to get started.

Growing up as identical twins, Brooke and Gabriella were extremely close. At least, they were when they were with family or it was just the two of them. Brooke was more of the intellectual type, while Gabriella tended to enjoy more physical activities. Brooke could typically be found curled up with a book, and Gabriella preferred being outside, often spending time working or playing with animals.

Being a teacher had been Brooke's dream for as long as she could remember. As a child, she could be found "teaching" a classroom full of dolls about any and every subject imaginable. Whatever Brooke was learning, she shared with her "students." As soon as she learned to read, her mother Juliette's role was changed from story teller to story listener. Each night Brooke read bedtime stories to Mommy along with the host of stuffed animals and dolls surrounding her.

It was probably inevitable that friends would compare her with her twin sister. Unfortunately for Brooke, she felt like she always came out on the losing end. And, unlike most of their other siblings, because they were twins, they were often given gifts they were expected to share. Lots of times, Brooke just wished she could have her own things. She just wanted something she could say was *mine* and not *ours*. But somehow it didn't ever seem to work out that way very often. Sometimes it felt like having a twin was about the same as having a shadow that would never leave you alone.

The boy troubles started when they were only in their early teens. Likely due to her more outgoing nature, Gabriella was the more popular of the two girls. At fourteen, Brooke still tended to be a little more bookish and shy. She wasn't ready to even *think* about having a boyfriend. Gabriella, on the other hand, had several boys: Ralph, Jeremy and Steven. Each wanted to be linked with her and labeled as her "boyfriend."

Bad Case of Lovin' You

When Gabriella finally chose Jeremy over her other suitors, Steven quickly announced to Gabriella that he "loved Brooke instead." When her twin told her about it, Brooke found it a little strange, considering the fact Steven had never even *spoken* to her. Gabriella chose Jeremy because she liked the way his name sounded with hers.

"Gabriella and Jeremy. Don't you think that sounds a lot better than Gabriella and Ralph or Gabriella and Steven?" she'd asked her sister. Then Gabriella told her twin about Steven's confession of his "love" for Brooke like it was supposed to be a compliment or something. Brooke didn't see it that way at all. She was more annoyed than flattered, and things just seemed to go downhill from there.

Over the years, Brooke came up with a strict rule. She only went out with a guy *after* he knew she was an identical twin. Once that was out in the open, she refused to go out on even a single date until she'd personally introduced her potential suitor to her more outgoing sister. After that, it was Brooke's decision, not the prospective beau's, whether or not she would date him *after* the meeting with her sister. With uncanny precision, she always just *knew* if there was going to be some sort of problem. Brooke quickly ditched any guy who seemed to be drawn to Gabriella's more outgoing personality. She also eliminated those who were overly enthusiastic about how much alike in appearance the girls were.

The bottom line was, when it came to men and dating, Brooke was quite conservative. Her twin Gabriella had always been the one who went through men like water. They were both beautiful women, but Brooke had always held herself to a higher standard. She'd barely dated in high school and had kept potential suitors at bay during most of her college years as well. Unlike most college students, she went to school for the sole purpose of getting an education, and not for the parties and drinking. She'd lived at home, rarely went to the abundance of parties to which she was invited. And, on top of everything else, she preferred iced tea and lemonade over the taste of most alcoholic beverages.

The one time she'd allowed herself to really fall for a guy, it was a complete disaster. She'd met Marcus during her freshman year at UC-Boulder, and he was drop dead gorgeous. He quite literally swept Brooke off her feet at the fraternity party Gabriella talked her into attending between their first and second semester.

Brooke and Gabriella were standing side by side when the handsome young man spotted them from across the room. Watching him make his way through the crowd, Brooke thought, *Here we go again. Another conquest for my outgoing twin*, and turned her back to the Greek god. It was a total shock when she felt a tap on her shoulder. She turned to find herself face to face with the very same fraternity boy she'd been watching only moments before.

"Hi. I'm Marcus."

He was holding out his hand. Not knowing what else to do, she shook it and replied, "Hello, Marcus. I'm Brooke." She then grabbed her sister's shoulder, spun her around and said, "This is my twin, Gabriella." She was surprised when after he and Gabriella exchanged greetings, he immediately put his focus back on Brooke.

"I don't think I've seen you around campus before. Did you just start here?" he asked.

"No, not really. This will be my second semester, but I don't live on campus. I live at home ... with my parents." With what she'd heard about frat guys she figured that would be the end of the conversation.

"My folks live too far away for me to still live at home. This is my second year at the Pi Kapp House. I lived at home the first two years and went to community college back in Montrose. I wanted to go to an APA accredited school to get my psych degree. My dad went here, and he was a member of Pi Kappa Phi. I think that's why he wanted me to come here; it was important to him I join too. Otherwise, I'm not sure I'd have gotten into the whole Greek thing."

Her estimation of him grew, and she looked at him with fresh eyes. He wasn't much taller than she was. Usually, guys of his height weren't attracted to her or her sister in the first place, but the fact they stood eye to eye didn't seem to bother Marcus. From the looks of his arms and well-defined chest, however, he must have spent time in the gym lifting weights. She thought his muscular frame might have contributed to his apparent self-confidence.

"Are you a football player?" Brooke asked.

"I was back in high school. A couple of colleges offered me football scholarships. I was more interested in what the schools had to offer in terms of classes than I was in playing football."

Before their conversation could go any further, Brooke was jostled from behind. A fight had broken out, and people were moving to get out of the way. Marcus positioned his body between her and the increasingly tense crowd. The next thing she knew he turned and swept her off her feet into his arms. Within seconds he was heading toward the door at the rear of the building.

Once they were outside, away from the fray, Brooke remembered Gabriella. "My sister!"

"I'll get her." He'd run back into the fraternity house and come out pulling Gabriella behind him. As soon as the twins saw each other they embraced.

"Are you all right, Gabby?" Brooke asked.

"I am thanks to this guy." Gabriella gave her most adorable look of gratitude to Marcus. Brooke felt a familiar sinking in the pit of her stomach. It was the same one she always got when she was unceremoniously dumped for her more flamboyant sibling.

But Marcus surprised both sisters by putting his arm around Brooke and saying to Gabriella, "When Brooke said I needed to help you, that's what I did."

That was the beginning of what Brooke believed would be a 'til death do us part" relationship. He was a serious student, a psychology major with plans to pursue advanced degrees. She'd given him her heart and her virginity. They studied together, rode bicycles on the many wonderful trails in the Boulder area, and done lots of other fun things couples in love do. She'd introduced him to her entire family and everyone seemed to like him a great deal. Life was good.

Marcus finished his undergrad classes. Then he left to go back to Montrose for the summer to work at his father's accounting firm. She should've known there was something wrong early on. The time between phone calls got further and further apart, and their conversations got shorter and shorter. When Brooke suggested she come visit him for a weekend, he had some excuse as to why it just "wasn't a good time." When the fall semester started, he finally got around to breaking the news to her. Even though he'd been totally faithful to Brooke, he just couldn't seem to get past the strong attraction he also felt for her twin sister. He'd tried to ignore it the whole time they were dating, but his guilt finally got to him. He'd been sharing his feelings with his former high school sweetheart, and the flame between them had rekindled. Now, his old girlfriend was pregnant and they were getting married. He wouldn't be returning to UC-Boulder.

Since then, she'd gone on a few dates ... very few. It wasn't that she didn't get asked out fairly often. She simply wasn't interested enough in anyone who asked to bother putting herself through the emotional work and potential heartache of dating any of them. Several of the male teachers at Summit Middle School, where she'd been teaching since she graduated from UC - Boulder, made flirtatious overtures toward her. But none of them made her want to break her steadfast rule of not dating co-workers.

Dr. Zackary Carter was the first man in a very long time who had her even thinking *just maybe.* Maybe it might be worth it to open her heart a tiny bit and explore a relationship once again. And now she'd made a total fool of herself by letting the old rivalry with her sister tarnish the relationship before it even began.

Once she got back home, Brooke called Jane and rescheduled their visit to Tom's Tavern/SALT. They'd go on the weekend when neither of them would have to be concerned about interruptions from work. The two women had become good friends, and Brooke was looking forward to spending some time together. Perhaps she and Jane could discuss what happened on her disastrous not-really-a-date with Dr. Carter. Besides being a good friend, Jane was also a counselor and might be able to help Brooke better understand her out of control behavior. Not that it would do any good as far as her now thwarted crush on the handsome young doctor. But maybe she could avoid doing anything quite so stupid in the future.

"It's probably just as well," she said to her reflection in the mirror. "You've got lots of things going on at school. Just keep your focus on your work. Everything has a way of working out for the best."

Brooke's abrupt departure left Dr. Zackary Carter in a real quandary. This was the first time in *years* he'd met a woman he was really interested in. It was rare for him to take a few hours away from his career and give some of his rather sparse spare time to a woman.

After his break up with Miranda he poured himself completely into his studies and then his career. From time to time he'd go out with a group of fellow doctors or residents for drinks. Occasionally he'd hook up with a good looking chick for a one-nighter. If the girl wanted or expected more than that, she was destined for disappointment. He never took anyone to his place and made it a rule to never give out his phone number. Any numbers received from his conquests were summarily deposited in the "circular file" underneath his kitchen sink. As soon as he cleaned out his pockets at the end of the evening or the next morning the slips of paper went into the trash.

Brooke Adler was altogether different. Not only had he taken the time to make a phone call and *ask* for her number, he'd *programmed* it into his cell phone. After what, in his estimation, had been the absolute *best* kiss he'd had *ever*, she'd freaked out and walked away like he had the plague or something. Interestingly enough, instead of making him want to chalk her off as a nut case, he was even more intrigued.

What is it that makes you tick, Brooke Adler? He'd never been attracted to women who were *easy*. In fact, he loved a challenge, and Brooke Adler was proving to be one of the most complicated and difficult to understand women he'd ever met ... as well as one of the most beautiful. Plus there was that underlying current of sensuality that had come briefly to the surface when their lips met.

He was certain her response to him hadn't been planned, but had been the instinctive reaction of a naturally sexual and seductive woman. He was also certain she did *not* see herself as such. Their kiss had been intense ... perfect. There was no doubt in his mind. He could clearly sense her desire, her need for more ... for him. Yet once she recognized she'd *lost* control, she immediately pulled back.

Oh, Brooke, how wonderful it's going to feel to be with you when you lose control completely ... to watch you come apart in my arms. I can hardly wait.

He smiled inwardly. A moment later he chuckled at himself as he thought, *I'll bet my jaw was hanging open like the Grand Canyon when she got up and walked out on me.* Almost without thinking he lifted his glass, tilted his head back and drank down his still cold, craft brewed beer. *There's definitely way more to this woman than meets the eye. A twin, huh?* He then picked up her virtually untouched beer. The taste of her was still on the rim where her lips had been when he took a sip of the light pilsner. With each swallow he savored the memory of the passion she'd been unable to hide in the kiss they'd shared. *This just might be a lot of fun. In fact, I'm sure of it. Watch out, Brooke. Whether you realize it or not, you've just thrown down the gauntlet, and I'm up for the challenge.*

After finishing both of their drinks, he left a generous tip for the waiter. Whistling softly he walked back toward his car. En route, he noticed a florist and was hit with a bolt of inspiration. Stepping inside, he ordered a bouquet of flowers featuring a bird of paradise. He quickly scrawled a note to be included and requested next morning delivery to Miss Brooke Adler at Summit Middle School.

Chapter Three

Brooke was down in the dumps as she stood in front of the mirror in her bathroom the next morning. She frowned at her reflection as she carefully applied the small amount of makeup she wore to school each day. With her parents' help, she'd been fortunate to purchase a wonderful family home in the North Broadway – Holiday neighborhood in Boulder. With its three bedrooms, two and a half baths, a big front porch, an unfinished basement and an attached garage, it was much more than a single woman needed, but she had plans for the future.

John Adler had set aside funds for each of his nine children to help them with the down payment on their first home, and Brooke had taken advantage of her father's generosity. Even with that, she wouldn't have been able to afford the home, if not for someone else's less than fortunate circumstances. The home had been foreclosed upon during the housing crisis, and Brooke was able to buy it substantially below its value.

Anita Louise

When she bought her house, she envisioned herself with the husband and children who would one day make it truly a home. She could almost hear the voices filling each room with love and laughter. But it didn't look like she'd hear those voices in anything but her imagination any time soon. With reluctance, she'd decided to do her best to forget about the handsome and deliciously sexy Dr. Zackary Carter. After the way she'd left him at the restaurant where they'd met the day before, she assumed the likelihood of hearing from him again was somewhere between zero and nil.

Instead of continuing to wallow in her misery, she looked at her reflection and gave herself a sincere pep talk. "Brooke Adler, you know what you do as a teacher is very important, don't you? Every day you're making a positive difference in your student's lives. Not only are the young people whose lives you touch better people because of you, you're a better person because of them." She smiled. Speaking positively to herself always made her feel better.

There were plenty of things for her to do in her role as a seventh and eighth grade teacher at Summit Middle School. Enough that she shouldn't have any problem keeping her mind on her lessons and students, and *off* the gorgeous doctor. In addition to the classes she taught in English and Language Arts, she'd also been helping out with the school play for the last couple of years. It required quite a bit of what otherwise would have been her free time, but she loved it.

Casting, props and a myriad of other tasks were part of the process of putting on a play. But the first challenge was deciding what play to perform. Last year they presented the musical *Annie,* and it was a huge success. However, students who were not musically inclined were, necessarily, excluded from the cast. And even though they could help with the behind-the-scenes work it wasn't the same as being on stage. Therefore, this year they were doing the play *Our Town*. It was a classic play and it ended in a way that left both the actors and the audience with something to think about.

Brooke was a very conscientious teacher. She made it a point to get to know the majority of her students quite well every year before school ended in June. Mary Beth Silvers had been in Miss Adler's Language Arts class last year. The pretty little blue-eyed blonde, now an eighth grader, was her student once again. Both teacher and student liked each other a lot. Not only was the girl bright and well mannered, she was also the daughter of one of Brooke's friends from high school.

Brooke had known Shelly Silvers, Mary Beth's mom, as Shelly Blake when they were students at Boulder High School. In addition to hanging out with the same group of friends, Shelly would often come to Brooke's house to study. Not only did the young women share a lot of the same classes, they were both practically straight A students at BHS.

With nine children in the family, there were always plenty of people at the Adler house. Juliette and John Adler were not overly protective parents, but they preferred to know where their children were and who they were with. Consequently, an open door policy was adopted at the Adler home. The basement was equipped with ping pong, billiards and other game tables for year-round use. In the summer the volleyball area and outdoor pool were very popular. All the

Anita Louise

amenities meant that most of the time, friends preferred to come to the Adler house. The rules were clearly posted.

ADLER
FAMILY RULES
RESPECT EACH OTHER
Be Kind

Always tell the truth

TREAT OTHERS

AS YOU WISH TO BE TREATED

LAUGH OUT LOUD

Be Happy ~ Keep your Promises

Do Your Best * *BE GRATEFUL*

KNOW THAT YOU ARE LOVED

Reminiscing, Brooke smiled to herself. Her younger brother Luke was in eighth grade when she and Shelly were juniors in high school. Usually Luke was nowhere to be seen when Brooke's friends came to the house, *except* when Shelly would show up. Both girls clearly understood why he was always hanging around the older kids whenever the pretty girl with the long blonde hair was in the group. The young boy's presence was either grudgingly tolerated or totally ignored by practically everyone except Shelly. She always took time to acknowledge him. Ignoring the subtle jeers of her classmates, she spent time talking to the eighth grade boy with the obvious crush.

"Whadda ya doin' talkin' to that little punk?" Brooke's smile quickly faded as she recalled the voice of Shelly's then boyfriend and now husband Nathan Silvers. Unlike the rest of Brooke's friends, Nathan had little tolerance for Luke's schoolboy crush.

Shelly started going out with Nathan Silvers during her junior year at Boulder High. Nate was a senior and a star football player. At first, everyone thought Shelly had made quite the catch landing one of the most popular guys in school, especially an upper classman. Brooke accepted the fact the jock would be a part of the group that showed up fairly regularly to the Adler home, once the pair started dating.

Nathan Silver's grades weren't all that good. But he managed to get into Colorado State University on a football scholarship. However, his college education ended early. Before he finished his freshman year, he was cut from the team. Even during and after the time he went to CSU, Nate and Shelly continued to date off and on. They argued a lot and it seemed like they were broken up as much as they were together.

When Shelly came to school with a black eye in her senior year, she told everyone it was an accident. She said she'd run into the bathroom door in the middle of the night. No one really believed it. There was a rumor going around that Nathan had developed a drinking problem after he lost his scholarship and had to drop out of college. It was quite a scandal when Shelly disappeared from Boulder High shortly before graduation. The rumor that Shelly Blake and Nate Silvers had gotten married proved to be true, and Mary Beth was born eight months later.

Now Brooke was a little concerned about Mary Beth Silvers. The girl's grades had been dropping steadily for the past few months. In addition, the student's normally sunny disposition had seemed to dim considerably. Shelly Silvers usually came in for parent-teacher conferences, but had missed the last one. High school was a long time ago, but Brooke still remembered Shelly's black eye.

There would be a rehearsal for the play after school today. Mary Beth was cast in the role of Mrs. Soames in, *Our Town*. It wasn't a huge role, but Brooke knew it would give her an opportunity to see the girl outside of class. Hopefully, it would also give Brooke the chance to talk with Mary Beth privately. Brooke hoped to gain some insight into what might be going on in her student's home life to warrant the changes she'd observed.

Pulling on gray slacks with a muted pattern along with a long-sleeved burgundy cowl neck sweater, Brooke surveyed her appearance in the full length mirror. She'd wear the jacket to match her slacks until it got too warm in the classroom. Even though there was no strict dress code at school, Brooke tended to wear more conservative clothing than some of the other teachers. She'd always been taught and still believed it was better to err on the side of caution, especially when it came to your job.

She chuckled to herself as she hopped into her minivan and thought of her soon-to-be sister-in-law Jane Barloc. One of the many things Brooke and Jane had in common was their enjoyment of bicycling. Jane and Brooke became good friends when Jane asked for advice on a vehicle to transport her bicycle to the many trailheads in the Boulder area. They'd gotten a kick out of the fact that both of them drove minivans even though neither of them were mothers ... yet. The final word had been said in unison and caused them to laugh uproariously.

Bad Case of Lovin' You

Summit Middle School was less than ten miles away from Brooke's house, usually only a fifteen to twenty minute drive. School started at eight, and she always gave herself more than enough time, typically arriving approximately an hour before school started. Even though it was a short trip, it still gave Brooke's mind enough time to slip back to Dr. Zackary Adler ... the one person she'd told herself to forget about.

She'd been to a number of her brother Aaron's personal growth and development seminars. Now she recalled one of the demonstrations he'd used to illustrate "ironic process theory." The concept said that the more you try *not* to think about something, the more likely it is you *will.*

Aaron had stood in front of a room filled with several hundred professionals. "I'd like you all to help me with a little thought experiment," he said. "Okay?" The audience had murmured and nodded their agreement. "I want you to close your eyes, and imagine an elephant with a very distinguishing characteristic. It's *pink.* Get as vivid a picture as you possibly can. How large are the elephant's ears, its trunk? Does it look like an elephant you'd see in the zoo, or does it look more like a cartoon ... maybe Dumbo?" He waited silently for a moment. "Got it? Great! Now open your eyes, and whatever you do, *don't* think about the pink elephant."

A buzz started in the audience. Someone spoke up, "Hey, that's not fair. Now you've got that pink elephant stuck in our minds."

Aaron smiled indulgently. "No, I don't have the elephant stuck in your mind. You do. I had you do this experiment for a reason. You've probably heard the advice, 'just don't think about it,' after something less than wonderful has happened. Perhaps you've even said that phrase to yourself. However, you've just proven that suppressing your thoughts doesn't really work. Until you *replace* the thought with something else that can completely absorb your attention, your mind will continue to return to the unwanted thought."

Well, at least while I was thinking about Aaron's 'ironic process theory,' Dr. McDreamy left my mind for a couple of seconds. She sighed and gave in.

How could she possibly forget the most wonderful, fabulous, exciting and exhilarating kiss she'd ever experienced in her entire life! Just picturing the look in his eyes as he leaned forward and stroked her cheek gave her goosebumps. Sighing softly, she recalled the feel of his hand in her hair, gently pulling her mouth to his. Her body tingled as she relived the moment his lips touched hers. She'd had no choice. Hers was a response as ancient as time. Never before in her life had she experienced the kind of heat that ignited between them.

She was a school teacher, a sensible, responsible adult. And she was experiencing the feelings of an adult, not some adolescent crush. She'd thought she was in love with Marcus, but what she felt for Zackary Carter was so much more. Never before had she *wanted* a man so badly. When he kissed her something *happened* to her. For the first time in her life, she'd wanted to forget all about being responsible and sensible. She wanted to deepen their kiss. She wanted to know how it would feel to have his hands on her and to have her hands on him. She wanted him ... all of him ... every inch of him.

Desire.

Now, for the first time, she understood it clearly.

It was a good thing she'd driven the same route to school so many times it was like being on auto-pilot. She was almost stunned when her car seemed to turn itself into the parking lot. She looked around and blinked several times.

Back to the real world, she thought. She exited her vehicle and entered the building that had become something of a second home. *It's going to be much easier to keep my mind off Dr. Zackary Adler now that I'm at work. Isn't it?*

Brooke went directly to her classroom and got busy. She did her best to keep her thoughts from drifting back to the doctor who was such a delightful distraction. Unfortunately, the time spent daydreaming about him last night had prevented her from finishing the work she'd taken home with her. There were still a few more essays to review before school started.

She sat down and began poring over the students' papers. Brooke liked to give assignments that challenged the students to think about social and ethical issues. This time they were to write a one to two page essay on the importance of honesty in relationships. Most of the written responses were typical of young teens and pre-teens. Their youth and immaturity was clear in their words.

Brooke smiled to herself as she wrote positive and encouraging comments along with the necessary corrections to grammar, spelling and punctuation. Amber Stanton had written, "If you're not honest, no one will welcome you into their group. You'll lose friends and end up being alone because no one will trust you." Johnny Martindale wrote, "A dishonest person is disbelieved and hated by all. If we are

Anita Louise

dishonest with ~~are~~/our friends, the life of the dishonest person becomes miserable."

Mary Beth Silvers' was the next paper Brooke picked up. Usually the girl turned in papers that were neatly and carefully written. It was obvious even at first glance, this paper was an exception to what Brooke had come to expect. The paper was wrinkled and stained, and the girl's normally precise handwriting was almost illegible.

What is going on with you, Mary Beth?

Before she was able to even get started on reviewing Mary Beth's paper, the bell rang and students began to filter into the classroom. Putting the stack of papers off to the side, Brooke stood and smiled as she prepared for another day as a middle school teacher.

Classes began. Students filed in and the morning flew by. Brooke was more than ready by the time her lunch hour rolled around. As she walked from her room to the teachers' lounge, she was confused by the looks and comments from the other teachers.

"It's not your birthday, is it?" one of her colleagues asked.

"Who's the lucky guy?" said another.

Yet another asked, "What haven't you been telling us, Miss Adler?"

Finally, she grabbed the arm of Mrs. Finnegan, the math teacher who was about the same age as Brooke. "What in the world is everyone talking about, Molly? What's going on?"

"Well, I guess you haven't been in the office since you came in this morning. Have you?" Molly winked with a twinkle in her eye.

"No. I had some work to catch up on so I went straight to my room. Why?"

"If I were you, I'd stop in the office before you go to lunch. You can fill me in later." With a little wave, Molly Finnegan walked down the hall.

Without hesitation Brooke turned on her heel and headed to the building office. Before she even opened the door, she saw the stunning flower arrangement featuring the exotic bloom of a bird of paradise through the glass. As soon as she walked in, Mrs. Erikson, the school secretary, spoke up. "What a lovely arrangement, Miss Adler. Is this a special occasion?"

"You mean, that's for *me?*"

"It sure is. It was delivered about an hour after school opened. Everybody who's been in the office has been admiring it."

"Who's it from?" Brooke asked.

"Why heavens, I'm the one who should be asking *you* that question, my dear. In fact, I will. Who sent you that exquisite bouquet, Miss Adler?"

Brooke's hands were already reaching for the card enclosed with the flowers. "I have no idea, but I guess we'll soon find out."

Opening the card she read, "The Bird of Paradise is a magnificent bloom. You are just as lovely and even more magnificent than this, or any other flower. It is also used to indicate exciting and wonderful anticipation. It is with wonderful anticipation I look forward to spending more exciting times with you again in the near future. Sincerely, Zackary."

"Well, who's it from?" asked the curious secretary patiently.

Mumbling more to herself than to Mrs. Erikson, she replied, "The last person in the world I would have *ever* expected." Sliding the card back into its envelope, she then tucked it safely into her pocket. Remembering her manners, she added, "A friend, Mrs. Erikson. The flowers are from a friend."

Brooke felt like she was in a fog. Therefore, it was easy to ignore the stares and questions as she carefully carried the arrangement back to her classroom.

Wonderful anticipation? Exciting times? Really? How did I get so lucky? I didn't think he'd even want to speak to me, let alone see me again after the way I behaved.

Sitting in her deserted classroom, she looked at the beautiful flowers. As her finger stroked the delicate blooms, her thoughts turned once again to the kind and generous man who'd sent them.

Chapter Four

When Zackary Carter submitted his application for admission to the University of Washington – School of Medicine in Seattle he was apprehensive. Less than four percent of applicants who applied were actually admitted. But now he was almost more nervous than he'd been back then. Only this time his nerves had nothing to do with his usually all-consuming career. Instead, it was because of a certain tall and slender middle school teacher.

I wonder what she thought of the flowers. The note? He'd been so confident when he ordered the arrangement to be delivered to her school. But now he was second guessing himself. *I'm almost positive she's as attracted to me as I am to her,* he thought. *Surely her abrupt departure didn't mean she's not interested.* Now, wondering what her reaction was to the undoubtedly unexpected gift from him was nerve wracking. Ever since he'd driven away from the Pearl Street Mall, he'd been asking himself these and other questions.

Anita Louise

Time and again, he replayed and analyzed his meeting with Brooke. *You certainly couldn't call it a date, could you?*

Fortunately, he was back at the hospital now. The emergency room was busy as usual which meant he had very little time for thoughts about the intriguing school teacher. It was common for him to work ten to twelve hours a day. He'd been assured his time in the emergency room would be limited to three to four days a week, but five was more the norm. Today wasn't much different from most. Auto accidents, sports injuries, chest pain, severe headaches, high fever and other symptoms brought a hundred or more people of all ages into emergency at Foothills Hospital every day.

It was early evening, nearing the end of his shift. Walking through the emergency room doors was what he assumed to be a mother and her teenage daughter. They were similar in appearance and both had long blonde hair. The daughter held her face in her hands and was crying uncontrollably. The older woman was limping slightly. She had her arm around the girl's shoulders, apparently doing her best to provide comfort. From where he stood, it wasn't possible to determine the cause of the younger female's distress. He kept the pair in his sights as they approached the nurses' station. Then he casually moved closer so he could hear the conversation.

"How may we help you?" the nurse asked.

"My daughter. She tripped and fell. We're afraid she's broken her nose."

When the girl lifted her head, her nose was bleeding and her face was swollen.

"Your name please, and your daughter's name. Here's a form you'll need to complete, and we'll need your insurance information as well." The nurse's badge said Nora Raynor. She was calm and efficient as she handed a clipboard to the woman.

"I'm Shelly Silvers, and this is my daughter, Mary Beth." The woman took the paperwork from the nurse. Then she dug in her purse, apparently looking for the information requested.

"You can have a seat. We'll call you as soon as we can." The nurse's demeanor softened as she spoke directly to the teen. "I'll get you a cold compress, and the doctor will be with you shortly. Hang in there, sweetie." An intern evidently saw what was going on. As the nurse stood, she was handed a thickly folded, soft cloth wrapped around a small ice pack. "Here you go. Hold this gently to your face."

The girl's sobs turned to whimpers. She reached across the desk and took the package. "Thank you." Flinching as she placed the compress to her face, tears rolled down her cheeks.

"Come on, Mary Beth. Let's go sit down for a minute so I can get this paperwork filled out."

After the two disappeared into the waiting area, Dr. Carter walked up to the intake desk.

"What do you think, Nora?" he asked the nurse.

"Not sure. You just never know these days. I'm pulling up the family records right now. I'll let you know what comes up. You want to handle this one?"

"Yeah. *Damn.* I hate to see kids come in looking like that. Sure sends up a red flag. Let me know what you find. I'll check on the girl as soon as you get them into the exam area." He returned to the exam area to make sure the previous patients were being cared for. As he did, he thought to himself, *I hope to God it really was an accident that caused that girl's injuries.*

As they walked into the waiting room Shelly Silvers did her best not to limp. It was bad enough she had to bring Mary Beth into emergency. Sure, her hip hurt where Nate had knocked her down. And the bruises were probably already forming on her arm where he'd grabbed her to throw her out of the way. But, if she let on she was hurt too all hell would break loose, both here and at home.

Up until recently, Shelly had been able to put herself between her husband and their daughter. But it seemed like ever since Mary Beth had become a teen, he'd been more and more determined to "show that girl who's boss" with his fists.

"You okay, honey?" she asked her daughter.

"It *hurts.* Oh, Mom, why does he *do* this?"

"He doesn't mean to, sweetie. It's just he's been having some trouble at work, plus he just hasn't been feeling all that good lately."

"You always make excuses for him! Well, I don't have to. You can lie if you want to, but I'm telling the truth."

"Mary Beth, you know how much I love you. I always have and always will do anything in the world I can to protect you. But the *truth* is if you tell them your Dad did this to you, you'll be taken away from us ... from me. As soon as you tell them, you'll go into foster care and your Dad might go to jail. Is that really what you want?"

"No, but ..."

"Honey, just tell them your room was a mess. You tripped over some clothes you left on the floor and hit the corner of your dresser when you fell. Okay?"

"But, Mom." Her cry was plaintive and forlorn.

"It's for the best, Mary Beth. You trust me, don't you?"

"Of course, I do, Mom, but ..."

"No buts. Just remember; no matter what they ask, you just say, 'I tripped over some clothes on my bedroom floor and hit the corner of the dresser when I fell.' Just say the same thing over and over. Got it?"

"Okay, 'I tripped over some clothes on my bedroom floor and hit the corner of the dresser when I fell.' I got it." She sighed and slumped while holding the cold compress to her swollen nose.

Shelly Silvers patted her daughter's shoulder reassuringly, "It'll be all right, Mary Beth. We'll figure something out. Don't you worry. We'll figure something out." With that she returned to completing the many forms the nurse had handed to her.

Shelly Blake was only seventeen when she'd gotten pregnant, and she was scared to death. At first Nate urged her to get an abortion. When she told him she was going to keep the baby, he surprised her. He professed his love and asked her to marry him. She was overjoyed and thought she'd found the proverbial silver lining in the storm clouds. Those clouds seemed to have been following her for years. Shelly could hardly wait to get out of the house where she lived with her mother and the step-father who drank too much. It was usually when he was drunk that he made inappropriate overtures to his teenage step-daughter. Shelly never bothered to say anything to her mom. Mom was

Anita Louise

usually drunk right along with her husband. It probably wouldn't have made any difference anyway.

Nathan was a high school senior and a popular jock when he'd first taken notice of Shelly. She'd been absolutely thrilled. When Nate got a scholarship to Colorado State, she figured that would be the end of it. But instead he'd told her he needed her even more. At Boulder High Nate was a big fish in a little pond, but such was not the case at CSU. He told Shelly he didn't like college. It didn't take much to figure out why. In high school he was the star athlete who didn't have to worry about his grades. But in college he was sitting on the bench and was expected to pass all of his classes.

Shelly had been looking forward to attending CU-Boulder after she finished high school. Even though it meant she'd have to live at home a few more years, it was worth it. She'd applied for and received scholarships to cover most of her tuition and books. She planned to work full time while going to school. But when she got pregnant, her dreams of a degree in education faded away like a puff of smoke.

Luckily, Nate was able to get decent employment as a wood worker at the Longmont Millwork Company. The trade didn't pay much to start, but it didn't require a college degree or any experience either. He didn't really like it, but it was a job. Shelly worked as a waitress during the dinner hour after Nate got off work. Both of their paychecks together made it possible for the three of them to live in a small two-bedroom apartment.

We were happy once, weren't we? She couldn't really remember. She hadn't even had the baby yet. She'd been so excited about moving out of her mom and step-dad's house into the tiny apartment with Nate.

"It's a cute little place, don't you think, Nate?"

"Cute? If you call old and cramped cute, I guess so."

"Honey, I know you're used to a lot nicer, but things will get better. Once the baby's born, I can work things out so I can go to school and get a teaching job. It'll be perfect! My school schedule and our daughter's will be the same. Everything'll work out perfect. You just wait and see."

"Perfect? To begin with you're having a girl instead of a boy, so how's that *perfect?*" he sneered.

"The next one will be a boy. I'm sure of it."

"Next one? Are you kidding me? Do you know how much it costs to raise a kid these days? You should've gotten an abortion like I told you to. Then we wouldn't have to worry about any of this. I'm going out. Have fun in this dump you call a 'cute little place.' I'll see ya later. Don't wait up for me."

She waited up anyway, but when he'd come home drunk, it was even worse than when he was sober. After that, she was mostly just glad when he was out with the boys. Being alone was better than being with a man who blamed her for ruining his life. Somehow he seemed to have forgotten he'd lost his football scholarship *before* she'd gotten pregnant.

Nathan had an abundance of demeaning names he used to label his wife. None of them were too creative. Fat, ugly, stupid, and lazy were a few of his favorites. It'd taken several years after Mary Beth was born for him to move from verbal to physical abuse. And it had only been recently he'd started trying to take his discontent out on their daughter.

Shelly frequently thought about and even tried to get out of the verbally and emotionally abusive relationship she'd always had with her husband. But there always seemed to be a reason to stay. Her own mother encouraged her to "work things out." In addition, her pastor told her time and time again God hates divorce. As a woman of faith, how could she flaunt God? Of course, Nathan promised more than once that he'd change. He told her he loved her and never meant to hurt her. But the biggest reason was money. They could barely make it on both their incomes as it was. How could she possibly get by on her own?

None of those excuses mattered after the first time he'd gotten physically abusive. It started out as pushing and shoving. When he held her up against the wall, his hands had left bruises on her arms. The first time he struck her across the face, she knew she had to get out. Shelly had sworn to herself right then and there, the abuse she'd lived with as a child would end. There was no way she was going to allow her own daughter to watch the same crap she'd had to deal with while growing up.

Shelly started keeping a secret rainy day fund. At first, she didn't know what she was going to do with it, but it didn't take long to figure it out. Mary Beth was in school much of the day and was also involved in after school activities. Plus, Nathan was either at work or out drinking with his buddies most of the time. Of course! School.

Shelly did her homework and learned about using CLEP, the College-Level Examination Program. It would allow her to test out of a number of the otherwise lengthy and expensive courses she needed to graduate. In addition, she'd been taking one or two classes at a time year round ... ever since Nate hit her the first time. She studied in the library and left her books in her locker at work. She'd have enough credits for her bachelor's degree by the end of the semester. Her student teaching was the only challenge left to overcome. Somehow she'd figure that one out too.

She was almost smiling in spite of the current circumstances when a voice brought her out of her reverie.

"All set?" The deep male voice caused Shelly to flinch, and she looked up. Seeing the white lab coat of a doctor, she relaxed slightly.

"Oh, yes. I guess I was daydreaming a little bit. I'll just take these back up to the nurse."

He put his hand gently on her shoulder. "That's okay. You stay here with your daughter. I'm the one who'll get a bunch of those papers from the nurse anyway." He reached out his hand. "I'm Dr. Zackary Carter."

He seemed nice enough, and he was certainly good looking. But Shelly knew better than to judge a book by its cover. She hadn't come this far only to have her daughter taken away from her ... especially now that she could see the light at the end of the tunnel. She extended her hand.

"Hello, Dr. Carter. I'm Shelly Silvers, and this is my daughter Mary Beth. She had a little accident in her messy room. Didn't you, Mary Beth?" Shelly squeezed her daughter's shoulders reassuringly.

Looking at her mother and then to the doctor, the teen repeated the line she'd been coached on. "Uh, yeah. I guess I must've slipped on some clothes or something on the floor in my bedroom, and I fell."

"Wow, looks like that 'fall' is going to give you quite a shiner," Dr. Carter said sympathetically.

"Yeah, I guess I'm just clumsy. At least that's what my Dad always says."

Anita Louise

Shelly stiffened. "Oh, you know he's just teasing you, Mary Beth. Your Dad loves you. He'd be real proud of how brave you've been since you fell and hit your face on the dresser." Turning her attention to the doctor, she continued. "My husband Nathan, Shelly's Dad ... he'd have been here with us if he could. But he got called into work. Isn't that right, Mary Beth? You remember how worried your dad was when he couldn't come to the hospital with us, don't you?"

The girl just shrugged and looked at the floor. "Yeah. I guess."

"Well, let's get you into the examination area, shall we?" said the doctor.

Shelly thought she heard a note of sincere kindness in his voice. She stood and put her arm around her daughter once more. "We're ready, doctor."

Dr. Zackary Carter didn't believe the mother's story for a minute. It was clear there was more here than met the eye. He was required by Colorado law to report his suspicions. He'd already contacted local law enforcement. An officer was headed to the hospital emergency room. He'd seen these kinds of cases before, and felt compassion for the woman and her child. Although he didn't have to, he wanted to at least give the mother a head's up. He gently ushered her away from her daughter's earshot.

"You know, Mrs. Silvers, this just doesn't look right to me. As much as I'd like to believe you, your daughter's injuries are inconsistent with your description. Do you want to tell me what really happened?" He could see the panic in her eyes, even though she quickly tried to cover it up with bravado.

"I don't know what you're talking about. Why do you have me over here away from my daughter? She needs me. She's hurt, and she needs to have her mother by her side. I need to be with her instead of standing over here talking nonsense with you." She started to move back toward where her daughter was seated on an examination table.

"Mrs. Silvers, I'm required by law to report any suspicions of the abuse of a child under the age of eighteen."

She stopped. He watched her shoulders slump. When she looked up, he could see she was on the verge of tears.

"Please, Dr. Carter. I just need a little more time. Please, don't call anyone. Not yet."

"I had no choice. But if you tell me the truth, I might be able to help."

"You already did it, didn't you? You already called someone. Are they going to take my daughter away from me? Please. You can't let them take my daughter away from me." Her tears were falling unchecked.

"First things first, Mrs. Silvers. Let me take a look at your daughter and make sure she's going to be all right. When the officers get here, we'll go someplace where we can all talk in private. Okay?"

She sniffed, wiped her eyes and seemed to regain a degree of control. "You're right. Of course. Mary Beth is most important. Yes, please, do what you need to do to make sure she's going to be all right. We'll deal with everything else later." She hesitated a moment. "And, Dr. Carter, please call me Shelly. I don't much like being called Mrs. Silvers anymore."

He nodded. They both returned to the examining area where Mary Beth sat with the now warming compress still held to her face.

Shelly Silvers went directly to her daughter's side and put an arm around her. She whispered into her child's ear, "Everything's going to be fine, Mary Beth. Mama's here and we're going to get through this together, you and me. Don't you worry about a thing, baby. Everything's going to be just fine."

Officer Luke Adler was behind the wheel of the squad car. His partner Monique Hix was riding shotgun. They arrived at the Foothills Hospital Emergency Room a little after nine p.m. He hated these kinds of calls. But he and Monique had been working child abuse cases together with the Boulder PD for over three years now. They were a great team.

At six foot six and two hundred twenty-five pounds, Luke Adler not only *looked* like a force to be reckoned with ... he *was*. Although he was younger than six of the nine Adler children, he was the most formidable of the family members. Growing up, he'd often been called a "gentle giant." He'd joined the Boulder PD after completing his tour of duty with the Navy. His inherent compassion and the discipline he'd developed in the military worked together to make him a better office with the Boulder PD. He had both the mental and physical toughness necessary to be an outstanding police officer.

Monique Hix had worked very hard to become a highly respected member of the police force. Being black and female meant to her that she had to be twice as good at everything. She had a near genius IQ, and a tough but fair, no-nonsense way of dealing with people. She also worked very hard to make sure she had the physical strength necessary to handle any situation she and her partner might encounter. Her decision to become a police officer was partly because of her own difficult childhood. She knew what it was like to be treated unfairly. Therefore, she did whatever she could to make sure people were treated equitably.

"What do we have here, Monique?" Luke asked.

"Not much. Fourteen-year-old girl brought into emergency with her face all banged up. The doc isn't buying the story given by the mother and her daughter. I know I've said this a million times, but I'm glad the docs are required to report this crap these days. If they don't, *their ass* is in hot water. That means a lot less of these *bastards* are getting away with treating their kids like a punching bag."

"C'mon, Mo. Just because there's suspicion, doesn't mean there's been a crime. Innocent until proven guilty, remember?"

"Yeah, yeah, I know. But *you* know we're saving a lot of kids who used to slip through the cracks. I'm damn glad they're bringing the authorities in sooner rather than later." She shuddered inwardly remembering some of the children who didn't get the help they needed soon enough. Stories of everything from the loss of life to almost irreparable physical and emotional damage flashed through her mind. "I'd rather be alerted and have it be a false alarm. It's a lot better than some kid out there going even one more day being treated like a piece of garbage."

"You're right, Mo, and you're real good at getting to the truth." Luke sat quietly for a few moments. "You okay?"

"Me? Yeah. Sure. Of course, I am."

"Just because it's a teenage girl doesn't mean ..."

"Hey! Shut up, man," Monique snapped. "I know. I know. You know I've been doing this long enough I can tell the difference between a girl who's been molested and one who hasn't. I'm not making any assumptions, so just cool your jets. Okay?"

"Okay." Luke knew better than to push his partner any further. "Just give me a sign how you want to handle this one once we get in there."

"Okay. Will do."

Convinced his partner had her emotions under control, they drove the last couple of miles in silence. He parked the cruiser near the emergency entrance and the two officers walked in side by side.

"Hi, Nora," Luke said to the nurse who was manning the desk.

Looking up, she smiled brightly, "Oh, Luke ... I mean, Officer Adler, it's so nice to see you again."

Monique nudged her partner and whispered under her breath, "Hey there, pretty boy, remember this is official business, not a social call."

Luke repaid her nudge with an elbow to the ribs. "It's nice to see you too, Nora. Unfortunately, we got a call. We need to speak with Dr. Carter, please."

"Of course. I'll let him know you're here. Wait just a minute, please." The nurse nodded to one of her counterparts to take over the desk. She then walked briskly through the swinging doors to the patient area.

Monique took the opportunity to make a few more of what she knew would be unwelcome comments to her comrade. "So when you were in the Navy, I assume it was the proverbial 'girl in every port.' Now it's a nurse in every hospital, a waitress in every donut shop, and a sales clerk in every store. Hmmm? There must be a few I've forgotten." She smiled broadly at his discomfort.

"Just because you went off the deep end and married Lamar last year, doesn't mean I have to follow in your footsteps. Next thing you know you'll be telling me I have to find a new partner for a few months because you've got a bun in the oven."

"A bun in the oven? Are you kidding me? What century are you from, anyway, Adler?" Monique snorted. "A bun in the oven. Hmph." She paused, looking at him askance. "When Lamar and I decide to start a family, I'll be sure to let you know when I get *pregnant.* Not preggers, not harboring a fugitive, not eating for two ... pregnant, p-r-e-g-n-a-n-t."

"You're not, are you? Pregnant, I mean."

"No, damn it! Didn't I just say I'd tell you if I was. Man, you got ears, but you don't hear too good."

"Sorry, Mo. You don't have to get your drawers in a twist, you know."

Their friendly banter was interrupted by the appearance of Dr. Zackary Carter who spoke as he walked toward the officers. "Hi, Luke. Officer Hix. Thanks for coming over. Fourteen-year-old girl. Somebody got to her face pretty good. No evidence of sexual abuse, thank God. She's back there with her mother. I'm ninety-nine point nine percent sure Mom had nothing to do with it. In fact, the Mom's been doing her best to hide a limp. I'm thinking the perp is most likely the 'loving husband/father,' but both mother and daughter are singing the same song. The girl tripped over a pile of clothes on the floor of her room and fell into her dresser. I'm not buying it. That's why I called you guys."

"Thanks, Doc," Officer Hix responded. "You did the right thing. Can we talk to them now?"

"Sure. Follow me. Anything else you need from me, just let me know." Moving the drape separating the beds in the emergency room, Dr. Carter stepped aside. "Mrs. Silvers, this is Officer Adler and Officer Hix. They'd like to have a few words with you and your daughter."

As soon as he heard the name Mrs. Silvers, Luke Adler's heart skipped a beat. "Shelly?"

"Oh, my God. Luke."

Monique Hix stepped up. "Excuse us a moment." Grabbing Luke by the sleeve, she pulled him out of the confined space.

Chapter Five

"**Y**ou *know* this woman, Adler? This chick in every port shit has got to stop."

Luke could tell his partner really wished she could yell at the top of her lungs, but instead she'd whispered in the most intense voice he'd ever heard.

"Relax, Mo. Yes, I know her, from a very long time ago. She was friends with my sister Brooke back in high school. Actually, they were in high school, but I wasn't yet. There's really nothing to be concerned about here. Like I said, it was a *long* time ago." There was no point in telling his partner he'd had a huge crush on his sister's friend.

Monique Hix seemed to settle down a bit. "In any case, I think you better back off and let me take the lead on this. Last thing in the world we need is for some lawyer to claim we didn't do everything strictly by the book."

"You're probably right. You take the lead. I'll put my two cents in if it looks like there's anything I can do to help. Okay?"

Anita Louise

"Yeah, sure. Maybe she'll be a little more open because the two of you have some history."

"Ancient history, Mo. Ancient history," Luke assured his partner.

"All right. Ancient history. Still, keep out of it as much as possible. And we better make sure we have the doc there as a witness. He's the one who called us in on this."

The officers returned to the area where Shelly Silvers sat with her daughter. Dr. Carter was examining the girl, gingerly touching the area around her nose.

"With the swelling, it's very difficult to tell if your nose is broken, Mary Beth."

The teen, who'd been whimpering up until then, broke into tears and loud sobs. "I really *am* going to be ugly now. Oh, God, how am I ever going to be able to go back to school? And I was supposed to be in the play this year too. Now everything's ruined!"

Shelly Silvers spoke up. "Now, Mary Beth, don't be so dramatic. First of all, you're beautiful. You're my gorgeous, beautiful, wonderful daughter and nothing's going to change that. You might need to take a little time off school. But don't worry, we'll make sure to get all your assignments from your teachers so you can keep up. And you're still going to be able to be in the play. It'll take a little while, but you'll be back to normal real soon. Won't she, doctor?"

"Yes, she will, Mrs. Silvers."

"Please, call me Shelly. It makes me feel so old when you call me Mrs. Silvers. Besides ..."

Officer Hix spoke up. "Besides what, Mrs. Silvers?"

"Oh, nothing. It was nothing."

Bad Case of Lovin' You

Before the conversation could progress any further, Dr. Carter interjected, "We're going to need an image of Mary Beth's nose, just in case. I've asked Nora to send an orderly to take her to X-ray. He should be here any minute now." Mary Beth girl looked expectantly from the doctor to her mother. "I'm sorry, but your mom can't go with you for this one."

Shelly Silvers patted her daughter's hand. "You'll be fine, sweetie. I'll be right here when you get back."

Just then, a young man peeked through the curtain. "X-ray?"

"Yes, Frank," Dr. Carter responded. "Please take Miss Silvers down. Have them do a workup on her nose. Bring her back to the patient conference room. That's where we'll be. Thanks."

"Mom? Should I ...?"

"Shhh, baby. It's okay. We'll talk about everything later. Right now, you just do what the doctor says. Go get your pretty little nose looked at. Everything's going to be just fine. Don't you worry."

The mother and daughter hugged each other, and Shelly kissed her child gently on the cheek. They reluctantly drew apart and held each other's hands until Mary Beth left with the orderly.

Shortly after their departure, Officer Hix spoke up. "Dr. Carter, we know where the conference room is located, but it would be appreciated if you would show us the way. We're going to need to get a statement from you as well. First, we'd like to talk to Mrs. Silvers while her daughter's elsewhere. But it would be very helpful to have you present as well."

"Certainly. I understand," Dr. Carter responded. "I'll make sure Nora knows I won't be available for a while. Unless there's a huge emergency, I'm at your service."

Monique Hix turned to Shelly Silvers. "Mrs. Silvers, follow me please."

"Of course," Shelly said softly.

Luke followed his sister's old high school friend down the hall. He noted her slumped shoulders and slight limp. *The Shelly Blake I remember was so vibrant and happy. She was always ready with a smile and words of encouragement for everyone. I can still see the old Shelly when she interacts with her daughter, but that's about the only time.*

Once in the conference room, Shelly was asked to sit at the head of the table with Dr. Carter on her right and Officer Adler on her left. Monique Hix remained standing.

After a few moments of uncomfortable silence, Officer Hix began speaking. "First of all, Mrs. Silvers, we want you to know we appreciate your cooperation. Let's begin with the basics." The next few minutes were spent putting preliminary information into the report: name, date, current location, location where incident occurred. Monique Hix then continued. "Just like you, our primary concern is your daughter. You love your daughter, don't you, Mrs. Silvers?"

"Why of course I do. What a silly question to ask." She looked at Luke Adler and inquired, "Am I being accused of something, Luke?"

"Of course not, Shelly," Luke replied. "This is just routine. Dr. Carter called and asked us to come here. In fact, he said it looked to him like your daughter might not be the only one who was hurt this evening. Isn't that right, doc?"

Bad Case of Lovin' You

Zack Carter nodded and looked directly at Shelly Silvers. "Yes, that's true. It looked to me like you were limping a little when you came in with Mary Beth. I'm usually pretty good at spotting that sort of thing. Are *you* okay, Shelly?"

The apparent concern coming from both the doctor and her old friend seemed to be Shelly's undoing. "No. No, I'm not okay, and yes, I was doing my best *not* to limp." She broke into sobs and put her head down on the table in front of her.

Officer Hix spoke up once again. "Mrs. Silvers, please, just tell us what happened."

Shelly sat up straight. "No, I can't. I'm sorry, but I just can't do that right now."

"Of course you can, Shelly," Monique Hix replied. "That's the only way we can help you. That's the only way we can protect you and Mary Beth."

The tears were streaming down Shelly's face. "You don't understand. I'm not ready yet."

"You're not ready yet? What do you mean, you're 'not ready yet?'" Officer Hix asked.

Shelly sniffed and said, "I've been going to school. I'm almost done. Then I'll have my degree and I'll be able to get a job ... a *good* job. I won't be stuck just waiting tables."

Luke's curiosity got the better of him, and he could no longer sit silently. "What are you going to do, Shelly? What kind of a job do you plan on getting?"

She looked up at him and smiled weakly. Her crying had abated somewhat. "A teacher. I'm going to be a teacher like Brooke. Mary Beth just loves the class she has with Miss

Adler. In fact, she tried out for the school play because her favorite teacher was involved."

"That's great, Shelly," said Luke. "Brooke will be so happy to know how much Mary Beth enjoys her class. She'll also be thrilled to know you're going to follow in her footsteps. You'll be a great teacher." When Luke finished speaking, he felt more than saw his partner's disapproval.

Monique Hix spoke again. "Mrs. Silvers, we're all just pleased as punch that you're going to be a school teacher," she said sarcastically. "However, the fact remains your daughter has been severely injured. It's been reported to us as suspected child abuse. Under these circumstances, it's our responsibility to protect the child."

Zackary Carter had been sitting quietly, watching and listening carefully. Hearing the name Brooke got his attention. "Luke. Luke Adler. Oh, my gosh. You're related to Brooke Adler?"

"Brooke's my sister. How the heck do you know my sister, doc?"

"I met Brooke last month when Mrs. Adler, your mother, was hospitalized," Dr. Carter responded. "I'm surprised I didn't put two and two together before now. In fact, I'm amazed I didn't see you during the time Mrs. Adler was in the hospital, Luke. There were so many Adlers hanging around, it looked like a family reunion."

"I was there," Luke said. "We must've just missed one another somehow."

"Excuse me, folks." Monique Hix appeared to be a bit exasperated, and she spoke with authority. "So sorry to interrupt your little tete-a-tete, but we've got a job to do here. Can we get on with it, please?"

The smile on Luke's face faded as he sat back in his chair.

"Yes, of course," Zack Carter stated apologetically.

Shelly Silvers gulped and asked, "What's going to happen now?"

"There's no way we can allow Mary Beth to return to the home where we suspect the abuse occurred until we do a complete investigation," Officer Hix stated. "Is there someplace else you and your daughter can go? Relatives? A friend's home?"

"No. Not really," Shelly responded. "A few years after my step-dad died, Mom ended up remarrying. Harold's a nice man. They're both retired so they moved to Arizona. They love the warmer climate."

"What about friends? asked Monique. "Mrs. Silvers, if you don't have any place you can take your daughter, we'll be forced to put her into foster care. Surely, there must be someone."

Shelly spoke through her tears, gulping for air periodically as a person drowning in pain and fear. "What am I going to do? Mary Beth needs me. She's hurt enough already. Oh, God, what are we going to do?"

Luke had been doing his best to keep quiet after the proverbial slap on the wrist by his partner. But when a possible solution popped into his head, he couldn't keep his mouth shut. "I have an idea."

Monique Hix rolled her eyes and looked at him askance.

Ignoring her, Luke continued. "What about Brooke? She's got lots of room, and she's known you since high school. I know she wouldn't want Mary Beth to end up in foster care."

The look on Shelly's face was one of hope. "Do you really think she'd let us stay with her for a while?"

"You better figure out something." The tone of Officer Hix's voice was completely professional as she said, "Because until we've had time to do a thorough investigation, Mary Beth Silvers will *not* be allowed to stay in the home where the alleged abuse occurred. This is going to have to be resolved before we can let you leave here with your daughter, Mrs. Silvers."

Luke leaned forward and spoke softly. "I know my partner's not going to like this much, since I'm on duty here. But I'm going to give Brooke a call. You hang in there, Shelly."

She looked at Luke with tears in her eyes. "Thank you. Thanks for thinking of Brooke. Whatever happens, I really appreciate it."

Chapter Six

Brooke Adler had just finished one of the most challenging days of her teaching career, and it had nothing to do with her students. She kept being distracted by the flower arrangement sitting on her desk along with the intriguing note tucked in her purse.

In one class she'd been conducting a lesson on adjectives and adverbs. "Adjectives further describe, or modify, a person, place or thing in a sentence," she said. "For instance, if you wanted to make the sentence 'The flowers sat on the desk' more interesting, what adjectives might you use?"

One student called out, "The beautiful flowers sat on the desk."

"The pretty flowers sat on the desk," said another.

"The fragrant flowers sat on the desk," said a third.

By the time her students finished calling out descriptive adjectives for the amazing, awesome, unusual, delicate, graceful, lovely, stunning flowers sitting on her desk, her head was practically spinning. And, of course, hearing all those descriptions shifted her thoughts almost completely away from her classroom full of students. Instead her head was filled with images of the handsome, amazing, awesome, considerate, remarkable doctor who'd sent the arrangement.

It wasn't all that unusual for a married, female teacher to have flowers delivered to school. Typically they were from her husband, fiancé or steady boyfriend for her birthday, anniversary, or some other special occasion. But Brooke was an unmarried teacher who, as far as every person in the building knew, wasn't even dating anyone. And it was highly unusual to receive such an unexpected gift for *no reason whatsoever*.

Practically every single teacher, student, para-pro, and custodian in the building showed up in Brooke's classroom to see the flowers. Those same individuals also made comments and asked questions that Brooke was totally unprepared to answer.

Molly Finnegan commented, "Seth and I would love to meet him. Finding new couples to go out with is always fun."

Another teacher asked, "Who's the mystery man, Brooke?"

"From the looks of this arrangement, you're going to want to hang on to this one. Bird of Paradise is a beautiful, but very expensive flower," said Mrs. Erickson.

By the end of the day, Miss Brooke Adler could hardly wait to grab her treasured gift, plus a stack of papers to correct, and head out the door. The quiet solitude of her car was a great relief.

Bad Case of Lovin' You

By carefully wedging her precious cargo between other items in the back of her van, the flowers made it to her house on 18th Street safely. Once inside, she moved the arrangement from the kitchen to the living room to her bedroom and, finally, back to the kitchen. The Bird of Paradise now occupied the center of the table. She sat nearby with her phone in her hand. Ever since she'd gotten home, she'd been enjoying the blooms thoroughly. She would alternately touch, sniff, and simply gaze at their beauty.

Thank God she'd had the presence of mind to program his number into her phone when he'd called her yesterday. *Yesterday? Was it really only yesterday Zack called me? Just yesterday that we met at the brewery? That we kissed?*

"That I acted like a total idiot?" she said out loud. Sighing, she stood and walked to the mirror hanging next to the back door. Speaking to her reflection, she said, "Okay, so evidently he either *likes* idiots, or he didn't see my behavior as quite as horrible and stupid as *I thought* it was. Either way, he sent me the beautiful flowers sitting right there on my table. Common courtesy dictates I call and thank him. So that's what I'm going to do. Right now. I'm dialing his number." *Oh, geez ...* brrrring, brrrring ... brrrring, brrrring ... brrrring, brrrring ... brrrring, brrrring.

"You have reached the voice mail of Dr. Zackary Carter. Please leave your message and I'll get back to you as soon as possible."

Darn! "Oh, uh, hi Zackary. It's Brooke, Brooke Adler. I'm just calling to say thank you for the beautiful flowers. Um. I was totally surprised ... pleasantly so, of course. Uh, well,

Anita Louise

call me back please. Thanks again. Bye." *Phooey! I probably sounded like a total idiot once again. Oh well.*

Brooke shrugged and headed upstairs. Within minutes she was wearing a pair of comfortable blue jeans and an old CU-Boulder sweatshirt. Thick socks and slippers completed her usual at home look. Once back in the kitchen, she again admired the Bird of Paradise standing regally at the center of the arrangement.

The teakettle on the stove whistled. She smiled as she poured the steaming hot liquid into the vintage teapot she'd picked up at a garage sale. A cup of tea with a little lemon and honey was part of her daily after school routine. Today she was fortunate to have a slice of homemade banana bread to enjoy with her tea. One of the teachers brought the treat in to share with the rest of the staff, and Brooke brought the little delicacy home.

She settled herself at the kitchen table, sipping her tea and nibbling on the bread. The day's mail sat next to her: electric bill, a couple of sale fliers from Macy's and Victoria's Secret, a free dinner for listening to some financial planner talk about saving for retirement ... the usual.

Leafing through the sale fliers, Brooke's eyes lit upon a lacy black bra with very skimpy, not-quite-thong panties to match. *I wonder what the good doctor would think of these. Would you be surprised to find out how much I enjoy wearing these almost sinfully sexy undergarments?* In her mind Dr. McDreamy was staring at her with lust filled eyes. Brooke was clad only in tiny strips of lace covering strategic parts of her body, and she lounged gracefully across her eyelet lace bedspread. She opened her eyes. *If only I really was as sexy and sensual as the women I read about.*

Bad Case of Lovin' You

Brooke was a romantic at heart. She'd grown up seeing the love and respect her mother and father felt for each other first hand. Theirs was a love that had produced nine children. And now her parents had been married for forty years. Yet it was still common to see them holding hands and stealing kisses when they thought no one was looking.

In her late teens, she began reading romance novels. Even today love stories continued to fill her bookshelves. When she'd met Marcus, it seemed as if her own tale of true love was playing itself out. But the pain of his betrayal left her wondering. Was it only in works of fiction that the heroine actually enjoyed a happy ending?

Dr. Carter might be shocked by her choice of lingerie. But, he might also be amazed to learn that Marcus was the first and only lover she'd allowed herself. *Maybe my love of skimpy, lacy bras and panties is my way of hiding the fact I'm turning into the proverbial spinster school teacher. Next thing you know, I'll probably have the irresistible urge to get a cat ... or two ... or ten.*

She laughed at herself and spoke to the Bird of Paradise that somehow seemed to be listening. "Well, the truth is I am a teacher, and I've got work to do." Pushing herself back from the table, she emptied the teapot and rinsed her cup. Then she settled back down to finish grading papers. It was more than two hours later when she set her school work aside. Her solitary dinner included salmon, rice pilaf and a small salad. After eating, she tidied up and then finished the schoolwork she'd brought home.

The paper written by Mary Beth Silvers captured her attention for an inordinate length of time. Her student seemed to be struggling with self-esteem issues. In addition, the girl hinted at possible abuse in the home. Brooke had grown up with Mary Beth's mother Shelly and found it hard to believe her old friend was anything but a loving mother. On the other hand, Shelly's husband Nathan Silvers had never been one of Brooke's favorite people. She decided to make it a point to contact Shelly Silvers. Brooke needed to discuss her student's writing and the concerns the girl's words had brought up with the child's mother.

Deciding what to do next gave Brooke a sense of direction, and allowed her to set her concerns aside at least for now. It was getting late and she'd completed what needed to be done before tomorrow's day at school. After finishing her nighttime routine, she climbed into bed. This was her opportunity to escape into the current romance novel she was reading, *Words of Love*. The story was set in the southern United States in the 1800s and although published in the new millennium, the language was that of a much earlier time.

When Lady Constance awoke, she realized, once again, she was ensconced in her marriage bed alone. Her restless sleep had been filled with sensual dreams caused by the unwanted, yet unappeased cravings for the handsome plantation owner who was, by law, her husband.

Her father Lord Teasdale had gambled away the family fortune. To him, marrying his daughter off to the wealthy American had been his only choice. It didn't matter how

much Constance protested. Now the shores
of her homeland were thousands of miles
across the sea.

Brooke was interrupted as the cell phone next to her bed sounded its cheery tune. She answered almost immediately when she saw it was her brother.

"Brooke? It's Luke. I'm at Foothills Hospital."

"Luke? What's wrong? Are you okay? Is Mom okay?"

"I'm fine. Mom's fine. This has nothing to do with the family."

"Then why are you at the hospital? And why are you calling me now? It's almost ten o'clock at night."

"It's police business. I'm here with Shelly and Mary Beth Silvers."

"Oh, my God. Is Mary Beth all right? Is her mom all right?"

"Actually, Mary Beth's not all right. She's got a broken nose. Shelly's pretty shook up too."

"Oh, no! That's terrible. But why are you calling me?"

"Brooke, we suspect Nathan Silvers is the cause of Mary Beth's injuries. We can't allow her to go back there until we've had time to do a full investigation."

"Of course, you can't. I can see that, but I still don't understand why you're calling me at ten o'clock at night."

"It was my idea, Brooke. Shelly didn't really want me to call, but they've got no place else to go. Can Shelly and Mary Beth stay with you for a while, maybe a few weeks or so?"

"Yes, of course. Shelly and I have been friends for years, even if we haven't stayed in touch that much since she's been married to Nate. And Mary Beth is one of my favorite students. I've actually been a little concerned about her recently."

Luke sighed with relief. "Thanks, Brooke. I know how much this means to Shelly and to Mary Beth. They've got a rough road ahead of them for a while."

"I'm happy to help, Luke. I've got two extra bedrooms just waiting for them. Give Shelly my address and send them on over. I'll be waiting."

"Okay. By the way, Dr. Carter told me to say 'hello' to you for him."

"Zackary Carter? He did? I'm confused. What's he got to do with this?"

"He was the physician on duty when Shelly brought Mary Beth in. He's the one who called Monique and me in on this. Is there something going on between you and the doc I should know about?"

"Can it, Luke. If and when there's something in my private life you should know about, you'll be the first one I'll call. Until then you can just keep your police nose out of my personal business."

"All right, already. Right now what's important is that Shelly and Mary Beth have someplace to go. I know they both appreciate it. And, Sis?"

"Yeah, Bro?"

"I appreciate it too. Shelly needs a friend right now. Thanks for helping her out."

"No problem. When should I expect them?"

"Less than an hour. Doc Carter's done with Mary Beth. And Monique and I have everything we need for tonight. We'll follow them to your house ... make sure everyone gets there safe and sound."

"Okay. I'll be looking for them."

"Thanks again, Brooke."

"It's okay, Luke. You're welcome. G'nite."

"G'nite, Sis."

Brooke was in the middle of putting fresh sheets on the beds in the guest room when her phone rang again. Putting it up to her ear she asked, "What'd you forget, Luke?"

"Hi, Brooke. It's not Luke. It's Zack. Zack Carter."

"Oh, my gosh. Zack! Hi."

"I'm sorry to be calling so late, but I knew you were up."

"Yeah. I'm really sorry to hear about what's going on with the Silvers," Brooke said. "Mary Beth's a sweet girl, and I've known Shelly since high school."

"That's what Luke said. Sure is nice of you to take them in on such short notice, Brooke."

"Like I said, Mary Beth's a sweetie. I'm happy to help." Brooke paused and took a deep breath. "I don't know if this is the right time or not, but I have to tell you how much I appreciate the flowers. They're absolutely beautiful."

"Yeah, I got your message," Zack replied. "I'm glad you like them."

"Of course I do. They're gorgeous, and totally unexpected."

"Sorry about sending them to your school, but I didn't have a home address for you and I remember you saying you taught at Summit Middle School, so ..."

Anita Louise

"Oh, don't be sorry. It gave the entire school population something to talk about today." She rolled her eyes and chuckled softly.

"Were you surprised?" he asked.

"Shocked would be a better word, actually. In addition to saying thank you, I should also be apologizing for my behavior yesterday. In fact, I'm going to do that right now." She cleared her throat. "Dr. Carter, would you please accept my apology for my abrupt departure yesterday? I truly am very, very sorry."

"Brooke. It's okay. Really. There's no need for you to apologize. Was I surprised? Yes. Would I like to talk to you about it? Sure. Whenever you're ready, but I'm in no rush."

"Geez, Zack, I don't know what to say. Are you always this understanding or has it just been a really long time since you've kissed a girl?"

He burst out laughing. "That's what I mean, Brooke. You're so *you.* You're so natural and funny ... and a *very* good kisser."

It was a good thing he couldn't see her face, because it was probably redder than some of the accent flowers in the arrangement he'd sent. After taking in a couple of gulps of air, she finally managed to say, "You're not so bad yourself."

She heard him chuckle again.

"Why thank you, Miss Adler. Since it seems we've joined a mutual admiration society, how about we get together again. We can see if we can make the second kiss even better than the first."

"Sure. Yeah. Okay. When?"

"How about Saturday night? We can do something traditional, like dinner and a movie. How does that sound?"

"That sounds nice ... very nice. But I have to warn you, I don't do scary and I don't do violence. As long as you're okay with comedy or romance, we're good."

"Romance, huh? I like the sound of that," he said. "How about I pick you up about seven?"

After sharing the necessary information regarding the location of her home, Brooke hesitated slightly before speaking once again. "Zack?"

"Yes, Brooke?"

"The note."

"What about the note?" he asked.

"The note was almost better than the flowers. You're pretty magnificent yourself, Dr. Carter."

"Am I?"

"Yep. You sure are. Pretty magnificent. Not only because of the flowers and the note, but for calling Luke and his partner about Mary Beth. That can't be the easiest thing in the world to do."

"It might not be the easiest, but it's the *right* thing to do. I'm glad you liked the flowers, Brooke."

"I loved them. See you Saturday, Zack. G'nite."

"Good night, Brooke. Sweet dreams."

Chapter Seven

Brooke stood somewhat nervously near her front door waiting for her unplanned guests to arrive. She knew Mary Beth had been hurt, but didn't know how seriously.

This was the first time in over ten years of teaching she'd had to personally deal with the abuse of one of her students. The statistics regarding child abuse were pretty bad: three million reports every year, affecting over six million children. Plus adults who were abused as children were much more likely to have issues with drugs, alcohol, depression, unintended pregnancy and lots of other things that made life even more challenging than usual.

Even though it was late, Brooke had hot chocolate, tea, and coffee ready. She'd had some ready-to-bake cookie dough in the freezer. So now her home was filled with the smell of freshly baked chocolate chip cookies.

Nothing like cookies fresh out of the oven to help soothe whatever hurts, she thought.

When she saw headlights turn down her street, Brooke flipped on the porch light and opened the front door. Peering through the glass in the storm door, she watched as the car pulled to the curb. A few moments later, Shelly emerged from the driver's side. Brooke watched her high school friend walk around to the passenger's door, open it and then stoop down. Evidently Mary Beth was reluctant to get out of the car.

Brooke stepped out onto the front porch and waved. "You've got the right house," she called. "I'm here. Come on in,"

Shelly Silvers stood and held her hand out to the person in the car. Brooke watched her fourteen-year-old student move as if she were an elderly woman. The teacher's heart ached. *Oh, God, what has he done to her?*

Hand in hand the mother and daughter walked up the steps. Mary Beth's head hung down limply. Brooke held the door open and stepped aside. "Come in, come in, please."

Shelly Silvers looked at her hostess through tear stained eyes. "Oh, Brooke, thank you so much. You have no idea how much we appreciate this."

Embracing her friend, Brooke replied, "I'm so glad Luke called me. Anything I can do to help you and Mary Beth, it's truly my pleasure. I just wish the circumstances were a little more pleasant." Turning to her student who was still staring at the floor, she asked, "Mary Beth? Are you all right, honey?" Brooke could barely suppress the gasp in her throat when she saw the swelling and discoloration caused by the bruises on the girl's face. Opening her arms she said, "Oh, Mary Beth, sweetie. Poor baby."

"M-m-Miss Adler."

Anita Louise

The strength of the thin arms around her surprised Brooke.

"I can't go to school like this," Mary Beth cried. "What am I going to do?" Her tears had turned to sobs.

Brooke held her student tenderly, patting her back and smoothing her hair. "Don't you worry about school, Mary Beth. Right now the most important thing is you and your Mom are here, and you're safe. Everything's going to be all right." She turned to Shelly. "You're both going to be just fine. You can stay here with me as long as you need to. I've got plenty of room, and I'd love the company." She held the girl away from her slightly and used her finger to gently lift the child's chin. "Do you smell the cookies I baked for you?"

Mary Beth sniffed, "Yeah, I think so. You baked cookies? For us?"

"Well, the truth is they were already made up in the freezer. All I had to do was put them in the oven, but they're still warm. I have hot chocolate too, or whatever else you want to go with them. Sound good?"

"Okay. I guess. Mom?"

"Sure, honey. Let's just get our coats put away and we can all sit down in the kitchen for a little while." Shelly smiled weakly at Brooke. "You really didn't have to go to so much trouble."

"It's no trouble, Shell. Give me your coats, and I'll hang them up in the front closet." Brooke smiled and gave her friend's shoulders a squeeze. "It'll be a little like the sleepovers we used to have as kids. Is there more stuff in the car?"

Shelly shook her head. "No. Nothing right now. We thought we'd be going back home." She hesitated. "I guess

I'll have to go back there and get at least a few of our things tomorrow. I'm not really sure how to handle all this."

"It'll all work out, Shelly. Just give it time. Come on in the kitchen, and let's talk."

Mary Beth and her mother followed Brooke through the dining room toward the rear of the house.

"I really like your house, Miss Adler."

"Thanks, Mary Beth. I like it too. It's bigger than I need right now, but someday I hope to have a daughter just like you. Maybe a little brother or sister for her too. For now, I'm glad the two of you can help me fill up a couple of these empty rooms. There's a bedroom for each of you. I'll show you when we go upstairs."

As soon as they walked into the kitchen, Shelly commented on the flowers. "Wow! What a beautiful arrangement. I love Bird of Paradise. It's such an elegant flower."

"Thanks," Brooke replied. "They really are lovely, aren't they?"

Shelly raised her eyebrows in question. "Special guy?"

"Maybe. Too soon to tell. We can talk about that another time. Okay?"

"Sure. I didn't mean to pry," Shelly said.

"You're not prying, Shelly. In fact, it'll be nice to have a girlfriend to talk to."

"What about your sisters? You talk to *them*, don't you?"

"Of course! Gabby and I are super close. We talk all the time, but when it comes to men ... well, let's just say that's the area where we're probably the most different."

Anita Louise

"What about your younger sisters?" Shelly asked. "What were their names again?"

"Olivia and Whitney. I think they're actually almost closer to each other than Gab and me. They're less than two years apart in age, and they were surrounded by our brothers. I talk to both of them, of course, but we're not all that close. Other than Gabby, I think I'm closer with some of my brothers than I am to my other sisters. What about you, Shelly?"

"I'm an only child like Mary Beth. I never knew my real dad, and my step-dad died several years ago. Mom got remarried last year. She and her new husband retired to Arizona. Mary Beth and I see them a couple of times a year ... an occasional call on Sunday evening, that kind of thing. It must be great to have a big family like yours."

"Yeah. It is pretty great most of the time." Brooke looked over at Mary Beth who'd been listening while quietly munching cookies and sipping hot chocolate. "You okay, sweetie?"

"I guess so. Do I have to go to school tomorrow?" The look on the teen's bruised and swollen face was somewhere between panic and desperation.

Brooke stifled an unexpected chuckle, and somehow managed a serious tone when she said, "It's up to your mom. What do you think, Shelly?"

Shelly Silvers put her hand gently over her daughter's. "No, you don't have to go to school tomorrow. In fact, I'm going to have to call in to work tomorrow myself. There are a lot of things we've got to get settled."

"How am I *ever* going to be able to go back to school?" Mary Beth cried. "I can't go looking like *this*. I look like some kind of *freak!*"

"Shhh. Don't talk like that, Mary Beth," Shelly said. "Dr. Carter said your nose isn't broken. You're going to look just as beautiful as ever in a couple of weeks."

"A couple of *weeks?*" Dropping her head onto her arms folded on top of the table Mary Beth Silvers began to cry once again. "This is all my fault! I'm so sorry, Momma."

Shelly Silvers got up and put her arm around her daughter. "No it's not, Mary Beth. None of this is your fault."

"If I wouldn't have talked back to Daddy like that, none of this would have happened."

"Honey, it's okay," Shelly reassured her child. "Lots of teenagers talk back to their parents. You didn't do anything I didn't do when I was your age."

The girl looked up with tears running down her face. "I love you, Mommy." Mary Beth stood and wrapped her arms around her mother's neck.

It was almost an hour later by the time Brooke cleaned up the kitchen and crawled into bed. She'd had to practically force Shelly and Mary Beth out of the room.

"Let me clean up, Brooke," Shelly had insisted.

"Not this time, Shelly. You and Mary Beth have had a rough evening. Besides that there're still a few things in front of you that you're going to have to handle. They may not be all that easy either. Let me do this for you now, and you two get some rest."

"Thanks, Brooke. You'll never know how much this means to me ... to us." Shelly gave her friend a sincere hug.

Mary Beth was next. "Miss Adler, I always thought you were a great teacher. Now I know you're a great person inside and out."

Teacher and student hugged, and Brooke felt a bond was forged that would never be broken.

Brooke couldn't go to sleep right away. She needed to fill her mind with something more pleasant than the picture of a young girl recently beaten by her out of control father. She picked up the romance novel sitting next to her bed and continued her reading.

> *Constance Teasdale had arrived only two weeks earlier, after an arduous three month journey across the seas to Magnolia Plantation. Against her wishes, the wedding had taken place almost immediately. She felt fortunate to have been able to defer the consummation of their vows. Now, the heat and humidity of northern Georgia in July caused her batiste nightgown to cling to her bosom. As Constance pulled the fabric away from her breasts, she found herself wondering when he would insist upon the completion of their marital union. Thus far, theirs was only a titular relationship.*

Brooke sighed at the thought of "marital union." Her life as an adult female had held little romance thus far, and it'd been a very long time since she'd been intimate with a man. Marcus was the only male she'd allowed into her bed and into her heart. The memory still hurt, but oh, how she longed for a strong, loving relationship ... for the commitment of a marriage.

A few minutes later she put down her book and turned off the lamp next to her bed. She'd accomplished her goal. Brooke's imagination was filled with longing looks from a handsome man, more specifically one dark haired, gorgeous doctor, before she fell fast asleep.

It'd been a long time since Zack Carter had taken a woman out on a date. He hadn't been in a serious relationship since he split up with his fiancée. For the most part, he was celibate, but there were times when, as a man with needs, he just felt like he had no choice. So over the past several years, he'd managed to hook up with a good looking woman on occasion when he was out with the guys. *Well, at least their bodies were hot*, he recalled. And at the time, that was all he really cared about.

He'd never brought any of his conquests to his home. It was either go to their place or a hotel room. If he couldn't get the heck out of there whenever he was ready, forget it. The last thing in the world he wanted was to wake up in the morning with some strange woman in his bed. However, when he pictured waking up with an extremely attractive school teacher next to him it was entirely different. The idea kept getting better the more he thought about it.

It'd been so long since he'd gone out on a real date, he was almost nervous about it. There was only one person in the world he felt confident enough to call and ask a few questions. His mom.

Nancy Carter was the most amazing woman he'd ever known. Zack had just turned five and his brother Dylan

Anita Louise

was almost seven when she was widowed and left with two boys to raise. If it wasn't for the pictures his mother would often pore over with her boys, Zack would've had practically no memory of his father. He wasn't sure if the vague memories he had of the big, handsome man with a ready smile and a warm hug were real or simply created through the stories his mother shared.

Nancy Carter had shown Zack the meaning of unconditional love. There wasn't anything she wouldn't do, no sacrifice she wouldn't make to see to it her boys were taken care of. Without a shadow of a doubt, he knew he wouldn't be a doctor, if not for his mother's encouragement and belief in him. She'd also taught him to believe in himself. He'd learned to be patient by watching his mother's tolerance for his own missteps along the way. She was quick to praise and recognize his accomplishments, both big and small. Now he was a person who recognized and appreciated the positive actions he saw in others. Yes, Mom was the person he needed to speak with today.

She picked up after the first ring. "Zack! How wonderful to hear from you, sweetie."

"Hi, Mom. You sound great, as usual."

"Of course I am, honey. There's always so much to be grateful for, if we just look for it, isn't there?"

"Yes, there is, Mom. You keep telling me that, and you know, you're more often right than not. In fact, that's part of the reason I'm calling you."

"Oh, wonderful. There must be something new and exciting, or some*one* special and exciting in your life right now. Who or what is it?"

"It's a some*one*. Her name's Brooke, Brooke Adler."

"Brooke ... that's a lovely name, so peaceful and serene. It's been too long since you've had a special someone in your life, Zack. Do you think it's possible with Brooke?"

"It's really too soon to tell, Mom, but I did ask her out."

"I'm so happy to hear that. When and where? Tell me more. Please, tell me more. Do you have time to come over for a while? I'd love to see the look on your face when you talk about her. I'd get a whole lot better sense of how you feel and where this might be going if I could see you in person."

"I know, Mom, and I'd love to see you too, but I really don't have any time to spare at all. I'm taking her out tomorrow night for dinner and a movie. It's funny, in some ways she's a little bit like you."

"How so?" Nancy Carter asked.

"When I suggested a movie, she said, 'I don't do violence or scary.' She only agreed to a movie that was either a comedy or romance. Sound like anybody you know?" He chuckled.

"Humph. She sounds like a very intelligent young woman to me. Why would anyone want to put any more images of horror or violence than we're already subjected to in life into their minds? It's beyond my comprehension. We get more of what we focus on, so why in the world would anyone want more yucky stuff in their lives?"

"Yucky stuff, huh? Your scientific terminology is amazing, Mom."

"You know what I mean, young man," she said in mock sternness.

"I do, Mom."

Anita Louise

"I like this Brooke girl already," Nancy said. "Am I going to get to meet her soon?"

"Hopefully one of these days, but I really don't know how soon it might be."

"So why is it you called me, anyway, Zack?"

"You know, Mom, I think all I really needed was to hear your voice and to have you confirm exactly what I was already thinking."

"Zack?"

"What, Mom?"

"I love you, honey, and if Brooke's as smart as I'm already thinking she is, she's going to love you too."

"Whoa, whoa, whoa! Nobody said anything about *love*."

"Don't rule it out, sweetheart. Love is a precious gift. Grab it when it comes along and hang on tight. Enjoy it for as long as you can."

"It's a *date*, Mom. Just a date."

"We'll see. Are you working on Sunday?"

"Sure am. Why?"

"Well, let me know the next time you're *not* working, and you can come over for dinner. I'll invite Dylan and Kaylee too. If you want, you can bring Brooke. I'd love to meet her."

"Thanks, Mom, but I think it's definitely too early to be bringing her home to meet my mother, let alone my brother and his new bride too. After all, tomorrow will be our first *real* date."

"What do you mean by that? Have you already gone out with her?"

"Kinda," Zack replied. "We met for a drink down on Pearl Street, but quite honestly it didn't go all that well."

"How so?"

"Mom, I've got to go."

"Okay. I get it. I'm being too nosy. So sue me. All I want is for you to be happy, and this is the first time you've called me about a girl since ... well, you know."

"I know. If it gets more serious with Brooke, you'll be the first to know."

"Promise?"

"Yes, Mom. I promise. Really, I've got to go now."

"Okay, Zack. Thanks for calling. I love you, honey."

"Love you too, Mom. Bye."

"G'bye, son."

Zack smiled and shook his head after he hung up the phone. Leave it to Mom to invite the first girl he's dated in a million years over to a family dinner right off the bat. Brooke was definitely the kind of girl he'd be proud to bring home and introduce to his family, but it was simply too soon for anything like that. However, he did trust his mother's instincts, and so far Brooke was scoring pretty darn high on the Nancy Carter scale. It was a good sign.

Of course, there was no way he could tell his mother how much he wanted the pretty school teacher in his bed. That was also a good sign.

He'd been attracted to Brooke from the first moment he'd seen her in the hospital. Their eyes had locked, and there was an instant connection. And the kiss they'd shared sitting in the sun outside the West Flanders Brewing Company definitely warranted a repeat performance. Her initial response had been genuine and natural. She possessed an innate sensuality, yet she seemed totally unaware of how sexy her prim school teacher persona was to him. Zack was more than anxious to explore her hidden depths. He could hardly wait to taste her lips again, and to continue on to savor other even more delicious parts of her body.

He certainly didn't expect her to be the kind of girl he could take to bed on the first date. However, there was something to be said for the proverbial thrill of the chase. The wooing of Brooke Adler was a challenge Dr. Zackary Carter was looking forward to.

He was a generous lover, and it was his desire to give Brooke more pleasure than she'd ever before experienced. Her enjoyment was even more important to him than his own. He wasn't just interested in having sex with her. His plan was one of seduction.

Brooke Adler, you're going to love every minute of it. And so am I, he thought.

Chapter Eight

Brooke awoke to the aroma of freshly brewed coffee. It smelled delicious and made it easier than usual for her to roll out of bed. After slipping her feet into fuzzy slippers and wrapping herself in a comfortable robe, she followed the scent down to the kitchen.

"Ummm. That smells wonderful," Brooke said.

Shelly turned from the counter where she was standing at the sound of her hostess's voice. "I wasn't positive if you drank coffee in the morning or not, so I took a chance. There's hot water too, if you'd prefer tea."

"I do enjoy my afternoon tea, but in my opinion, mornings require coffee. Thanks." Brooke smiled at her friend as she poured herself a cup and added stevia, her favorite natural, no-calorie sweetener. "Mary Beth still asleep?"

"Yeah. Poor kid."

"Do you want to talk about it?" Brooke asked.

"There's not really a lot to say," Shelly replied. "You remember Nathan, don't you?"

Anita Louise

"I do, but the truth is I never knew him all that well. In fact, after you started dating him, I didn't see as much of *you* anymore either. I guess I just figured you two were so in love, there was no room left for anyone else."

"I thought so too in the beginning. After a while, not so much. It started to feel like he wanted to control me. Where was I going? Who was I going with? How long was I going to be gone?" Shelly brought her own cup of coffee over to the table and sat across from Brooke. "We'd end up arguing about it. We broke up several times, but he'd always be so sweet afterward. He used to write me these poems, apologizing for hurting me and telling me how much he really loved me." She smiled weakly and shrugged. "His poetry would never win any awards, but he seemed so sincere. Said I was the only one who'd ever really loved him, and he couldn't live without me. That kind of stuff."

"You were young," Brooke commented.

"And then I got pregnant with Mary Beth. Funny. At the time I thought having a baby would make everything better, but it didn't."

"What happened?"

"I learned later that when Nate was a kid, his dad used to smack him around. I guess it's pretty common for abused children to become abusers." Shelly shrugged. "It didn't start right away. I mean, at first he'd just yell and slam things around. I guess after a while that wasn't enough so he started throwing things. Somehow or another it went from slamming and throwing *things* around, to slamming and throwing *me* around. That's when I knew I had to get out, so I started stashing money away. Supporting Mary Beth and myself on a waitress's salary wasn't going to cut it. I started taking online classes a few years ago. Plus I was able to test out of some of the basics. That saved me a ton of time and money."

"Good for you, Shelly. You should be proud of yourself."

"How can I be proud of myself? I should have gotten Mary Beth out of there before he had a chance to hurt her. It's one thing for him to take out his anger or whatever it is on me, but something else entirely to take it out on his own daughter. I totally don't get how he could possibly hurt his own child."

"I don't understand it either, Shelly, but unfortunately, it happens all the time. Give yourself some credit."

"I almost made it. My student teaching will be the last hurdle. I should have my degree at the end of next semester. The plan was to have a good paying job *before* leaving Nate." Shelly shook her head. "Why couldn't he just leave her alone for a few more months? Wasn't it enough he hurt me? Why'd he have to go after Mary Beth?"

When she looked up, Brooke saw the tears glittering in Shelly's eyes. Reaching across the table, Brooke covered her friend's hand with her own. "It's going to be all right, Shelly. And I want you and Mary Beth to stay here with me. A few weeks, a few months ... longer if need be."

"Oh Brooke, that's so kind of you, but we can't impose on you that way."

"Nonsense. Having the two of you here is no imposition. I grew up in a house filled with people. Actually, I've been a little lonely rambling around in this place all by myself. You'll be doing me a favor by staying here with me."

Anita Louise

Shelly smiled as her tears spilled onto her cheeks. "I ... I don't know what to say."

"Just say, 'We'd love to stay with you, Brooke.' That's all I want to hear."

Shelly did as her friend requested. "We'd love to stay with you, Brooke."

Brooke stood up decisively. "Perfect! Now that's all settled. I have to get ready for school." She paused. "What grade do you want to teach, Shell?"

"Middle school. Math and science. I always loved those subjects back in middle and high school. Teaching is the only career where I figured I could do something I really enjoy and get paid for it. Next semester is my last one. It's my student teaching. I'm really looking forward to it."

"Do you know where you'll be doing your internship yet?" Brooke asked.

"No, not yet. Hopefully, it'll be a middle school somewhere here in Boulder."

"Hey, wouldn't it be cool if your internship was at Summit? We could ride to school together!"

"Are you kidding? That would be super fantastic." Shelly paused. "In fact, tonight before I go to sleep, I'm going to start visualizing us riding to work together. It would be absolutely wonderful to work at the same school as you, Brooke. Whether you know it or not, even though we're the same age, you've always been a role model for me. Being around you and your family was always so nice."

"Thanks for the compliment, Shelly. I got awfully lucky to be born into the Adler family. They're a pretty special group of people."

"They certainly are."

Bad Case of Lovin' You

"By the way, I don't know if it would help or not, but if you need a recommendation or reference or anything, I'll be happy to give you one."

"Oh Brooke, you're the best. I just don't know how to thank you enough."

"Just keep doing what you're doing. Take care of yourself and that beautiful daughter of yours. Okay?"

"You bet." Pushing her chair back, Shelly walked around the table, and gave Brooke a heartfelt hug.

Nathan Silvers woke up in a very bad mood. He had a terrible headache, and his stomach was empty. He needed to eat. Food always helped after a night of heavy drinking.

"Shelly! I'm hungry. How come I don't smell my breakfast cooking?"

He listened for the sounds of his wife scrambling around like she always did when he told her to do something. Silence.

Where the hell is that bitch?

When he looked over at the side of the bed where his wife should've been, it was empty. That wasn't all that unusual. Seemed like half the time that worthless piece of crap for a wife slept on the couch. He couldn't remember the last time they'd had sex. Plus she'd turned into a real ballbuster lately.

She practically went ballistic when I let that whiney little brat Mary Beth have it last night. Shit, a man deserves respect in his own house, doesn't he? There's no way some snotty teenager's gonna smart off to me and get away with it. She'll know better than to talk back to me next time, by God.

Anita Louise

His stupid ass wife Shelly had wanted to take the girl to emergency. He'd told her it was totally unnecessary. Hell, back when he was in middle school, he'd walked around with a fractured bone in his arm for a couple of days before the school nurse finally insisted he get an x-ray. He'd been knocked down by his dad so many times he'd lost count. But the beatings ended when Nate got into high school. By then, he was as big as his old man, too big for his father to smack him around anymore without getting as good as he gave.

He wasn't like his old man. That son of a bitch just whacked his wife and kids around for the fun of it. Nate never *meant* to hurt his wife or his daughter. It was just that they made him so damn mad! If they'd just do like he told them ... if the both of them would just learn to keep their goddamn mouths shut, he wouldn't have to shut their mouths for them.

So he'd smacked the girl around a little bit last night ... no big deal. *The little brat got what she deserved. I'll bet the damn bitch went ahead and took the little piece of shit to the hospital anyway ... even after I told her not to. Can't' even go to sleep in your own damn house. Probably should've tied their asses down so I could get some friggin' rest. Goddamn it! Don't they know going to the damn hospital could land me in a heap of trouble? F***in' kids today. Seems like they can get away with talking any way they want to their parents. Then the minute you do something to shut their damn mouths, it's you that's in trouble instead of them.*

He walked into the kitchen. Eight o'clock. Shit. He should've been at the plant an hour ago. Opening the refrigerator, he picked up a gallon of milk and slugged down a few gulps. There were still a half a dozen donuts left over from yesterday sitting on the counter, so he shoved one in his mouth.

Looking down at his chest he brushed the crumbs off his shirt. There were a couple of spots on it, but it still looked okay. Even though he hadn't bothered to change his clothes before hitting the sack last night, there really wasn't time to do anything about it now. He was going to catch hell as it was for being late again.

As he walked out of the house, he slammed the front door ... hard. Then he hopped into his truck. Silver's Silverado. It was black and it was a *bad ass* vehicle. He smiled. Man, he loved that thing! There was nothing like flying down a dirt road on a hot summer night with the windows rolled down and the radio blasting. He took good care of his truck, and it *never* talked back to him. Chuckling at his own joke, he turned the key in the ignition. The engine roared to life. He'd just thrown it into reverse and put his arm across the back of the seat when he looked out the rearview mirror.

Shit. Cops. He couldn't go anywhere with their goddamn cruiser right behind him so he put it in park. With the motor still running he rolled down his window. "Morning, officer. I'm running a little late. Gotta get to work. You mind moving your car outta the way?"

The police officer looked at him sternly. "Nathan Silvers?"

"Yeah, that's me, but like I said, I'm running late for work. Can we do this another time?"

"Mr. Silvers, do you know why I'm here?"

"Nope. No idea." Nate thought of a funny joke he'd heard and chuckled. "You sellin' tickets to the policeman's ball?" The officer didn't say a word. Nate grinned and continued. "You're supposed to say, 'That's the firemen's ball. Policemen don't have balls.' Get it?"

"Mr. Silvers, this is no joke. Are your wife and daughter in the house?"

*Damn it. Those f***in' bitches again.* "No, sir. Neither of them."

"Where are they, then?"

"Uh. I guess my wife's at work and Mary Beth's at school."

"You're not sure?"

"Pretty sure. Yeah." Nate looked at his watch. "Yeah. It's past time for Mary Beth to be in school. Shelly works all kinds of hours. She must be at work. I don't know where else she'd be."

"Mr. Silvers, we'd like you to come to the station and answer a few questions."

"Questions about what?"

"Your wife and daughter." The policeman showed no emotion. "We'd like to ask you some questions about your wife and daughter."

"What the hell is this? Has something happened to my wife ... my kid?"

"Are you going to come down to the station willingly, Mr. Silvers, or do we have to get a warrant?"

"A *warrant!* Are you kidding me? A warrant for what? I ain't done nothin'."

"Mr. Silvers, this would be a lot easier and maybe save you some embarrassment if you'd cooperate. I'd hate to have to come back here and cuff you in front of your neighbors."

Bad Case of Lovin' You

"This is f***ing bullshit! Look, I gotta go to work. If you want me to come down to the friggin' station when I get off, I will. Okay?"

"What time can we expect you, Mr. Silvers?"

"I get off at three. I can probably be there by about four. Okay?"

"That'll be fine, Mr. Silvers. If we don't see you at four, we *will* be back here with a warrant. Is that clear?"

"Whatever. Yeah, sure. Now will you get your damn cop car outta my driveway so I can get to work?"

The officer tipped his cap. "See you at four, Mr. Silvers." With that the man in blue walked back to his cruiser and left.

When Mary Beth Silvers walked into the kitchen, she saw her mom and her teacher hugging each other. She'd looked in the mirror before coming downstairs and the face looking back at her was pretty horrific. Her swollen nose was covered with a metal brace and tape crossed her cheeks and forehead. Both of her eyes were black and blue. Her right eye had red lines of broken blood vessels running across the white and was barely open. Thankfully it was the worst of her two, normally beautiful, blue eyes.

The two women broke apart and looked at the teen. Her mom spoke first. "Good news, Mary Beth. Brooke wants us to stay here with her at least until next semester's over. Then hopefully, I can get a teaching job. I might just have to sub until next fall, but who knows, maybe something more permanent will come up before then."

"That's great, Mom." Mary Beth's response was less than enthusiastic. She stood motionless, looking at the floor.

Anita Louise

Brooke looked at Shelly and moved toward the teen. Putting her arm around the girl's shoulder Brooke said, "Good morning, Mary Beth. I hope you slept okay. I've got to run upstairs and get ready to go to school. You and your mom should talk. Help yourself to whatever you want to eat."

After Brooke left the room, Shelly motioned to the chair recently vacated by her friend. "Come on, Mary Beth, sit down. Do you want a glass of milk or some juice?"

"Yes please. I'll have some juice." The teen sat down and laid her head down on her arms.

Placing the glass of orange juice in front of her daughter, Shelly gently squeezed her child's shoulders and said, "Everything's going to be all right, sweetie."

As much as she appreciated her mother's positivity, the teen was angry and afraid. She pushed the comforting arm away. "How can you say that? Everything's *not* okay, and saying that it *is* doesn't change a thing!"

Shelly moved to the chair next to her daughter. After sitting quietly for a few moments, she responded calmly. "You have every right to be upset, Mary Beth, and I can't blame you. The fact is there's nothing we can do to change the past. What's done is done. We just have to deal with it, and do our best to create a better future ... a future where the kind of thing that happened last night never happens again."

"But what about Daddy?"

"What your dad did was wrong, honey. You know it. I know it. And as much as he might not want to admit it, your father knows it too. When someone does something he knows is wrong, but does it anyway, there's a price to pay. There's always a consequence to whatever we do. Good actions bring good consequences, and bad actions bring bad consequences. That's just the way life works."

"I don't want Dad to go to jail. He didn't mean to hurt me this bad. He just lost his temper."

"I'm sure you're right. He *did* lose his temper, and he probably *didn't* mean to hurt you. But the fact is he *did* hurt you. And *no one* has the right to do what he did ... to you or anyone else for that matter."

"What's going to happen?" Mary Beth asked.

"I don't really know, baby. What I *do* know is everything happens for a reason. And even when bad things happen we can look for the good. There's an old saying, 'Life is ten percent what happens and ninety percent what you *do* with what happens.' We're going to find some good in this whole situation and make the best of it we possibly can. You okay with that?"

"I guess so. What about school? Please don't make me go to school looking like this. I *can't*. I just can't, Mom." She was practically crying.

"Well, you certainly don't have to go to school today, and tomorrow's Saturday so you've got another couple of days off after that. Let's think about it. And we can talk about it some more over the weekend. Okay?"

"Okay, Mom." The teen thought for a moment. "What about my stuff?"

"We're going to have to get our things from the house and bring them over here. Your dad's going to be pretty upset about us moving. I'm not exactly sure how to handle all that yet. That's one of the things we're going to have to deal with today." Shelly stood once again and put her arm around her daughter's shoulders. Planting a kiss on the top of her

Anita Louise

child's head, Shelly repeated her earlier statement. "Everything's going to be okay, honey. I promise you."

This time Mary Beth stood and turned into her mother's arms. "I love you, Mom."

"I love you too, honey. So very much."

Brooke called her brother on her way to school. "Hey, Luke, it's Brooke. Hope I'm not calling too early."

"Hi, Sis. I'm up. Everything okay with Shelly and her daughter?"

"Everything's fine. I'm really glad you called me last night. In fact, I told Shelly this morning they can stay as long as they like. As much as I love my house, after living at Mom and Dad's all those years with tons of people around, it's been kind of lonely being the only one there. I think I'm going to like having their company."

"That's great, Brookie. Let me know if there's anything I can do to help."

"There's nothing in particular I need," Brooke said, "but I did hear Shelly and Mary Beth talking this morning about getting their personal belongings from their old place. What if they run into Nathan? Couldn't that be a problem?"

"Yeah, it could be. I know for a fact we sent a car over there this morning. Nathan Silvers was majorly pissed off, but he's supposed to come in voluntarily at four this afternoon for a little chat. If not, there'll be a warrant issued, and we'll go out and arrest him. You can't go around beating up your kid these days and expect to get away with it. It's bad enough how many wives *and husbands* end up being the brunt of their spouse's anger and frustration. If the spouse won't press charges, there's not much we can do in those cases. But when it's a kid that's another story. I could probably have a car meet them over at the house. Why don't you have Shelly give me a call and let me know what time they're going over there, and I'll set it up."

"Thanks, Luke. That makes me feel a whole lot better. Hey, you're coming to Aaron and Jane's party next weekend, aren't you?"

"Wouldn't miss it," Luke replied.

"I think I'll see if Shelly and Mary Beth want to come."

"They might not want to, Brooke. It's going to be a while before the girl's face is back to normal. Besides, I don't know if Shelly's going to feel like partying that soon. It'd be nice to see her under better circumstances though."

"You're right, but I'm going to ask anyway. If they want to ... great. If not, that's okay too."

"Sounds good, Sis. Talk to you later."

Brooke smiled as she hung up. *He's such a good man,* she thought, *wise beyond his years.*

Her next phone call was to Shelly Silvers. Brooke told her friend about the police going to Nathan's house. Brooke also repeated Luke's suggestion of police protection while Shelly was picking up their things. Shelly agreed it was a wise precaution. Brooke felt that moving Shelly and Mary Beth's belongings was another positive step in them making a clean break to a new and better life.

Almost before she knew it, Brooke was walking into Summit Middle School. She thought to herself, *Oh my gosh, the last twenty-four hours have been crazy! Was it really only yesterday morning I got those beautiful flowers?* It was a relief to allow her mind to drift to the most pleasant of

Anita Louise

thoughts ... those of the very kind and very handsome Dr. Zackary Carter.

It wasn't every day you met a man as good looking as Zack who wasn't also full of himself. In fact, Zack seemed to be just the opposite. He seemed to always be thinking about someone *other* than himself. Maybe that was why everyone genuinely liked him. He had a way of really listening and people felt understood as a result. Obviously he didn't just accept things at face value. Otherwise he'd never have bothered to contact her again considering how she'd behaved after that mind blowing kiss. Rather than writing her off as some sort of an ice queen, he'd not only sent her flowers , but had asked her out on a *real* date.

Dinner and a movie ... the classic first date. Brooke sighed. *What am I going to wear? Will he kiss me again?*

The sound of the bell announcing first hour forced her to come down from the clouds and plant her feet firmly on the ground of Summit Middle School. Once the students started moving through the halls, Brooke had no choice but to keep her mind focused on her classes.

It was third hour, and she was taking role. When the name Mary Beth Silvers came up, Brooke knew there would be no response. Her mind drifted back to all the craziness happening outside of school. She wondered how her student was dealing with the situation. Having an almost idyllic childhood herself, it was difficult to imagine what Mary Beth might be feeling.

Maybe I can give Shelly a quick call during my lunch hour and see how everything's going. Right now, however, Brooke was in the middle of a typical day at school. There was no time for anything but her responsibilities as a teacher.

Chapter Nine

Dr. Zackary Carter sipped a cup of hot coffee while enjoying the view from the sliding glass door to his deck. A ring of snow circled the tops of the majestic peaks in the distance. Farther down, the slopes were blanketed with green pines and bare limbs. It wouldn't be long before spring would fill the stark branches with blossoms and leaves.

He felt fortunate to have the next couple of days off work after last evening's events. There was no way he would ever understand how anyone, let alone a parent, could hurt an innocent child. Mary Beth Silvers wasn't an infant or even a toddler. She was a young girl on the verge of womanhood, yet she *was* still very much a child. Shelly Silvers clearly loved her daughter. It seemed she'd been doing her best to protect the teen. Zack deduced the husband had been abusing his wife for quite some time. However, once the man moved to harming the child, tolerating the intolerable was, apparently, no longer an option.

Bad Case of Lovin' You

Fate had a funny way of working. Zack and Luke Adler had met on the several sad occasions when Zack's profession forced him to call in the police. The relationship he and Luke developed was one of mutual respect. Zack always felt like, under different circumstances, he and Luke might become good friends. Now that he knew Luke was related to Brooke Adler, that possibility might be greatly increased.

The sudden flash of desire at the thought of Brooke Adler was unexpected. Zack reflected back on how she'd instinctively responded to his kiss. It wasn't until her realization of where they were and what they were doing that she stiffened, withdrew and ran. *Maybe she's one of those women who needs to give herself "permission" to feel sexual.*

He did his best to remind himself it was only a kiss. One that was abruptly cut short by the recipient, but his body refused to listen. For now he would go to the gym and relieve some of his energy by lifting some extra heavy weights.

Zack had plans for Brooke Adler. When he picked her up for their date tomorrow night, they'd start where they'd left off. This time he'd make sure the setting was much more private. Enough to keep her focus on him and the sensation of his lips on hers, instead of their surroundings. Hopefully, his spare time would soon be filled with interesting afternoons and evenings with a very beautiful and innately sexy school teacher. And that was something he was definitely looking forward to.

Shelly Silvers made sure her daughter was following the prescribed procedures for her injury. Dr. Carter had given Mary Beth a prescription for pain relief. In addition, he'd instructed them to apply ice around the girl's eye area in ten minute intervals for the next twenty-four to forty-eight hours. When she was resting, several pillows were used to make sure Mary Beth's head remained elevated. The pillows helped to limit swelling by keeping blood flow to the area at a minimum. Getting plenty of rest was emphasized. That was why Shelly decided her daughter should stay in bed instead of going back to the house to retrieve their belongings. At first Mary Beth was reluctant to agree. Not wanting to be seen in public was the deciding factor in the teen's going along with the plan.

After Brooke left, Shelly made sure to tidy up the kitchen. By the time she finished, the already neat space was totally spic and span. When she found a dust cloth and furniture polish under the sink, her next project was to make sure the living room sparkled. Rugs were shaken. Floors and furniture were polished to a high gloss. The guest bathroom also received her attention once she and her daughter had taken their showers.

It was a little after noon by the time she finished. Shelly smiled as she looked around Brooke's lovely home. Suddenly her smile faded when she second guessed herself. *Brooke's not going to think I did all this because her place wasn't clean enough, is she? Maybe I should've asked her first before doing all this. The last thing in the world I want to do is offend her after all she's done for me and Mary Beth.*

Shelly's thoughts were interrupted by the sound of her cell phone. Seeing Brooke Adler as the caller was a relief. "Hi Brooke. I'm so glad you called. How's your day going?"

Bad Case of Lovin' You

"That's what I was about to ask you, Shelly. Everything all right with you and Mary Beth?"

"As good as can be expected. She's resting right now. I finally talked her into staying here while I go back to the house and get our stuff. Luke's going to have a squad car meet me there in about an hour. I'm really glad you suggested it. I was pretty nervous to go over there by myself. I know I'm going to have to face Nate sooner or later, but right now I'm just not ready for it."

"It was Luke's suggestion," Brooke said, "so if you want to thank somebody, thank him. I hope you're not trying to do too much. This whole thing has got to be a lot of stress on you too."

"It is, but I handle pressure better when I keep myself busy. In fact, I'm glad you brought it up. I hope you don't mind, but I did a little extra cleaning around your house. I mean, it already looked great. I just gave it a little extra polish. I hope that's okay." Shelly waited expectantly for Brooke's reply.

"Of course it's okay, Shell. You certainly didn't have to, but it's very much appreciated. I keep the place picked up pretty well, but housework has never been one of my favorite activities. Anytime the urge to clean strikes you, just go right ahead. I want you and Mary Beth to totally make yourself at home. Mi casa, su casa."

"Thanks, Brookie. There's no way I can ever show my appreciation enough for all you've done for me and Mary Beth." Shelly was fighting the lump in her throat signaling she was about to cry.

"You're more than welcome. I'd like to think if our roles were reversed, you'd do the same for me. Even though we lost touch for a number of years, I've always considered you a good friend."

"Me too, Brooke. Wish we could have reconnected under better circumstances, but ..."

"I'm just glad we reconnected. It's like the old saying, 'Every cloud has a silver lining.' Having a dear friend like you back in my life is a huge blessing. Anyway, I just wanted to give you a quick call during my lunch break. Gotta go now. I'll see you this afternoon."

"Yes you will, Brooke, and I'm going to have a nice dinner ready for you too."

"That'll be great. Thanks."

As soon as she hung up the phone, Shelly went to check on her daughter. Mary Beth was lying on the bed just staring into space. "You okay, honey?"

Mary Beth shrugged ever so slightly before responding, "Yeah. I guess so."

Sitting on the edge of the bed next to her child, Shelly stroked the hair on her daughter's head gently. "It's going to be okay, sweetie. I know it doesn't feel like it right now, but everything's going to work out. We can't always see it when we're smack dab in the middle of the mess, but God is good all the time. He can make a way even when it looks like there is no way. Our job is to have faith and trust."

"You say that kind of stuff all the time, Mom, but where's it gotten you? Your situation isn't a whole lot better than mine ... other than the fact you don't have a broken nose and a couple of black eyes." The girl sniffed and looked at her mother bleakly.

Shelly smiled. "Believe it or not, I'm actually quite happy. Don't get me wrong, I *never* wanted to see you get hurt. But the truth is things haven't been all that good with me and your dad for a long time now. That's why I've been going to school, but not letting your father know about it. Sometimes it makes people feel better about themselves if they think someone else is worse off than they are. Your dad never finished college. Whenever I talked about getting a teaching degree, he seemed to find a way to talk me out of it. Finally, I just *knew* it was something I needed to do for myself, no matter what anyone else thought."

"Don't you love Daddy anymore, Mom?"

"Your daddy will always hold a special place in my heart, baby girl. If it wasn't for him, I wouldn't have *you*. And you're the best thing that's ever happened to me in my entire life." She paused before continuing. "You going to be okay on your own for a while? I've got to go and get our things, and I'd like for us to have things organized before Brooke gets home."

"I'll be fine, Mom. I'm not a baby, you know." The resurgence of her daughter's teenage surliness was almost good to see. It was a sign she was slowly, but surely returning to normal.

"I know you're not a baby. But no matter how old you get, you're always going to be *my* baby, so you might as well get used to it." Shelly hugged her daughter gently before leaving the room. From down the hall she called to her daughter. "Brooke's going to bring your books and assignments home with her today, so you'll be able to stay current with your work."

Mary Beth's sarcastic, "Oh *great,*" put a smile on Shelly's face.

It only took a few minutes before Shelly was in her car on the way to her future ex's home. She hadn't filed for divorce yet, but had definitely made up her mind to do that as soon as her finances would allow.

No doubt, Nathan would try his old tricks of profuse apologies, gifts and poems in an effort to get her to change her mind. It wasn't going to work this time. She'd threatened to leave before, after he'd taken out whatever was bothering him on her. Now that he'd extended his violence to their daughter, there was no going back. Shelly still hoped Nathan would do something about his out of control temper. In addition to ruining their marriage, it got him into trouble in other areas of life as well.

When Shelly arrived at her former residence, there was a police car waiting in the drive. She pulled in and opened the garage door with her remote, parking her ten-year-old Volvo wagon near the entrance. She was grateful for her vehicle. It had over a hundred thousand miles on it, but still looked good and ran like a top. Shelly was glad to see that the officer who'd been sent to her soon-to-be ex's was tall and muscular ... just in case Nathan showed up. Her husband might not be the sharpest knife in the drawer, but he wasn't foolish enough to mess with a policeman. Especially when the officer was younger, bigger and stronger than him.

"Good afternoon, ma'am. I'm Officer Montgomery. I'll stay right here in the drive until you've finished gathering your things. Let me know if you need any assistance."

"Thank you so much, Officer Montgomery. I'll do this as quickly as I can."

Once inside the house, Shelly gathered together every piece of luggage she could find. Starting with Mary Beth's room, she moved her daughter's belongings from dresser drawers to suitcases. Each suitcase was stuffed to the point where Shelly had to sit on the top to close them. Since she hadn't thought about bringing along any boxes, garbage bags served to hold pictures, trinkets and other items from the walls and other surfaces. With every load she moved from the house to her car, it felt as if a burden was being lifted from her shoulders.

Once Mary Beth's room was emptied, Shelly moved on to the master bedroom. It was strange to walk in and see all of her husband's things lying about. Picking up after him would be a chore she'd gladly leave behind. It was almost as if he was deliberately sloppy. Early in their marriage she'd told him how she liked things neat and organized. His tone had been mocking and the look in his eye belligerent. He threw his dirty t-shirt on the floor and scoffed, "I do too, so make sure you keep my things picked up."

After packing all her clothing she looked around the room. Her wedding picture stood on top of one of the dressers. It seemed like an eternity since she'd looked that young or that happy. When she'd told Nathan she was pregnant, his first response had been to encourage her to get an abortion. It'd been a pleasant surprise when he'd asked her to marry him, after she refused to destroy the life growing inside her. She'd believed once they were married and had a child together, they would grow closer.

Unfortunately, that was not the case. Nathan seemed to resent everything. He didn't like his job. He didn't like their apartment. He didn't like the fact she was pregnant. When she'd tried to get him to put his hand on her growing stomach to feel the child moving inside her, he'd screamed at her, "I don't want to touch you. You look like a fat cow!"

Although their first few years weren't idyllic, Shelly was committed to making their marriage work. While Mary Beth was an infant, Nathan was earning enough money to allow Shelly to stay at home with her baby. The only jobs she could find didn't pay enough to justify her working anyway. As her own little girl grew from infancy to a toddler, Shelly brought in a little extra money by watching another child in her home. That ended the day after the parents were late picking up their daughter. Nathan had come home to two crying babies, and one of them wasn't even his.

Once Mary Beth was old enough to be put to bed and stay asleep for the night, Shelly felt comfortable working afternoons as a waitress. Nathan was home most evenings so they didn't have to pay for a babysitter. Shelly always made sure Mary Beth was well fed and sleeping soundly before she'd leave. It would practically break her heart when she'd come home to find her husband passed out on the couch with the television blaring, while her little girl lay in her room crying.

Nathan's drinking had increased gradually over the years. He'd gone from a couple of beers a night to downing a six pack and then even more. After that he'd started drinking vodka. He chose it because he thought the booze couldn't be detected on his breath as easily as most other liquors.

Shelly wasn't sure when his drinking had gone from excessive to totally out of control. All she knew for sure was he'd gotten to the point where he was drunk more often than he was sober. As his drunkenness increased, so had his abusiveness. She'd been listening to his verbal abuse for years. But when he started using her as his personal punching bag, she knew it was time to get out. That was when she'd started to devise her escape plan.

If only I could have kept him away from Mary Beth for a few more months. I was so close to having everything set up just the way I planned!

She shook her head and then shrugged resignedly. She'd just thrown the last of her things into the back seat of her Volvo. After much deliberation, Shelly finally decided to take her wedding picture with her. It wasn't that she really wanted it. She just didn't want to leave any part of herself at Nathan's house. As far as the household furnishings went, he could keep them. They were all hand-me-downs or expedient purchases from thrift stores anyway. She'd decided the next time she moved into her own place, every piece was either going to be brand new or chosen carefully for its classic beauty and usefulness.

It'd taken Shelly more than three hours to pack and load up her car. Officer Montgomery had been patiently waiting the whole time. Just as she was thinking, *Thank God I didn't need police protection*, she heard the familiar sound of Nathan's souped up truck. He pulled into the driveway behind her car and jumped out.

"Hey! What's going on here?" Nathan shouted.

Officer Montgomery placed his body between Shelly and her husband. At the same time, the officer placed his hand on his pistol. "You Mr. Silvers?"

"I sure as hell am, and this is *my house.*" He looked at Shelly with fire in his eyes. "What the hell have you got in that piece of crap car of yours?"

The policeman spoke up. "Mrs. Silvers has only been removing her personal belongings from the premises. I believe she was just about finished. Am I right, Mrs. Silvers?"

"Yes, Officer Montgomery. I've got everything I need, and I'm ready to go. If you'll please ask Mr. Silvers to move his vehicle, I'd like to leave now."

"Go where?" Nate Silvers snarled. "Where the hell are you going to go, Shelly? You *know* you've got *nowhere* to go. So you might as well haul all that junk of yours back in the house where it belongs. You're my *wife. Remember?*"

Ignoring her husband, Shelly moved to get into her car. Nathan lunged and grabbed her arm.

"I *said* you ain't going *nowhere,*" Nathan screamed." Now get your ass back in the house!"

As Shelly struggled to remove herself from her husband's grip, she heard Officer Montgomery's voice. "Mr. Silvers, take your hands *off* Mrs. Silvers. Get back in your truck and move it out of the way. Your wife is ready to go, and she's leaving *now*. I suggest you do as requested."

Nathan's face was red and he was breathing heavily. "Do you mean to tell me she can come in *my house* and take whatever she damn well pleases? What about *my rights?* Don't I have something to say about it?"

The officer responded calmly. "She only took her personal belongings, Mr. Silvers."

"How the hell do you know that? Huh? Did you watch her every minute? How do you know she didn't rob me blind?"

"Mr. Silvers, if there's anything missing of value you can make a report. Once we have it, we'll look into it."

"Make a report? This is *my* f---ing house! You ought to be arresting this bitch instead of sitting here watching her take all this stuff out of my house. Look at her goddamn car. It's *loaded!*"

Shelly knew better than to attempt to talk to Nate. Trying to reason with a man who was totally out of control was pointless. Doing her best to ignore him, she got into her car and locked the doors.

When Nathan reached for the car door handle, her concentration was so focused, she barely flinched. Blocking out whatever epithets her husband may have been screaming, Shelly started her car. Keeping her hands on the steering wheel, she waited as calmly as possible.

Within minutes she heard the screeching of tires as Nathan backed out of the driveway and sped off. Officer Montgomery knocked on her window and motioned for her to roll it down. Doing as requested, she extended her hand through the opening. "Thanks so much for being here."

"I'm glad I was here, Mrs. Silvers. I'll be putting this in my report. I take it your husband doesn't know where you're staying."

"No. He doesn't."

"I think it's best you keep it that way, Mrs. Silvers."

"You're right, Officer Montgomery. I totally agree, and I plan to do exactly that. Thanks again."

"No problem, ma'am. Happy to be of service."

Nathan Silvers was very careful to keep his distance as he followed his wife's old Volvo.

If that bitch thinks she can just walk out on me like that with no consequences, she's even more stupid than I *thought. Next time I see her I'll make sure there're no f***in' cops in the way.*

Chapter Ten

When Brooke walked into her house she was greeted by the aroma of what was, most likely, a delicious meal simmering on the stove. A fresh pot of coffee along with what appeared to be a batch of homemade cookies sat on the kitchen counter.

No wonder men enjoy having a stay-at-home wife. I could get used to this. Lifting the plastic wrap from the plate of cookies, she grabbed one and took a bite. *Yum! Oatmeal raisin ... and they're still warm.*

"Shelly? Mary Beth? Where are you two?"

Brooke heard the sound of feet running quickly down the stairs. A few seconds later, Shelly rushed through the kitchen door.

"Hi, Brooke. I didn't hear you come in."

Covering her mouth, which was filled with delicious sweetness, Brooke replied, "You're spoiling me, Shell. And if you keep feeding me goodies like this when I get home, I'm going to be forced to buy a whole new wardrobe ... in a larger size."

Shelly's smile faded. "Oh, I'm sorry, Brooke. I should have known you wouldn't want fattening snacks in the house. I promise I won't do it again."

"Oh no you don't. You better promise me you *will* do this again. Just not every day. Next time, you can show me your terrific cookie recipe. Maybe we can bake together on a Saturday or Sunday afternoon. Then I can take whatever the three of us don't devour over the weekend to school with me on Monday. That way the temptation will be gone, and I'll get brownie points with the staff." She gave her friend a big smile and surveyed the sparkling clean kitchen. "The place looks great. Did you have time to go over to Nathan's and get your things?"

"Sure did. And it's a good thing Luke suggested having an officer there. Nate showed up not two minutes after I put the last load in the back seat of the Volvo."

"Yikes. How did that go?"

"Not so good. As you might expect, Nate was not happy. Of course, he accused me of taking *his* things. Honestly, Brooke, I didn't *want* anything out of that house except Mary Beth's and my personal belongings. It's funny, The only thing I felt was 'ours,' Nate's and mine, was our wedding picture. I almost didn't take it, but I didn't want to leave anything there to remind him of me. Not that he'll really miss me anyway. I just didn't want to leave any piece of *me* there."

"Oh Shelly. I wish I could have been there with you ... for moral support if nothing else."

"I'm glad you weren't, Brooke. If you'd have been there, he might figure out Mary Beth and I are staying here with you. Now that we're out of there, I feel a real sense of relief."

Mary Beth came down from her room and joined them for cookies. There was milk for the teen and tea for the adults. Between sips and bites the three discussed when Mary Beth would need to return to school. Brooke brought home all of the teen's books and assignments for the following week. A few tears and twenty minutes later, all three agreed to Mary Beth being "home schooled" until it was possible to cover her bruises with make-up, probably about two weeks. Once that decision was made, Brooke brought up something else she'd been wanting to discuss with her friend.

"You remember my brother Aaron, don't you, Shelly?"

"Of course I do. He was only a year ahead of us in high school. Very good looking too, as I recall. Of course, every single person in your family is so attractive they could be a model." Shelly paused. "Just curious. Did anyone end up going that route?"

"As a matter of fact, Whitney, the baby of the family, has been modeling since she was fifteen. She's done really well ... been on several magazine covers over the years. Now she's twenty-six. Not long ago she started her own modeling agency. It's already off to a good start. She's a pretty smart cookie. I'm sure she'll be successful regardless of what she does."

"I'm not a gambler, but I'd be willing to bet on that. From the looks of it, success must be in the Adler family genes."

Anita Louise

"I don't know about that, Shell. Being a school teacher isn't exactly what most people would call the pinnacle of success."

"Not so fast, my friend. That all depends on your definition of success. In my book, if you're doing what you love, you're successful. Money's nice, and we all need to feel secure, but how much you get paid isn't most important as far as I'm concerned. Family. Love. Happiness. Those things are on the top of my list."

"You're right, Shelly. I totally agree. Thanks for the reminder. I know it's only been a short while, but I'm really enjoying having the two of you here." Brooke reached out and grabbed a hand of each of her guests and gave them a sincere squeeze and a smile.

"Thanks, we're glad to be here," Shelly replied and Mary Beth quietly nodded her agreement. The trio sat in silent gratitude for a few moments. Then Shelly tapped the heel of her hand to her forehead. "I'm such a doofus. You were getting ready to say something about your brother Aaron, and I totally got you off track. Sorry about that. So what's up with Aaron these days?"

"Actually, he's getting married," Brooke said.

"That's great!" Shelly replied. "I'm so happy for him. What's his fiancée like?"

"Jane's wonderful. She was my brother Connor's counselor. About a month and a half ago Connor's car was in the shop. He sweet talked Jane into driving him up to my folks' house for their fortieth wedding anniversary celebration. That's where Jane met Aaron, but the story gets even more interesting."

"Really? What happened?"

"You remember where my folks live, right?

"I sure do," Shelly said. "Gorgeous place way up in the mountains overlooking town."

"Well, somehow Jane's car almost slid down the side of the mountain. She was in a pretty serious accident and ended up in the hospital. Aaron saw her headlights off the side of the road and called an ambulance. To make a long story short, Aaron ended up taking care of her when she got out of the hospital. One thing led to another and now they're getting married. Pretty cool, huh?"

"Very cool. Sounds like a romantic love story." Shelly sighed wistfully.

"Here we go getting off track again." Brooke grinned. "There was a reason I told you all that. I'm hoping the two of you will come to Aaron and Jane's engagement party next Saturday."

"Oh, I don't know, Brooke. It's super nice of you to invite us, but that's a family thing. I'm not sure it's appropriate for Mary Beth and me to be there."

"Nonsense. You've known me and a bunch of my brothers and sisters, including Aaron, for over ten years. Now that you're staying here with me, it's almost like we *are* family. Please say you'll come."

Shelly looked at her daughter. "What do you think, Mary Beth?"

"I don't know, Mom. You go. I'll just stay home."

"Honey, if you don't feel up to going, I'll stay home with you." Shelly patted her daughter's hand.

"Maahm," the girl whined, "I'm not a little kid, you know. I *can* stay home alone."

"I know you can, sweetie. I just don't want you to feel left out."

"Fine. I'll go, as long as I don't still look like I just got out of a fist fight."

Brooke chuckled inwardly as she watched the interplay between mother and teenager. "I'm glad that's settled because I've got something else going on. And I'd like *both* of you to help me." Shelly and Mary Beth looked at Brooke expectantly. "Well ..." Brook paused dramatically. "I have a *date!* Tomorrow night. With a very hot guy who I happen to like a whole lot. In fact, he's the one who gave me the flower arrangement in the kitchen with the Bird of Paradise in it."

Mary Beth smiled for the first time since coming to Brooke's house. "How'd you meet him? What's he like? Where're you going? What are you going to *wear?*" The teen's questions were bubbling out like soda from a freshly shaken can.

"As a matter of fact, you both know him. It's Dr. Carter, the doctor you saw in the ER the other night. His first name's Zack. I met him a while ago. Jane introduced me to him when Mom was in the hospital. He was somewhat responsible for Jane and Aaron getting together."

"How so?" asked Shelly.

"Aaron followed the ambulance and went with Jane to the hospital after her accident. Even though he'd just met her, he stayed with her *way* more than anyone would expect. As a result, Zack came to the conclusion they were a couple. He started giving Aaron instructions on how to take care of Jane when she left the hospital. As it turned out, she really *didn't* have anyone here in Boulder to help her out. So,

Aaron ended up taking her back to his house. And as they say, the rest is history."

Mary Beth spoke up. "Well, at least I won't have any reason to hide when Dr. Carter comes to pick you up. He's already seen how awful I look."

"Honestly, Mary Beth, a few bruises could never cover up what a truly beautiful girl you are ... inside and out. Please don't say those kinds of things about yourself. They're just not true."

"I'll try not to, Miss Adler. Mom's always saying that kind of stuff to me too, but Dad ... Well, he doesn't tend to give out too many compliments."

"When you squeeze a lemon, you get lemon juice," Brooke stated matter-of-factly.

"Huh? What do you mean by that?" Mary Beth asked.

"Your dad must not like himself all that much. A person only hurts another person when they're hurting inside. It's no excuse. But at least it helps to explain how sometimes people hurt the very ones they care about the most."

"Yeah. I guess." Mary Beth sat quietly for a few moments. "Can we not talk about this right now? It was a lot more fun talking about your date. Can we just go back to that for now?"

"Of course, sweetie. What do you want to know?" Brooke asked.

Shelly stepped in. "So tell us some more about what Zack's really like. I mean, we know he's a doctor, so he's all kinds of smart. And we've seen him. You're right. He's super good looking, but we need more. Come on, spill all the details."

"He's *adorable.* I nicknamed him Dr. McDreamy the first time I laid eyes on him. I love his super thick dark hair. It's the kind most women would love to have ... or would love to run their fingers through." Looking at Mary Beth, Brooke blushed and said, "Never mind what I just said." Mary Beth grinned as if she knew something more than a fourteen year old ought to know. Brooke cleared her throat and continued. "I guess you'd call his eyes hazel. Sometimes they look green and other times more brown. He *must* work out, don't you think? I mean, he's really built. Is it just me, or did you notice those big strong arms, wide shoulders, and narrow hips too?" *I'll bet there're other parts of him that are well developed too,* her wicked-self teased her.

"Even though Mary Beth was my primary focus," said Shelly, "it would've been next to impossible to totally ignore a man like your Dr. McDreamy. If we weren't at the hospital, it would've been kind of a hunk fest. I mean, with your doctor and your brother both there and all." Shelly sighed. "Tell us more."

Looking directly at Mary Beth, Brooke put on her stern school teacher face and used her classroom voice. "Now Miss Silvers, the conversations that take place in this house are *not* to be repeated in any way, shape or form to *anyone* at Summit Middle School. This is very private girlfriend stuff. Do I have your word?"

The three females sat silently for a moment. The teen then answered seriously, "Miss Adler, you know a bunch of stuff about me, Mom and Dad. Stuff I wouldn't want *anybody* at school to know. So I guess we're pretty much in the same boat. It's almost like we have our own secret club or something."

"It is, isn't it?" Brooke agreed. "We're a special group of women who care about each other a great deal. I've known your Mom since I wasn't much older than you are right now, Mary Beth. So we've been friends practically forever." Brooke smiled. "Now you and I have known each other through school for a couple of years too. As a teacher I do my best not to have 'favorites,' but I've liked you from the start. You always do your best, and it's nice to have students who participate in class like you do. Plus the fact you're a genuinely nice person. I'm glad you decided to get involved in the school play this year as well."

Mary Beth couldn't hide her pleasure at her mentor's words, and the smile on the teen's face confirmed it.

Shelly spoke up. "Back to Dr. McDreamy. Where's he taking you, and what are you going to wear?"

"He said dinner and a movie. That sounds great, but I don't know if it's pizza or filet mignon. I don't want to be too casual or too dressy either."

"How about the three of us go and rummage through your closet. We can put together the absolutely *perfect* first date outfit."

"That's a great idea, Shelly. Let's go," Brooke said.

The three females ran laughing up the stairs.

Shelly and Mary Beth sat cross legged on Brooke's bed. Brooke proceeded to pull practically everything out of her closet and dresser. The trio eliminated one outfit after another as being a little too informal or too elegant for Brooke's very important first date. Finally, all three agreed. She'd wear black leggings with super cute heeled boots along with a black tank top under a white, lacy, and somewhat sheer loose fitting shirt. Brooke would top it off with her favorite leather coat. It made her feel extra attractive and would bring everything together.

Once the vital decision of what Brooke should wear was made, they needed something to eat. The compatible group determined a large pizza with everything except anchovies was in order. A quick phone call to Brooke's favorite pizzeria with home delivery was a just reward for their decision making prowess.

"If Zack was thinking pizza for tomorrow night, I'm going to have to use my feminine wiles to gently move him to another choice," Brooke said. She then smiled slyly and pretended to twist her non-existent handlebar mustache, and the group dissolved into gales of laughter.

The only minor dissension came when they couldn't agree on which chick flick to watch while devouring their decadent dinner. Brooke's selection of *Gone With the Wind* finally won out.

Mary Beth had never seen the classic film, and it had been years since Shelly had viewed it. Brooke confessed to having lost count of how many times she'd watched the timeless movie. "I love all the history. And Scarlett and Rhett's relationship is so turbulent and yet so romantic. I can't say that I agree with everything Scarlett does, but she's got a spirit that's unstoppable. I like that."

Nathan Silvers had been sitting across the street from the house on 18th Street for almost an hour. His windows were already tinted to the maximum allowed by Colorado law. By slouching low in the seat he felt sure his truck appeared to be unoccupied. Now that he knew where his wife and daughter were staying, he'd be able to figure out a plan.

Shelly's always thought she was so damn smart. She must think I'm really stupid, but I'll show her. That dumb broad thinks I don't know she's been taking classes behind my back. Only reason I let her get away with it was I figured she could damn well make enough to support me for a change!

He sure as hell didn't need Shelly for sex. There were plenty of other women he could find to take care of that. Nathan never wore a wedding ring. He'd told his wife some bullshit about being afraid wearing a ring would make it more likely for him to get hurt on the job. The stupid bitch didn't have enough on the ball to even question him. Hell, he'd always had plenty of women. Being married hadn't really slowed him down all that much. He could get laid any time he wanted to, and he'd been getting a little on the side almost from the beginning. *Yeah, there're lots of women who know Nathan Silvers is pretty damn good in the sack,* he thought smugly.

Shelly'd been a pretty good lay before she got pregnant. But they weren't married more than a couple of months before her belly had started to get so big and ugly. After that, she had about as much sex appeal as a watermelon. *A man's got needs, after all, and I sure as hell wasn't gonna waste my skills on some lard ass pregnant cow.*

*When I find out who the son of a bitch is my old lady's staying with, that asshole's gonna be one sorry mother f***er. For all I know, she's been cheatin' on me for years. Goddam kid might not even be mine.*

Anita Louise

Nathan watched a guy with a pizza delivery sign on his car from "Boss Lady Pizza" pull up in front of the house where his wife was hiding out. He almost lost it. *That f***in' BITCH! Boss lady, my ass. I'll be showing her who's boss real soon.*

He had no choice but to slam the truck into drive and squeal his tires as he drove away. It was either that or follow the asshole pizza guy into the house and kick some serious butt. *I'll kick some ass all right, but not just yet. If that stupid bitch thinks she's seen the last of me, she's got another think comin'.*

Chapter Eleven

Dr. Zackary Carter stood in his kitchen clad only in workout shorts. He'd pulled the sweaty t-shirt off immediately after finishing his run. It was now hanging on one of the hooks in the laundry room he'd installed for just that purpose. After downing almost a full eight ounce glass of water, his body was beginning to cool down. But his mind was still racing.

He could hardly believe it. *What the heck is this about? I'm really nervous! When was the last time I was actually anxious about going out on a date? I honestly can't remember.*

As much as he racked his brain, he just couldn't figure it out. What was it about Brooke Adler that had him so discombobulated? Sure, she was attractive, but that could be said about hundreds of women he'd come into contact with since breaking it off with his fiancée. Something was different with Brooke. From the first moment he'd seen her, there'd been an instant chemistry. It was simply undeniable. *I wonder if my father felt like this when he first met my mother.*

Anita Louise

Where did *that* come from? All of a sudden, Zack wasn't liking the direction of his thoughts all that much. Dating a woman was one thing. Even *thinking* about her in the same context as his mother and father was another thing entirely.

On the other hand, contemplating how to *seduce* the lovely Brooke Adler was a subject he could warm up to. He loved the fact that she was tall. Her long, lanky body would fit nicely next to his.

A picture was suddenly clear in his mind. He was sitting at the table they'd shared at the microbrewery on Pearl Street. As she walked away, he noticed how her curves filled out the snug fitting jeans she wore. She was wearing a loose fitting sweater, but the baggy top couldn't hide the swell of her full breasts. His hands practically tingled at the thought of holding the soft globes.

He was fairly certain the attraction he felt for Brooke was reciprocated. From their first meeting, they'd seemed to be inexplicably drawn to each other. There was an unquestionable magnetism just beneath the surface of every look, every word they shared. The strength of her allure increased with even an accidental touch. And she'd seemed physically incapable of resisting when he'd gently pulled her mouth to his. Her response had been immediate and genuinely sensual. He was certain the sparks ignited that day could easily grow into flames.

How would it feel to have her naked and willing in his arms ... giving herself to him without reservation? There was no question in his mind, having her in his bed, writhing and moaning with pleasure was inevitable.

Bad Case of Lovin' You

His plan for seduction was simple. This time he would take it slow. He'd almost blown it by giving into the urge to kiss her in such a public setting. The flowers were a good way to restart their budding relationship. Whenever possible, he'd give her honest compliments. That would be easy to do when everything about her was exquisite and a complete turn on.

He remembered casually brushing a stray lock away from her face. Even though the interaction was perfectly innocent, the softness of her cheek and silkiness of her hair felt shockingly seductive.

Part of his plan included doing little things to keep him in her thoughts. He'd just finished sending her an email letting her know how much he was looking forward to their date this evening.

To: Ms. Brooke Adler
From: Dr. Zackary Carter
Subject: This evening

Brooke,

Just want you to know how much I'm looking forward to spending the evening with you. It's been a long time since I've experienced this kind of anticipation. You're a very beautiful and interesting woman. Getting to know you better will be most enjoyable.

BTW, while I'm sure you'll enjoy our dinner destination, it leans more toward the casual than the elegant. If you don't mind, we'll reserve a more sophisticated setting for another time.

See you at 7:00.

Zackary Carter, M.D.
Foothills Hospital

Anita Louise

Immediately after hitting "send" he began to second guess himself.

What if she thinks I sound needy? If she was expecting dinner at a fancy restaurant, is she going to be disappointed with the restaurant I've chosen? Will she think I'm being cheap by not taking her to an expensive place? What if she doesn't even look at her emails on the weekends? To alleviate at least one of his concerns, he followed up his email with a text.

Just wanted to make sure you got the email I sent you about tonight. ~ Zack

OMG, now I'm starting to sound like a love struck teenager stressing out over his first prom date! His fears were soon alleviated when he received a return text almost immediately.

How very thoughtful of you. I'll look for your email right away. Thanks! ~ Brooke

He breathed a sigh of relief. *She thinks I'm thoughtful. That's a good sign.*

Now it was time for a shower. He'd have to make it a much cooler one than usual. Maybe cold water would help him to get the very sexy thoughts he was having about a tall, dark haired school teacher out of his mind ... at least until later this evening.

"Shelly, Mary Beth, I've got lunch ready." Brooke carefully flipped over the perfectly browned grilled cheese sandwiches just as one of her house guests walked into the room.

"Smells yummy." Shelly peeked over Brooke's shoulder. "Please tell me there's tomato soup to go with those sandwiches."

"Of course! Isn't it a requirement?" Brooke joked. "Where's Mary Beth?"

"She's coming." Shelly lowered her voice. "I'm worried about her, Brooke. I know it's only been a couple of days, but she's really down in the dumps. I just don't know what to do."

"Have you thought about counseling? Not just for Mary Beth, but for you too. You know, both of you are going through some of the most traumatic events in anyone's life; divorce, moving, new job, health issues."

"I don't know, Brooke. I've always been able to handle things on my own. Talking to some stranger about my personal problems doesn't sound like it would do much good to me."

"You'd be surprised. We live in a different world today than it was when we were kids. A professional could help Mary Beth deal with all of the stuff that's going on. And I'm sure she'd be a lot more comfortable with it if you went too."

"Maybe. But I wouldn't have a clue where to look or who to call."

"We have referrals through the school, and my soon-to-be sister-in-law Jane is a counselor. Remember I told you Connor was going to her?"

"Maybe you're right, Brooke. Sometimes it's good to have somebody you can just vent to. When the person you're talking with can help you to understand how to deal with everything, it's probably even better."

"Counseling has helped Connor a *lot*. Not only has he matured, he seems to be able to handle life's little ups and downs much better than he used to. So many people, kids and adults, try to escape whatever discomfort they're feeling through less than positive means. You know, alcohol, drugs, even food ... anything to try to drown out what they can't understand."

Shelly tilted her head thoughtfully. "Looking back, I believe that's what Nate did. I noticed he started drinking more heavily right after he lost his football scholarship. Maybe if his parents had seen the signs, he'd be a different person today."

"Maybe. Right now there's nothing we can do to help Nathan, but helping Mary Beth *is* something we can do."

"You're right, Brooke. Would you mind giving Jane a call? I'm not sure if she's the right person for us, but it's someplace to start. Thanks."

"As a matter of fact, I'll be seeing Jane right after lunch. We're meeting at Tom's Tavern/SALT to finalize everything for the engagement party next Saturday. I'll talk to her. How much do you want me to tell her?"

"Domestic abuse. Divorce. I'm sure it's the kind of thing Jane deals with all the time. I just wish it wasn't happening to me and Mary Beth."

The teen walked into the kitchen when she heard her name. What she saw was her mother and one of the best role models she'd ever had, hugging each other once again. She smiled. "Hey, what's with you two?" Mary Beth asked.

"Seems like every time I see you, you're hugging. If I see you kissing I'm really going to get worried."

"Come here, my darling daughter. You need to be part of this love fest too."

Both Shelly and Brooke wrapped Mary Beth in their arms.

When the three separated, Brooke smiled and said, "The only person you might catch *me* kissing is that handsome, hunky doctor who's picking me up at seven this evening."

Nathan Silvers was getting bored staring at the house where he knew his wife was staying. *Damn cop shows make this whole stake out thing look so goddam glamorous. This ain't nothin' but sittin' on yer ass doing nothin'. I'm gonna go get a beer.*

He figured no one in the house on 18th Street would notice the squealing tires when his black pickup truck with tinted windows drove away. And so what if somebody did? He wasn't doing anything wrong. Just keeping an eye on his wife. He certainly had a right to do that, didn't he?

Shelly and Mary Beth looked at one another and smiled indulgently.

"For the tenth time ..." Shelly waved her arms like a symphony conductor as she cued her daughter and they said simultaneously, "you look *great!*"

Brooke blushed. "Sorry. I'm just so *nervous.* I know I shouldn't be, but ..." She looked at the grandfather clock standing in the corner of the living room once again. When she started toward the front window to peek out the curtains, Shelly spoke up.

"Stop it, Brooke. Just sit down and relax. He'll be here any minute. It's only ten to seven. A man shouldn't arrive too early. He said he'd be here at seven, and he will be."

"You're right." Brooke did her best to slow down her racing heart. She sat carefully on the edge of one of the two chairs in her living room. They were recliners cleverly disguised as wing backs.

Many nights she'd flipped up the footrest and curled up with a good book. A nice reading lamp was positioned between the two chairs. The furniture pieces were placed at an angle to take advantage of the wood burning fireplace in the middle of the room. *Just waiting for my other half to come and sit beside me on a cold winter night.* Standing once again, Brooke moved toward the kitchen. "I'm going to get a glass of water. Anyone want anything?"

"I'll go with you," Mary Beth responded.

Brooke was filling a glass with ice and water from the refrigerator when the teen tapped her gently on the shoulder. "Miss Adler?"

"What is it, Mary Beth?"

"You look beautiful, Miss Adler. I just want you to know I think you look beautiful."

After giving her a big hug, Brooke held the girl by the shoulders and looked her straight in the eye. "Thank you, sweetie. You are too, Mary Beth. Bruises and all. You're one of the most beautiful girls I've ever known. I'm not happy about the way it came about, but I'm *very happy* you and your mom are here with me. I'd have been a total wreck without you tonight."

The teen giggled. "It's kind of funny seeing an adult acting sort of like some of the kids in school. You know, talking about a boy they like and wondering if he likes them back ... all that stuff."

"Well, Mary Beth, in some ways the boy/girl thing and the man/woman thing isn't all that different. We're talking about liking someone and getting to know them ... figuring out if they like you too. You're only fourteen. I know some kids your age are doing things they're probably too young to be doing. If you have any questions or just want to talk, make sure you come to your mom or me. There's no way I'm going to do anything I'm not ready for with Dr. McDreamy or anyone else. I'm not, and neither should you. Always keep that in mind. Okay?"

"I will, Miss Adler. Thanks."

"Thank *you*, Mary Beth. You and your mom have been real life savers." The doorbell rang. "Oh, my gosh! He's here."

Zack Carter liked what he saw as he looked around. He stood under the roof covering the front porch of Brooke's house on 18th Street. It was a nice neighborhood that seemed to encourage a sense of community. All the houses had porches, many with rockers or swings. Some of the landings were empty of furniture now due to the cold weather. However, he could easily envision families sitting outside on a warm summer evening. Folks would be sipping their beverages, chatting with neighbors, and watching the children play.

Shelly Silvers opened the door. "Hello, Dr. Carter. Nice to see you again. Especially under much better circumstances than the last time. Come on in. Brooke will be right out."

"Hi, Shelly. It's good to see you too. Please call me Zack. How's Mary Beth doing?'

"Better. We've been following all your instructions. She talked Brooke and me into homeschooling for a couple of weeks. Can't say that I blame her. It's hard enough being a teenager without ... well, you know."

Brooke and Mary Beth walked in from the kitchen. Even though he'd just been talking about the girl, it was hard to take his eyes off the woman. He had an almost irresistible urge to quickly eliminate the space between them. He wanted to find out if her luscious looking mouth still tasted as good as it had the last time he'd had the opportunity to savor her lips. It was a good thing there were other people in the room. Otherwise he might've screwed up this second chance at taking it slow, and giving Brooke the space she apparently needed.

He cleared his throat and his thoughts before saying, "Good evening, Brooke. You look absolutely wonderful." He pulled a package from behind his back. "These are for you, but I figured you might want to share them."

"Chocolates? Thank you, Zack, but you really didn't have to," she responded. Her smile was completely genuine.

"I know, but I already gave you flowers. You know what they say, 'Sweets for the sweet.'" Not wanting to ignore the young girl standing there, he looked at the teen and spoke. "And that includes you, Mary Beth. How're you doing?"

"Okay, I guess. Miss Adler and I were just talking in the kitchen when we heard the doorbell. I'm going to my room now. Thanks for the candy. Have a nice night." The teen disappeared up the stairs.

Zack's medically trained eye observed that the girl seemed to be healing normally. Apparently she wasn't in the mood to chit chat.

Brooke spoke up. "Do you want to take your coat off and visit for a while? Or do we need to get going right away?"

"As much as I'd like to visit with all of you lovely ladies, I did make reservations. So, if you don't mind, we'd best be on our way."

"That's fine. Just let me grab my wrap." She walked to the closet and pulled out a black leather coat.

"Please, let me help you with that." The jolt he felt when their hands touched was unexpected and had nothing to do with static electricity. Had she felt it too? Their eyes met momentarily before she blinked and looked down. He watched her shake her head slightly, as if to clear it. When she lifted her head, she looked him squarely in the eye. Then she turned to allow him to assist her in donning the supple garment.

"Where're we going, or is it a surprise?" Brooke asked.

"I'll save surprises for another time. Tonight we're going back to Pearl Street. Griff's. Griff's Downtown Dining. Have you been there?"

"No, I haven't, but I've heard good things about it. Upscale, but casual. Sounds perfect." She headed toward the door. "Good night, Shelly. I probably won't be all that late, but don't feel like you have to wait up for me. See you in the morning."

Anita Louise

"No worries, Brooke," Shelly responded. "You and Dr. Mc ... um, Zack enjoy yourselves."

With all the formalities out of the way they headed out the door. Zack's mother had always been a stickler for being appropriately courteous with women. It was second nature for him to open, hold and close the door from Brooke's house. He then repeated the process as he helped her into his SUV.

"I like your house," he said once they were both settled in the vehicle.

"Thanks. I do too. It's a little more than I need right now, but it was in my price range. Besides that, I fell in love with it the minute I saw it."

"I can understand why. The whole neighborhood reminds me of the kind of home town every kid should grow up in. How long have you lived there?"

"Not quite a year. I moved in just before school started this past fall. Where do you live?" Brooke asked.

"I've got a condo. It's nice enough ... close to the hospital. That's one of the main reasons I bought it. That and the fact I have a pretty spectacular view of the Flatirons." He took his eyes off the road briefly and gave her a satisfied grin.

She smiled back. "The mountains are great, aren't they? Do you do any skiing?"

"Whenever I get the chance. Going to school, post-grad, medical school, residency, your first few years as a doctor takes a lot of time. It's put a serious crimp in a lot of the fun things I used to have plenty of time for."

"But you're glad, aren't you?" Brooke asked. "I mean, is there something else you'd rather be doing?"

"Nope. Absolutely not. Sure, right now the hours are long and I've got student debt up to my eyeballs, but I wouldn't trade it for the world. How about you?"

"I love teaching. I've always loved to learn. Always loved school. Sharing what I love with young people ... well, it just doesn't get much better than that."

"Middle school, right? Lots of changes taking place at that age. Must be pretty challenging at times."

"You're not kidding. It's a pivotal time for a lot of kids. I think that's why I chose it. At the end of the day, it's nice to go home feeling like you just might have made a difference in someone's life."

"I totally agree," Zack said.

Their conversation flowed effortlessly during the drive to the restaurant. Talking with Brooke was so easy. He'd never met anyone quite like her. She was, in his mind, quite a conundrum. At times she came across so confident and self-assured, yet she'd bolted like a scared rabbit after he kissed her outside the brewery. She was obviously bright and had a very quick wit. But she seemed blind to how very much he was interested in her. Smart and sassy. Bold yet shy. As he pulled up to the valet in front of Griff's, he smiled to himself and thought, *I really like this girl ... a lot.*

Chapter Twelve

G riff's Downtown Dining was a trendy restaurant with dark wood floors and worn brick walls. The aromas coming from the kitchen smelled marvelous, and walking hand in hand with Dr. Zackary Carter felt fabulous. Their drive from her house to the restaurant had been filled with laughter and interesting conversation. She almost wished their destination was farther away. She was so comfortable in the darkness of the warm car, riding with her handsome escort.

Brooke noticed Zack speaking to the attendant when he got out of the Jeep. It was a pleasant surprise when her attractive escort opened her car door instead of the valet who'd been standing there when they drove up. Brooke took his offered hand as she exited the vehicle. And it felt so *right* when he continued to hold her hand. She was a little disappointed when they were seated with only a moment's delay, because it meant he had to release her hand so he could pull out her chair.

Bad Case of Lovin' You

Their server was quickly attentive and brought ice water with lemon to their table. After a brief discussion, Brooke agreed to Zack's suggestion of a bottle of the Chateau St. Didier-Parnac Malbec from France.

Their waiter had just departed to bring their wine when Zack asked, "So, this is your first dining experience at Griff's?"

"Yes, and even though we just arrived, I like it very much so far." *Of course, the fact I'm here with you makes it all that much more enjoyable.* Brooke was not the flirtatious type, so giving voice to her attraction to Zack was something she wasn't inclined to do.

"I've been here a few times with colleagues from work," Zack said. "It's different. Instead of the traditional large meal, everything's served in fairly good sized appetizer portions. That way we can share and taste a number of different items on the menu."

"Sharing is good. I had to learn a lot about that growing up in a family of nine children." Brooke smiled as her mind quickly reviewed happy family times.

"Wow! The size of your family still blows my mind. It was just my mom, my brother and me for most of my childhood. My dad passed away when I was quite young. A good portion of my memories of him come from Mom showing pictures and sharing stories with my brother and me."

"Sounds to me like your mother did a pretty darn good job of raising two boys on her own. I'd like to meet her someday." She blushed. As soon as the words left her mouth, Brooke wished she could've taken them back. *OMG. He probably thinks I'm chasing him like a dog going after a bone.* She gulped, wishing the wine would arrive soon. At least then she could hide her embarrassment behind the round wide bowl of the stemmed glass. Instead she blurted, "I didn't mean ..."

"Funny you should say that, Brooke. My mother already asked me to invite you over."

"She has?" Brooke asked incredulously. "You mean, you've talked to your *mother* about *me*?"

"Oops. I guess the cat's out of the bag. Yep, sure did," he said a bit sheepishly. "I was on the phone with her and our date came up in the conversation. I just *had* to tell her about your comment on what kind of movies you like and don't like."

"Why?"

"Because when you said, 'I don't do violence,' it *totally* reminded me of Mom. She's the same way."

"Well, we can hardly turn on the tv or radio without hearing about all the violence that's happening around us. Why in the world anyone would want to subject themselves to any *more* violence is beyond my comprehension."

"That's what Mom says. She always says we get more of what we focus on, so we should focus on what we want instead of what we don't want."

"Your mother's a woman after my own heart. I totally agree. Now I *really* want to meet her, and I'm not embarrassed to say so."

"Okay. So, do you want to come with me to her house for dinner a week from tomorrow?" Zack asked.

Brooke was startled by his invitation. "Really?"

"Why not? Regardless of what happens with us, I think you and Mom would get along famously. What do you think? Is it a date?"

"Uh ... sure. Why not?" She reached out her hand to seal the deal. Instead of the handshake she expected, he took her fingers gently in his. He then drew her hand to his mouth. His eyes never left hers until he closed them momentarily as his lips touched her hand. The sensation of his lips on her knuckles sent tiny spikes of electricity up her arm. The energy then moved toward her core. She felt the tips of her breasts harden as with a cool breeze.

"Mom will be thrilled." Zack paused and looked deeply into her eyes. "I'm feeling pretty thrilled myself right now."

Hesitantly she replied softly, "Me too."

Just then the waiter arrived with their wine. After being offered the cork for approval, Zack nodded. A small amount of the dark liquid was poured into his glass. Brooke watched as he swirled and sniffed knowledgeably. Once their glasses were filled, the waiter backed away.

Brooke followed Zack's lead and lifted her glass.

As the crystal touched, he said, "Here's to possibilities."

"To possibilities," she echoed. They sipped. After a brief silence she spoke again. "Please. Tell me more about yourself. You said you have a brother. Older or younger?"

"Two years older. Dylan. He just got married a few months ago, on Christmas eve, to Kaylee."

"How romantic. My parents recently celebrated their fortieth wedding anniversary. They got married on

Valentine's Day. Sounds like a little romanticism runs in both of our families."

"Sure does. So, do you consider yourself one of those incurable romantics?" Zack asked.

"Maybe a little," Brooke confessed." Mom and Dad have sure set a great example of what I hope to have in a marriage someday. My brother Phillip and his wife Rachel have been together for about five years, and have been married three. Now they're expecting their first child. They seem blissfully happy."

"And now your brother Aaron and his fiancée Jane are tying the knot too. The first time I met them, I assumed they'd been together for quite some time. I guess, to a certain extent, I had a bit of a hand in putting those two together."

"You sure did! I was beginning to think Aaron was *never* going to get married again."

"He was married before?"

"Yes, but it was a long time ago. He was pretty young. She was actually a couple of years older than him. To be honest, I never really got to know her all that well. I have the feeling theirs was more a case of lust than love."

"Interesting," Zack commented. "I wonder what would've happened if they'd combined lust *and* love?"

All of a sudden Brooke's tongue felt really, really dry. Her brain was spinning off into some fantasy where lust and love came together and wrapped her and Zack in a warm, steamy embrace. Somewhere along the way their clothes had disappeared. In her mind she saw only the tangle of their naked bodies with limbs and tongues entwined.

She picked up her glass and took a long, steadying swallow. Pretending to savor the taste of the smooth, mellow claret allowed her to rein in her wayward thoughts. Finally back on planet earth, she moved the conversation back to safer ground.

"Dylan and Kaylee. How did they meet?" she asked.

"Theirs was no love at first sight story. They were both in college and dating other people when they first met. The way they tell it, they didn't even like each other very much in the beginning. I think they were really attracted to one another right from the git-go, but neither one of them wanted to admit it. They'd see one another at parties and stuff from time to time. Then they ended up working as servers at the same restaurant while they were still in college. Once she graduated, Kaylee got a good job in HR and married her high school heartthrob. But it turned out the high school sweetheart wasn't all that sweet. I don't think it even lasted a year."

"In a way, that's too bad," Zack said. "But it sounds like it turned out for the best. Seems like it's pretty rare for high school romances to result in long term marriages."

"Yeah. I don't think the ink was dry on the divorce papers before Kaylee was calling all her old friends at the restaurant asking about Dylan. He and his girlfriend had broken up too, so he and Kaylee ended up going out. They dated while he got his law degree, then lived together for a while. A couple of years ago they decided to have a family. So they wanted a more formal commitment. Thus the wedding on Christmas Eve."

Brooke had been spinning the stem of her wine glass around and around as she listened. There didn't sound like a lot of romance in the way Zack told Dylan and Kaylee's story. Now there was a question bubbling to the surface she simply had to ask. "Do you believe in love at first sight?"

He stopped. His eyes met hers and held. "That's a good question, Brooke. To be honest, I'm not a hundred percent sure. I guess I'd like to think so, and I'm willing to find out." He paused. "What about you? Do *you* believe in love at first sight?"

"Yes, I do. I think there are some people who are just *meant* to be together. My mother and father, Aaron and Jane ... even Phillip and Rachel. There was an instant connection with all of them."

"Mom says that's what happened with her and Dad too." He touched the fingers of her hand that rested lightly on the stem of her glass. "You know, this is the first real date I've been on in a very long time."

Brooke turned her hand so his much larger fingers rested in her palm and gently closed her hand around his. "Is it?"

"Yes, it is. Can I tell you something?"

"Of course. Anything."

"I was engaged once," Zack said. "A long time ago."

"You were? Do you want to talk about it?"

"No. I really don't. Let's just say she wasn't the right one for me after all and leave it at that for now. Okay?"

"Sure."

Their server returned. Brooke asked Zack to choose a sampling of his favorites from previous visits. She watched as he conversed with the waiter. She saw a genuine and kind man as he laughed and joked while making his selections. *I wonder what happened with his former fiancée.*

Bad Case of Lovin' You

Did he leave her or did she leave him? Was he in love with her? When Zack finished ordering Brooke asked, "Well, what're we having?"

"You mean you weren't paying attention?" He joked.

"I was watching you have all kinds of fun with our waiter."

"You mean, George?"

"George?"

"Yes, our server ... George. Heck of a nice guy. He's pre-med."

"Oh. That's nice, but you still didn't answer my question."

"We're starting with brussel sprouts."

"Brussel sprouts?" She thought she probably looked as skeptical as she knew she sounded.

"Yep. Flash cooked brussel sprouts with brown butter, hazelnuts and shallots."

"You're kidding, right?"

"Nope. And I'll bet you're going to love them."

"Okaaaay. What else?"

"Oysters on the half shell. They're an aphrodisiac, you know."

Brooke noticed a twinkle in Zack's eyes. "So I've heard. Okay, I don't think I want to hear any more. George can just bring whatever you've ordered, and I'll eat it."

"Ah, a woman after my own heart."

They chatted companionably until the food was served. Oddly enough, the brussel sprouts were delicious, as were the oysters, the short rib ravioli and duck confit. For dessert they had a mouth-watering apple pie á la mode drizzled with whiskey caramel sauce.

Brooke leaned back and patted her stomach. "Oh my, but that was good. I hope the movie's going to be able to keep me awake. What are we seeing?"

"You've probably already seen it, but it's a classic. Hopefully, one you like."

"Which one?"

"*Groundhog Day.* Is that okay?" Zack asked.

"Of course! I love it. It's one of my all-time favorites. Where's it showing?"

"Uhhhh, here's the thing."

"What? What's the thing?"

"Well, I couldn't find any really good, fun and funny movies playing anywhere. Soooo ..."

"Sooo?" Brooke looked at him warily

"So, I hope it's okay with you. We're going to my place to watch it. I've got popcorn ready to pop, wine, beer, soda, whatever you want to drink. I even bought some candy just in case: Milk Duds, M&Ms, and Raisinetes. Plus I have a seventy inch curved screen HDTV with surround sound that's to die for. It's almost *better* than the movies. You can pause it if you need to get something to drink or you have to go to the bathroom." He stopped and looked at her hopefully. "Okay?"

He'd been talking so fast, it would've been impossible to even *try* to stop him. Now it was Brooke's turn to test out the acting skills she'd been working on with her students in the school play. She crossed her arms over her chest and put on her best *you're in trouble with the teacher* face. "Really? Your house? On our first date?"

"I'll be a complete gentleman, Brooke. I promise." He made an X over his chest as he said, "Cross my heart."

"Well ..."

"Please?"

"Plain or peanut M&Ms?" she asked.

"Both. I bought both." He looked at her expectantly.

"Ok. Since you've gone to all that trouble ... two kinds of M&Ms, popcorn and everything else, I guess I don't have any other choice. I'll *have to* come over and watch the movie with you. Under *one* condition."

"Anything. What?" he asked.

She leaned forward and whispered, "Promise me you *won't* be a complete gentleman?"

"You really *are* a woman after my own heart, Brooke Adler. Let's get the check and *go.* George? Check please."

Chapter Thirteen

Brooke would have a very difficult time ever finding her way to Zack's condo again. She had absolutely no idea which way they went or what landmarks they passed during their drive. Her entire focus was on the man sitting next to her in the car. He'd hardly even touched her; only the few moments spent holding her hand and then gently placing his hand on her back as he escorted her from the restaurant. Still her hormones were racing. While his hands were firmly on the wheel and his eyes on the dark roads, she took the opportunity to admire his male perfection.

It looked like he'd shaved shortly before picking her up. There was barely a hint of stubble across his firm jawline. His dark hair was thick and fairly short without a definite part and stood up in spikey tufts. It looked like the kind of hair that would look good even when it wasn't perfect. *Like when he's just gotten out of bed or the shower.* That thought had her heart beating even faster than it was only a few moments before.

Zack's voice broke the silence. "Penny for your thoughts. You've been awfully quiet since we left Griff's. Everything okay?"

She certainly couldn't tell him she'd been fantasizing about his naked male physique. "Everything's fine."

"You sure?"

"I guess I'm a little nervous," she admitted.

"You've never seemed nervous with me before. Brooke, if you're uncomfortable going to my house, it's okay. They must have at least a dozen different movies playing at Century-Boulder. I'm sure we could find something you'd enjoy."

"No. Really. I *want* to go to your place. I'm glad you suggested it."

"You sure?" He took his hand off the wheel for a moment and reached over and put it on her arm. "I don't ever want to do anything you're not okay with."

His touch was reassuring. *It's not like he's planning on seducing me as soon as I walk into his living room.* While the thought should've made her feel better, instead she felt somehow disappointed. "Honestly, Zack, I love the fact you went to all the trouble to pick out a great movie, and get the candy and popcorn and all. Although the dinner at Griff's was so delicious, I'm not sure how much room my tummy's got left." She patted her middle for emphasis.

"I know what you mean. But it just seems like watching a movie almost *requires* popcorn. No matter how full you are."

"True. Are we almost there?"

He flipped on his turn signal. "Yep. We're here."

Anita Louise

Brooke noted the craggy outline of the Flatirons on the horizon. "I'll bet the view is fantastic in the daylight." When she turned to look at him, his eyes were focused on her ... not the mountains in the distance.

"It is, but I think the view is even more fantastic right now."

She felt herself blush and was grateful for the moonless night.

Pulling his Jeep into a spot in front of a closed garage door, he said, "Here we are." He quickly exited the vehicle. After opening Brooke's door, he offered his hand as she swung her feet to the pavement. Placing her hand in his, she stood and looked around as she waited for him to lead her into his home.

He squeezed her fingers gently. "Right this way, m'lady."

They walked around the garage and down a brick paver path to his front door. To the left of the entrance was a small patio, the furniture covered with snow. "Do you use this much in the nicer weather?" Brooke asked.

"Yes, I like this side of the house because it's totally private. Privacy is the one thing I find lacking by living in a condo. But, the deck facing the mountains is my favorite spot. When I can, I like to sit out there with my coffee in the morning and sometimes before or after dinner. Even though other people have decks on that side of the building too, most of the time I'm the only one out there."

"My place is just the opposite. There's lots of activity when I sit on the front porch, and the back yard is where I go when I want some privacy. I've only gotten to know a couple of my neighbors so far. When I first moved in last fall, I would sit out front almost every evening. There's usually some older kids playing catch and stuff in their yards or in the street. A lot of times there are people walking or riding their bicycles too. I like it. It's nice."

"Sounds like a real family friendly neighborhood."

"It is," Brooke agreed. "That had a lot to do with my decision to buy it. It's really more than I need right now. It would have been totally out of my budget if not for the fact I got it on a short sale. I feel bad for the family who lost it, but if I didn't buy it someone else would've."

"That tells me two things," Zack said.

"What?"

"One, you're a compassionate person."

"I'd like to think so." Brooke agreed. "If crying at sappy movies is any indication, I certainly qualify. What's number two?"

"You'd like to have a family one day."

"Yes, I would. I love coming from a big family. Since there were so many of us, we didn't go on a lot of fancy trips or always drive the latest model cars. But there was always plenty of love to go around."

When he opened the front door, Brooke completely understood what had drawn him to his home. Even on this dark night, she could see the shadowy outline of the mountains in the distance. Almost the entire back wall of his condo was glass, and the drapes were open.

"May I take your coat?"

"Of course." She shrugged out of her leather and felt a shiver of anticipation when his fingers lightly brushed the back of her neck.

Anita Louise

Opening the hallway closet, he hung her jacket and removed his own. "Make yourself at home," he said casually.

Brooke was drawn to the wall of windows and sliding glass door along the back of the room. She stood there admiring the view.

"Do you want more wine, or something else?" Zack asked.

"I think I've had enough wine, and I reserve my caffeine for the morning. How about a glass of water ... with lemon if you have it?"

"Would San Pellegrino with lemon work?"

"Perfect." Brooke could hear him rustling around after he disappeared into the kitchen. Soon the sound of popcorn exploding in the microwave filled the quiet room, followed quickly by the unmistakable aroma of the movie treat. She smiled to herself. As much as she wasn't the least bit hungry, the scent caused an involuntary salivation response. "Okay," she called. "You got me. I'm going to have to have some of that popcorn now."

He was grinning as he walked out of the kitchen holding two glasses of sparkling water with fresh lemon slices floating in them. "I was hoping you'd say that." Handing her a glass, he lifted his for a toast.

"You really like this whole 'toast' thing, don't you?" Brooke asked.

"As a matter of fact, I do. And I have, what I hope is an appropriate one for this most auspicious occasion."

"Auspicious, huh? Okay, let's hear it."

"May we have the good fortune to win a true heart, and the merit to keep it," he said.

She touched her glass to his and said sarcastically, "How many women have you used that line on?"

He paused and took a sip before answering solemnly, "You're the first."

Brooke had taken a sip of her drink. She almost choked when she heard his remark. "I don't know what to say."

"You don't have to say anything, Brooke. I don't even know why I said that. It just sort of slipped out before I could think. Don't get the wrong idea. I'm not really the romantic type. I just *like* you, Brooke. If it's okay with you, why don't we enjoy one another's company and see where it goes from here. Sound good?"

"I like you too, Zack, and yes, that *does* sound good."

"Great, shall we watch the movie?"

"That sounds good too ... *after* you bring that delicious smelling popcorn in here."

Zack nodded and they touched their glasses together once more.

Brooke took another sip of her drink and moved toward the sofa as Zack disappeared back into the kitchen.

Almost two hours later, Zack turned off the television. The gas logs in the fireplace provided the only light. Sometime during the movie, he'd put his arm around Brooke's shoulders and she'd snuggled in next to him. The empty popcorn bowl sat on her lap. Her head lay on his shoulder.

"I love that movie," she said wistfully. "I'm glad you chose it."

"I like it too. Confession?"

Anita Louise

She sat up a little straighter and looked at him. "Okaaay. What's your deep, dark secret?"

"That's my personal copy of *Groundhog Day*. I own it. I just watched it a few weeks ago."

"On Groundhog's Day," they said simultaneously.

Zack moved the popcorn bowl to the floor and put his other arm around Brooke. Pulling her closer he said, "You really are special, you know."

Brooke's hand moved soothingly up and down his back. "I'm glad you think so." She tipped her head up to look into his eyes and whispered, "I think you're pretty special too."

He took in her scent and allowed it to wrap around him. He wanted to breathe her in. Never before had he wanted so much to know a woman like he wanted to know Brooke. What were her dreams ... her secret desires? In what ways could he please her the most? He smoothed her hair away from her face and simply looked at her.

Her lips parted, but she uttered no words. Her tongue darted out and retreated as she softly bit her lower lip. When she smiled at him hesitantly a few moments later, he almost lost his breath. Words like beautiful and alluring were not enough to describe the woman in his arms.

After stroking his fingers across the soft skin of her cheek, it seemed only natural to cup her chin and bring her lips closer to his own. "Lovely," he whispered as their breath mingled, and he angled his mouth to meet hers. Her lips were soft. He could detect a hint of salt and butter from the popcorn they'd shared.

His hand drifted to her hip and pulled her closer. She splayed her fingers against his chest, and he could feel his heart beating against her palm. Her breath quickened as did his, and she moved her hand up to caress his neck. He loved the feel of her skin against his, and her full lips felt warm and oh so right pressed against his.

Brooke moaned softly and her lips parted slightly. Zack opened his eyes so he could watch her face as he ran his tongue across her mouth from corner to corner, testing. Savoring the taste of her, he deepened the kiss slowly, one degree at a time. Her lashes fluttered, and she released a sigh. He could see the throbbing of her pulse in her neck, just under her chin. He ran his fingers softly along her jawline and down her throat, where her skin disappeared into her blouse. Was it desire that brought the faint flush to her cheeks?

As much as he wanted to touch her everywhere, he sensed this was too important to rush. Somehow he knew this was about more than sex ... so much more than just smell, touch, taste. He allowed his fingers to skim along the neckline of the top she wore. Then he trailed a finger down the front of her arm, barely brushing the side of her breast. Her gasp and the instant peaking of her nipples were evidence of her arousal.

He covered her mouth with a hungry kiss. She opened her lips to him with a sigh. It was a good thing Brooke couldn't read his mind. Mentally he was slowly undressing her and covering every delicious area of skin with his lips, teeth and tongue as it was exposed. A rumbling groan escaped from his throat as his tongue tangled with hers. Her whimpers of pleasure enflamed his already burning desire.

Anita Louise

Shifting their position slightly, he lay down on the oversized sofa, taking her with him while continuing to plunder her mouth. Her hands moved into his hair and her breasts were pressed firmly against his chest. He could feel her heart beating wildly against his own. She continued to make soft sounds, as if unable to fight her own body's innately sensual response. When she adjusted her hips so the vee of her legs met his, he thought he might explode before even touching her naked skin.

Moving his hands down her back and across her hips, he arched his back in an effort to get even closer. Her response was to rock back and forth on his engorged member. Never before had he been with a woman who even fully clothed, turned him into a trembling mass of need.

Once again he turned their bodies in unison. She was now trapped between him and the back of the sofa. As she continued to grind her pelvis against his, he massaged her hip before allowing his hand to move up to her breast.

As much as he'd promised himself not to rush, it was almost impossible. He slid his hand over the fullness of her breast. The tip was taut, and he rubbed his thumb back and forth across it. Her body's needs seemed to override any reluctance she may have had previously.

Her hand moved to his breastbone. She began opening the buttons on his shirt exposing his bare skin. Then she was rubbing his chest and teasing his nipples as he had hers.

"*Brooke.*" He could barely speak, but he had to tell her. "You have to stop. I promised myself we'd take it slow, but if you keep this up I'll be forced to break my word."

Bad Case of Lovin' You

Both her hand and her body ceased moving, and her breathing slowed. She lay quietly with her head on his chest for a moment. Finally, she spoke. "You're right, Zack. I honestly don't know what came over me. I've never lost control like this before. Please forgive me."

"Forgive you? There's absolutely nothing to forgive. I must be out of my mind to have opened my mouth. The thing is, I never want you to think that whatever is happening between us is anything less than something special." He paused and smoothed her hair back from her face. "I want you, Brooke. I want to be with you very badly. I want to make love to you in such a way that will spoil you for any other man. But I was afraid if we didn't stop, it might ruin everything before it ever had a chance to really begin. I was afraid you'd never want to see me or speak to me again. And I certainly don't want to do anything that will ultimately put a wedge between us. Was I right?"

"Probably. I'm not sure I could have faced you if ..."

"I understand, sweetheart."

"It's still going to be difficult after what just happened," she confessed.

"Please don't say that, Brooke. Please. Just stay right where you are. Let me hold you for a while. I don't know where this is going to go, but I'd sure like to find out."

She didn't say a word. What she did do was turn her head to plant soft kisses along his neck and jawline. He wasn't sure, but he thought he heard her whisper, "Thank you."

Soon, her hand relaxed and her fingers splayed across his ribcage. Her head was resting comfortably across his chest, and within a few minutes he felt the tension leave her body. Her breathing slowed, and he could tell she'd succumbed to the sweet release of sleep.

A little voice popped into his head. "You some kind of fool, man? A gorgeous woman is ready and willing to have sex with you, and you tell her to stop? You must be crazy!"

If I'd have let her go through with it, she probably would've hated me in the morning.

He could almost see the little devil sitting on his shoulder shouting, "So what? She's hot, and she was hot to trot. There's plenty of other fish in the sea, fool."

She's different. I'm different when I'm with her.

"What kinda drugs're you on, bro? Different? Bah! What a bunch of hooey."

What if she's 'the one?'

"Now you talkin' smack, man. The one? Hah! There ain't no such thing."

That's where I think you're wrong.

Zack shifted carefully so as not to awaken Brooke, kissed her on the forehead and brushed the little devil off his shoulder.

The last thought in his mind before he dozed off was a personalized version of the toast he had made to her earlier. *May I have the good fortune to win a true heart, and the merit to keep it.*

Chapter Fourteen

When Brooke awoke, the room was dark. It took her a moment to remember where she was and whose arms she was in. At first she panicked as she realized that not only was she still lying on the couch in the living room of Zack's condo, but her date was still cuddled up next to her.

Oh, my God, what have I done? How could I have been so forward? That's just not like me at all. I wasn't drunk. What could possibly have come over me to make me act that way?

Never having sex with a guy on the first date was at the top of the list. If Zack hadn't stopped her ... well, she was pretty sure she knew what would've happened. She also wasn't sure if any other man would've had as much self-control as Zack had shown under the circumstances.

The memory of the passionate kisses she and Zack shared leaped vividly to the forefront of her mind. Their evening together had been the most perfect of her entire life. It started from the moment he entered her front door with the candy in his hand, and had been so kind and courteous to Shelly and Mary Beth. The restaurant he chose was cozy yet elegant, and the meal consisting of a series of oversized appetizers, was excellent. She thought back to how friendly he'd been when he talked with their server George. And, yes, the movie Zack had chosen was a romantic comedy, but it was more than just that.

The time loop aspect of *Groundhog Day* adhered to none of the rules or deadlines usually associated with time travel. The main character, Phil/Bill Murray was left to figure things out for himself, much like Brooke was trying to do in regard to her relationship with Zack.

Is there anything I would really want to change about last night if I could? Wasn't it unexpectedly wonderful to be so caught up in the sensuality of the moment that I actually let myself go so completely?

What did it say about Zack that he admitted to owning *Groundhog Day*? Not only that, but he admitted to watching it at least annually. *And* he'd suggested it for their first official date. One of the biggest themes of the movie was that nothing outside really changes, until you change yourself from the inside.

Yes, she decided, Zack was a very special guy. He was a man she definitely wanted to take the time to get to know better, and maybe even have as a part of her life for the long term. Since she was now feeling much better about what did and didn't happen earlier in their date, she began to plant gentle kisses along the side of his neck. His face was now covered with a fine stubble of whiskers. Her fingers traced his jawline, and he stirred. When he opened his eyes, she looked at him and smiled.

"It's awfully late. I really need to get home," she whispered softly.

"Brooke. Are you ...? Is everything okay?"

She answered his question by placing her hands on either side of his face. She kissed him in an innately sensual yet incredibly sweet way. "Wonderful. Everything was wonderful, Zack, but I really do have to go."

"I know you do." They moved together to an upright position. "I had a really great time," he said.

"I did too. Thank you ... for everything." Brooke pulled his face to hers once more. His mouth was ready for hers. Their kiss was warm and tender. The desire was still there, making her tremble ever so slightly. But now it was tempered with something more ... a sweetness and caring like she'd never before experienced.

"When can I see you again?" he asked.

"Soon. Let's talk later. Okay?" She looked at her watch. It was after two in the morning. "Right now, I've got to get home."

"I understand." He stood and helped her up. "I'll get your coat."

As he walked away, she looked out toward the mountains in the distance. The clouds had parted, and the moon cast a soft glow over their craggy peaks.

He came up behind her and enfolded her in his arms. His chest felt strong and solid against her back. She covered the arms encircling her waist with her own.

"They're beautiful, aren't they?"

"Sometimes I think the mountains are reaching for the sky, like they were destined to meet ... to kiss."

She turned in his arms and their lips met once more. He pulled her hips to his as she threaded her fingers through his hair. His mouth crushed hers, and their tongues met in a tangle of sudden need. He pressed his arousal into her heat and once again, a moan of desire escaped her lips.

"*Brooke.*" He captured her breast in his hand, massaging the soft flesh. "I want you, Brooke, and I *will* have you."

"Yes. I want that too. Soon," she whispered. She smoothed his hair and moved her lips to his bristled cheek. "Zack, I don't know what it is, but when I'm with you I want to break all my silly rules. I really do, but I can't. Not now. Not yet, but soon. Please?"

He stepped back. "It's okay, Brooke. I've got your coat right here." He picked it up from the back of the chair where he'd dropped it only a few minutes before, and held it up for her. She could sense his frustration as he put on his own coat. "Ready?"

"Zack, I ... I guess I just don't know what to say."

"You don't have to say anything, Brooke. I understand. I really do. Let's just get you home and we can talk later. Okay?"

Holding her hand he walked her out to the passenger side of his car and helped her in. They were both silent for most of the ride home. The porch light was on when he pulled to the curb in front of her house. When she started to open her car door, he reached out his hand.

"Let me. Please?" he asked.

"Of course."

Helping her out of the Jeep, he took her hand once more and walked her up to the front door. Taking both of her hands in his, he looked into her eyes. "This has been a wonderful evening, Brooke. I had a great time. The best I've had in a very long time."

"Me too." With their hands still clasped, they leaned in and shared a goodnight kiss. "Thank you, Zack. For everything."

"You're welcome, Brooke."

He watched as she put her key in the lock and opened the door. She stepped inside.

As she watched him walk back to the street and drive away, she blew him a kiss.

In her dream, Brooke was standing on the porch of her home laughing with a tall, dark haired man. There were children playing in front. Two of the boys in the group playing tag were her offspring. The man at her side had his arm casually around her waist.

"Dad!" one of the boys called. "Will you play catch with us now?"

The man gave her a squeeze and a kiss on the cheek before replying, "Sure, buddy." He then ran down the steps to join his sons.

It was the smell of frying bacon and coffee that somehow managed to entice Brooke from her wonderful reverie. She smiled to herself as she stretched and recalled how good her fantasy had felt. Was it possible the family she'd always hoped for ... everything she'd ever wanted might finally be closer to becoming reality?

Climbing out of bed, she donned her robe and slippers. Quickly she ran a brush through her hair, before following her nose to the delicious aromas coming from the kitchen.

Shelly stood at the stove. Mary Beth sat at the kitchen table with one of her school books open in front of her.

"Good morning, ladies," Brooke said cheerily as she walked into the room. "Sure smells good in here."

Turning from the stove and smiling, Shelly returned the greeting. "Morning, Brooke. How was your date?"

Brooke couldn't seem to stop herself from twirling around as if wearing a ball gown. "Wonderful. Absolutely wonderful."

Mary Beth looked up from her schoolwork. "You look happy, Miss Adler."

"I *am* happy, thank you."

Shelly turned off the burner and moved from the stove. She then poured a cup of coffee for her friend before giving herself a refill. "Breakfast can wait a little while. Come on, give us all the details." She sat next to her daughter who closed her text book and moved her papers to the side. "Sounds like your date was a success. Spill."

Brooke grinned. "We didn't really do anything all that special. He took me to Griff's Downtown Dining on Pearl Street. I'd never been there before, but I'll definitely be going back."

"What did you like best, Miss Adler?" Mary Beth asked.

"You're probably not going to believe this. And, by the way, please do your best to save Miss Adler for the classroom. At home, I'm Brooke. Okay?"

The girl smiled shyly. "Sure, Miss ... Brooke."

"What aren't we going to believe?" Shelly asked.

"Oh yeah. My favorite thing at Griff's was their brussel sprouts!"

Mary Beth made a face. "Yuck."

"You can't be serious," Shelly added. "I like them okay, but I sure wouldn't put brussel sprouts on my list of favorites."

"Really. You'd be surprised," Brooke said. "It's one of their specialties. We'll all have to go there one of these days, and you can both try them for yourself."

"If you say so, but there's no guarantee I'm going to like them," Shelly replied. "What else? Didn't you say he was taking you to a movie too?"

"I love the movies," Mary Beth chimed in. "Where'd you go? What'd you see?"

"We watched *Groundhog Day*. You remember that old movie with Bill Murray where he keeps repeating the same day over and over again?"

"Yeah, I remember it, but I didn't know it was showing anywhere," Shelly stated.

"Well, we didn't actually *go* to the movies. Zack has an amazingly huge television with all the surround sound paraphernalia at his house. He had popcorn and all kinds of candy too."

"Ohhh." Shelly drew out the word. "So you went to his *house,* did you? Aaaand? Do I need to ask Mary Beth to leave the room?"

"Of course not!" Brooke exclaimed. "Why would you need to do that? We watched the movie and talked. That's it."

"You sure about that?" Shelly teased. "Dr. McDreamy is awfully cute."

"Yes, I'm sure, and yes, he is. On top of that he's also a perfect gentleman."

"Are you going to go out with him again," Mary Beth asked.

"I think so. I hope so." Brooke paused. "Actually, I know so. He's going to be my date for Aaron and Jane's engagement party next weekend. And guess what else?"

"What?" was said in unison by mother and daughter.

"He's talked to his *mother* about me, and she wants to meet me. I think he's going to take me over to her house for dinner soon."

All three females were grinning from ear to ear.

Shelly raised her coffee cup and said, "I think this deserves a toast." Brooke lifted her coffee and Mary Beth her glass of juice. "To successful first dates. May they lead to many more."

They clicked their morning drinks together.

Not wanting to share any further information on her evening, Brooke changed the subject. "I'm starved. What's for breakfast?"

Shelly got up from the table and walked back to the stove. "Bacon, eggs, hash browns and toast. How do you want your eggs?"

Luke Adler was off duty so he was driving his Durango instead of a patrol car. His partner Monique Hix probably wouldn't approve of the route he'd been taking lately. But he figured what she didn't know wouldn't hurt her.

What he did on his off hours was none of her business anyway.

Recently he'd gotten into the habit of driving by Brooke's house on a fairly regular basis. She was his sister, after all. Of course, it had nothing to do with Brooke's new house guests. He just wanted to make sure everything and everyone was okay. Besides, Brooke was a single woman, and now there were three lovely ladies living there together. Under those circumstances, it seemed like it was more than just a good idea. It was practically his duty as a man and conscientious brother to keep an eye on things.

Luke had made it a point to talk to Colin Montgomery. Colin was the officer who'd gone over to Nathan Silvers' house after Luke turned in the report about what Nate had allegedly done to his daughter. Colin said that, ultimately, Silvers had been cooperative, but the guy was a little volatile. Silvers hadn't been in any serious trouble. But in Luke's book, any guy who hit defenseless people had a screw loose somewhere.

Being a police officer had some perks, and Luke had called in a favor. He'd asked the patrol car who covered the area where Brooke's house was located to drive by from time to time. Better safe than sorry. So far nothing had turned up.

He'd also checked the DMV records. Luke Silvers drove a black Silverado pick up. He'd let the patrol know that too. Spurned ex or soon-to-be ex-husbands sometimes did crazy things.

I wonder if Shelly's coming to the engagement party next weekend. The thought had crossed Luke's mind several times before. Only because he felt getting out and having some fun would be good for her. Maybe she'd bring her daughter too. Mary Beth seemed to be a very nice young girl. Brooke told him the teen was one of her students, and a good one at that.

Would it be too weird if I stopped in unexpectedly to say "hi" to everyone? Yeah, probably.

He cruised by the house slowly. Best to just get on with his day. Maybe he'd talk to Brooke at the engagement party about inviting him and some of the other siblings over for dinner one of these days. Potlucks were always fun.

Nathan Silvers woke up with a pounding headache. *Damn!* He'd intended to spend at least part of last night keeping his eye on the place where his wife and daughter were staying. He figured on a Saturday evening he might see someone coming or going from the place. But he'd gone to the bar after work and had a couple of drinks. When he got home it didn't seem like a few more beers and a shot or two would do him any harm. Next thing he knew the sun was streaming in, and he was still on the couch with the tv blaring.

Shit! If I catch that bitch goin' out with some other guy, there's gonna be hell to pay. The friggin' whore was most likely cheatin' on me the whole time we were married. That's probably why she was always so damn frigid in bed.

The fact he'd been seeing other women throughout his marriage meant nothing as far as he was concerned. The double standard was alive and well in Nathan Silver's head.

After popping a couple of aspirin, he managed to drag himself into the shower. He hadn't bathed in a couple of days, and figured the water might somehow help soothe his aching head.

Bad Case of Lovin' You

Looking in the mirror afterward, he smoothed back his hair to cover the spot on the top of his head where his hair was thinning. He smiled at his reflection.

Damn, Silvers. You clean up good. Why the hell would that dumb broad want anyone else when she had a stud like Nate Silvers? Some people are just too stupid for their own good.

The aspirin and shower had definitely helped. Now all he needed was a little food to calm his roiling stomach. The kitchen was a god awful mess and there wasn't much in the fridge. He decided to treat himself and go out to breakfast. Having to cook for himself had gotten real old real fast anyway.

Guess I'll have to find somebody else to cook for me now that my no good, cheatin' wife walked out on me. Since he didn't have any immediate prospects for that role, a restaurant would have to do for now.

An hour later he was walking out of the Village Coffee Shop, "890 square feet of reality surrounded by Boulder." The classic diner had been around since the seventies, and he'd been a regular for many of those years. He always got good food at a decent price, and they fed him fast, which was exactly what he needed this morning. *It wasn't noon yet, was it?*

After filling his belly it was time to go and check up on that sorry excuse for a wife.

He was feeling pretty good by the time he turned on to 18th Street. He'd washed his truck and had his favorite country station on the radio. When Freddy B.'s "She Only Bitches When She Breathes" came on, he almost had to pull over he was laughing so hard.

Anita Louise

Ain't it the truth? She was always hot to trot before we got married. Once she got pregnant, the bitch turned as cold as ice. It might have been all right if she'd a given me a son, but no. She couldn't even do that right. One good for nothin' broad in the house was bad enough. Shit, once that girl turned into a teenager, it was like havin' two women bitchin' at me all the time.

Hell, Shelly probably did him a favor by getting the f*** out of his life and taking her brat kid with her. Still, he better not find out she was messing around with anybody, or else he might have to hurt her just on general principles.

No broad's gonna fool around on me and get away with it.

Nathan knew he'd done absolutely nothing wrong. Everything had been entirely Shelly and Mary Beth's fault.

Now he sat parked a couple of houses down from where the woman who'd "done him wrong" was staying. He'd only been there about ten minutes when he saw a police car coming from the opposite direction.

*What the f*** are the cops doin' around here?*

He slouched down in the seat when the cruiser passed his vehicle ... low enough so it looked like there was no one in his truck. Once the cops were out of sight, he got the hell out of there.

*What the crap were those sons of bitches doing on this street? Were those mother f***r's following him?*

He was going to have to take some time and think about all this. There was definitely something fishy going on here. He'd figure out what it was, and then he'd find a way around it. In the meantime, he needed a drink.

Chapter Fifteen

Brooke was sitting at the kitchen table finishing up the work she'd brought home from school when Shelly walked in. The women smiled at one another.

"Almost done?" Shelly asked.

"Pretty close. I could use a break anyway. What's up?"

"I just got off the phone with my mom."

"How's she doing?"

"Fine. I told her about what's going on. She wants Mary Beth to come and stay with her for a while since she's not in school right now. Do you think that would be okay?"

"Sure. Why wouldn't it be?"

"I was just thinking about her school work. Do you think I need to make sure she's getting everything done?"

"Mary Beth's one of the most responsible students I have. I'm pretty sure she'll be fine. If she has any questions, she can always call and we can help her out over the phone." Brooke paused before continuing cautiously. "I don't know how to say this, Shell, but didn't you tell me once your folks had a bit of a drinking problem back in high school?"

"That's true. My mom and step-dad were pretty heavy drinkers. He was the worst. Guess you didn't hear about it, but he died quite a while ago. Cirrhosis of the liver's what killed him."

"I'm so sorry, Shelly. I didn't know."

"It's okay." She shrugged. "Mom was really messed up right after he died, but in a way it turned out to be a good thing. She got into counseling after he passed, and they helped her quit drinking. Eventually she met Harold and ended up marrying him. He's good *to* her and good *for* her ... doesn't drink a lick. They retired a few years ago and moved to Arizona. They love it there."

"That's good to hear. I'm glad things turned out so well for her."

"Yeah. Me too. Anyway, I told her I'd discuss it with Mary Beth and you and let her know."

"Have you said anything to Mary Beth yet?"

"Just before I came to talk to you. She's all excited. It's in the seventies in Tucson where Mom and Harold are. Mary Beth figures she can lay in the sun while she's there, and maybe get a tan. I think she's hoping it'll help hide whatever isn't totally healed before she goes back to school."

"Sounds like you've got things all worked out then." Brooke smiled. "And you know, Shelly, with Mary Beth gone you'll be able to come with me to Aaron and Jane's party next weekend."

"Do you really think I should? I don't want to horn in on a family celebration."

"Nonsense. Now why don't you call your mom back and then go help Mary Beth pack."

"Okay. Thanks, Brooke. You have no idea how much being here is helping both Mary Beth *and* me. There's no way we could ever begin to repay you."

"Don't worry about it, Shell. Like I told you before, I would hope you'd do the same thing for me if our situations were reversed."

"You know I would."

"Yes, I do. So let's get your daughter packed. Then tomorrow you and I can go shopping for new outfits to wear to the party. Unless you already have something you were planning on wearing."

"I've got nothing, and even if I did, I wouldn't turn down the chance to go shopping with you, Brooke. Sounds like fun!"

Brooke finished up her school work while Shelly called her mother back. Shelly's mom was thrilled at the good news. Mary Beth was excited to see her grandmother and Grampa Harold. He treated the teen with the same loving care as his blood related grandchildren. They were able to get very reasonable airfare from Denver to Tucson. Shelly would drive Mary Beth to the airport first thing in the morning.

The rest of the day seemed to fly by. Discussing what to pack took more time than actually putting things in suitcases. Shelly checked and double checked to be sure Mary Beth had everything needed to complete all of her school assignments while in Tucson.

Brooke got a kick out of watching and listening to the interplay between mother and teenaged daughter. When

Anita Louise

they asked her to intervene, she simply smiled and politely declined.

For the evening's entertainment the three females chose a romantic comedy that no self-respecting male would ever admit to watching. Of course, all three of them enjoyed every sappy minute of it.

It was while Shelly was tucking in her daughter who was "way too old to be tucked into bed by her mother" that Brooke's cell phone rang. It was Zack.

"Hello," she said cheerily.

"Good evening, Brooke. How was your Sunday?" Zack asked.

"Very pleasant, thank you. And yours?"

"I was at the hospital today. Nothing too dramatic, just the usual broken bones and stitches, a sick kid or two, plus there were a few heart attacks ... some fairly serious and the others more of a scare. Like an 'it's about time you started taking better care of yourself warning."

"Gee, Zack, all of those things sound pretty dramatic to me. If it was me or any of my loved ones in the ER with any of the things you mentioned, I'd probably be worried sick."

"True, but I guess when you work with that kind of stuff on a daily basis, it becomes more or less routine."

"I'm sure you're right."

There was a pause in the conversation before they both started to speak at once.

"I had a great ..." mingled with, "Last night was ..."

"Ladies first," Zack said.

"You really are a gentleman, aren't you?"

Bad Case of Lovin' You

"I try to be," he admitted. "What was it you were going to say?"

"I was going to tell you, I had a great time last night," Brooke replied. "What about you?"

"First of all, I'm glad to hear you enjoyed yourself. I was hoping you'd say that. And I was going to let you know that, for me, last night was pretty amazing. As near to perfect as a first official date could be, as far as I'm concerned."

"Really?"

"Absolutely," Zack said. "Please tell me you agree."

"Actually, I do, but I wasn't one hundred percent sure how you felt about it until just now. I mean, I did get a little carried away." She was glad they were on the telephone so he couldn't see how she was blushing.

"Just so you know, Brooke, you can get carried away with me any time you want to. And you can be sure next time there's no way I'm going to stop you. If anything, I'll probably be the one who has a hard time keeping myself under control." His voice dropped to a whisper. "Remember, I told you.... I *want* you, Brooke. Very much. And next time, holding back isn't likely to be on the list of options. Okay?"

Brooke felt her blush turn to the heat of desire. Her nipples were suddenly tingling and the warmth radiated down to her core. She had to swallow before she could speak. "Um, yes. That sounds ... oh, I don't know exactly what to say, but that's definitely okay with me, Zack."

"What time do you want me to pick you up on Saturday?"

"Well, since I'm kind of the one who's in charge of this gig, I need to get there pretty early. Do you want to meet me there?"

Anita Louise

"No way. I'll go early with you," Zack insisted. "I'm at your service. Anything you need me to do, just let me know."

"Heavens no! You're my guest. I don't want you to have to do anything." Brooke's practical mind then went into high gear. "Mary Beth is going to visit her grandma for a while so I'm pretty sure Shelly's coming to the party with me. I know she'd be happy to come early and help me out with any of the last minute details. In fact, it would probably be better if she and I rode together anyway. Honestly, Zack, it really would be best if you just met me there." Brooke paused, concerned he thought she was trying to push him away. "I mean, if that's okay with you."

"Can Shelly drive?"

"I'm sure she wouldn't mind driving, but why would I ask her to do that?"

"Brooke," he hesitated before continuing, "I want you to come home with me after the party." Silence. "Please, say something, Brooke."

"I don't know what to say, Zack. I mean, I'm flattered and all, and I want to. I really do, but it just seems so ... I don't know. So *planned.* The other night it was so spontaneous. It just *happened."*

"We don't have to *do* anything, Brooke. You can simply come over for a nightcap. We can turn on the tv and watch one of the late shows. I want you sitting next to me with my arm around you. That's all. If anything more happens, great. If not, that's okay too. All right?"

She hesitated before speaking. "All right. Yes. I'll ask Shelly to drive. I'll go home with you, but I'm not promising anything. What happened the other night ... the way I behaved. Well, I'm not really sure what that was all about. I'm not usually like that, so I hope you don't expect ..."

He interrupted her. "I don't *expect* anything from you, Brooke. If we get to my house and you tell me you want me to take you home before we even go in, it's okay. I'll turn around and take you right home. Do you trust me, Brooke?"

"Yes, I ..."

"What is it?"

"Gabriella will be there ... at the party. You'll get to meet her."

"Gabriella? You mean your sister?"

"Yes, my twin. The outgoing, popular, everybody loves her Gabriella."

"Oh, Brooke." His voice sounded sad ... disappointed. "I'm looking forward to meeting your twin, Brooke, but she's not *you.* I'm not interested in Gabriella or anyone else, Brooke. I'm interested in *you.*"

"You say that now, but how do you know? That's what Marcus said too," she mumbled almost to herself.

In her mind she could hear the voice of the boy she'd fallen for in college. He'd sworn Brooke was the only one for him. And then not only had he gotten back with his high school sweetheart, but he confessed to having the hots for Gabby all along.

"Marcus? Who's Marcus?" Zack asked.

"Oh, never mind. It's not important."

"I think it is. Brooke, we can't have secrets if we want this to work."

"I know. You're right, but if I tell you now, then I won't know ... How's this? I promise, if nothing happens at the

Anita Louise

party. If I end up going home with you, I'll tell you when we get to your house. Okay?"

"If nothing *happens* at the party? I don't understand, Brooke, but okay."

"I'm sorry, Zack. I guess now you're seeing the *real* me ... warts and all."

He chuckled. "Warts, huh? I'm pretty sure there's a cure for those."

"I must be sounding like an insecure teenager. God! I feel so stupid."

"Stop it, Brooke. You're feeling what you're feeling, and it's *okay*. I'm sure there's a reason, and when you tell me, I'll understand. For now, let's just look forward to having a wonderful time together on Saturday night. How's that sound?"

"Good. That sounds good." After a moment of hesitation she said, "And thanks, Zack. Thanks for being so understanding and not treating me like I'm some kind of weird-o. Even though *I* think I sound like some kind of weird-o."

He was chuckling as he said, "A weird-o with warts. Hmph. We're *really* going to have to work on your self-image, Brooke."

Now Brooke was chuckling too. "Okay. Enough already. I'll see you on Saturday."

"What time?" he asked.

"The party is supposed to start at eight, so any time after eight's okay."

"Okay if I'm a little bit early, just in case I can help with anything?"

She sighed. "If you insist. Yes. It's okay if you show up a little bit early, but if I have anything to say about it, there won't be a *thing* for you to do."

"Then I'll just stay out of your way. I'll make myself happy by watching you throw the best engagement party a brother and future sister-in-law could ever hope for."

"You're *good*, Zack Carter. I think I might just keep you."

"I certainly hope so, Brooke Adler. I certainly hope so."

Finding a bar that was open early on a Sunday afternoon was a bit of a challenge. But Nate finally found a little hole in the wall where he could get a cold one. He and the bartender were the only people in the place. The guy behind the bar was willing to bullshit with Nate for a while, but it didn't take long before he made some excuse about having "work to do." After that, Nathan Silvers was left alone with his thoughts.

What the hell were the cops doin' on that street where Shelly's stayin' now? There's no way they could be lookin' for me, is there?

There was a pool table toward the back of the bar. Nate decided to amuse himself with a little solo eight ball. After picking out a cue stick and giving it some much needed chalk, he racked the balls up nice and tight. He lined up his break carefully.

SMACK!

The balls went flying across the table. The solid seven and the red striped eleven ball each fell in different pockets.

Seven, eleven. This must be my lucky day. Take your pick, Nate. Stripes or solids?

After carefully looking over the table he decided on solids. With a little kiss off the thirteen he could easily sink the yellow one ball and leave himself perfectly positioned for the next shot.

Kiss off. Yeah, that's what that good for nothin' wife of mine can do.

He'd been playing pool since he was tall enough to see over the table, and he was damn good. As he watched the one ball drop into the corner pocket with satisfaction he thought, *Kiss off, hell. She can kiss my ass!*

With every shot he got more worked up.

After all I've done for that ungrateful bitch. Shit. I never should've married her in the first place.

SMACK!

He loved the sound of the pool balls crashing against each other.

SMACK!

She's got a hellava lot a nerve walking out on me like that.

SMACK! Two of his remaining solids fell right where he expected them to.

SMACK!

She's gonna have to pay for this. Leavin' like she did. Siccin' the cops on me.

He carefully lined up the eight ball. It would've been easy to sink it straight into the side, but there was no challenge in that. Taking his time he carefully calculated the angles to bank it off the side and back into the corner.

SMACK!

With a satisfied smile that didn't really look like a smile at all, he watched the eight ball roll neatly into the corner. He'd run the table.

She thinks she's so damn smart. Thinks she can walk away from Nathan Silvers without any consequences, does she? Well, she hasn't heard the last of me ... not by a long shot.

"Bartender! How about another beer over here?"

Chapter Sixteen

The house seemed much quieter than Brooke had become accustomed to now that Mary Beth was off visiting her grandparents. It was amazing how quickly Brooke had become used to having Shelly and her daughter living with her.

Kathy Braddock, Shelly's mom, called as soon as Mary Beth landed in Tucson to reassure Shelly the teen had arrived safely. After that, Shelly and her daughter spoke at least once a day.

It'd been Kathy and Harold's plan to take their granddaughter out and show her some of the local sites, but one look at the bruises on the girl's face changed their minds quickly. The pampering began immediately. While the teen loved being treated like a fragile princess, getting her schoolwork done was still a necessity. Luckily, the importance of personal responsibility was a value Shelly had instilled in her daughter from an early age.

Brooke was sitting at the table correcting papers, and Shelly was studying for one of her classes. Mary Beth had been in Tucson for only a few days. Both women were missing the girl and wanted to hear the teen's voice. Shelly happily agreed with Brooke's request to put the call with her daughter on speaker.

"Hi, honey. How's it going?" Shelly asked.

"Hi, Mom. Everything's fine. I do miss you though."

"I miss you too, baby. How about your school work? Brooke's right here. She said if you need any help just let her know."

"Hi, Brooke," Mary Beth chirped, "I'll let you know if I get stuck, but so far so good. I'm spending a couple hours a day working on my assignments, and I still have plenty of time for lying out in the sun."

"You're wearing sunscreen, right?"

"Of course I am, Mom. Grandma's a real stickler about it. She says she wouldn't have so many wrinkles today, if she'd used sunscreen instead of baby oil and iodine when she was a teenager."

"Teens just didn't know any better back in Grandma's day. What else are you doing besides lying in the sun? Are you getting any exercise? I hope you're not just studying and sitting by the pool all day."

"This is so funny!" Mary Beth exclaimed. "My first day here, I go down to the pool with Grandma and Grandpa Harold. For the first half hour or so we're the only ones there. You know ... nice and quiet. Next thing you know all these people start coming into the pool area."

"What was going on?" Shelly asked.

"Water aerobics! There must've been thirty people in the pool. At first I wanted to leave because I was embarrassed about the bruises. But Grandma and Grandpa

Harold wanted to stay for the class. Then they talked me into doing it *with* them."

"How was it?"

"It was actually *fun*. Can you imagine? A teenage girl with tape across her nose and a bunch of bruises on her face, in the middle of a bunch of old people with gray hair."

"I wish I had a picture of *that*." Shelly chuckled.

"You know, Mom, everybody was really nice. Most of them just ignored the bruises and treated me like a normal person. The ones who did ask, I just told them I had an accident. They were so nice about it. I guess this is a first for me. You know, spending time around old people. They're really very nice. Some of them even said they want me to meet their grandchildren."

"How sweet," Shelly replied.

"It'd be even sweeter if one was a really cute guy near my age." She giggled.

"You must be feeling better if you're back to talking about cute boys."

"Yeah, I guess, but I'd rather wait to meet boys till next time I visit here. Then I won't look so awful."

"Oh, honey, regardless of those bruises, you're still a beautiful girl."

"Thanks, Mom, but I think you almost *have* to say stuff like that. You know, since you're my mother and all."

Shelly was adamant in her response. "No, I don't. I've always believed honesty is the best policy. When I say you're beautiful, I mean it."

"Thanks, Mom. I love you."

"I love you too, Mary Beth. Say 'hello' to Grandma for me and I'll talk to you later. Okay?"

"K. Bye."

"Bye-bye." Shelly made kissing sounds into the phone before she hung up. "I sure do miss that girl," she said to Brooke with a sigh.

"I do too," Brooke agreed. "She's a great kid. You've really done a wonderful job with her, Shelly. You should be proud."

"I am. I'm real proud of my girl. I'd like it if she felt better about herself. She has a tendency to be pretty hard on herself."

"Hmmm. Sounds like someone I know," Brooke said pointedly.

"Me? Nah. I think I'm pretty good."

"You were pretty darn good at deflecting the compliment I just paid you."

"Huh?"

"When I said, 'You should be proud,' I meant you should be proud of *yourself.* You've done a good job raising Mary Beth. Of course, you're proud of her too, but give yourself some credit. You haven't exactly been in the best of situations since she was born, have you?"

"No. I guess not. I know Nathan was doing the best he could. We all do, don't we? I mean, we're all doing the best we can, given our view of the world. Nathan was always saying how this wasn't fair, or that wasn't fair. When something would happen and he didn't like it, he'd always find a scapegoat. It wasn't *his* fault. He'd blame me, Mary Beth, his parents, his coach in college, his boss, the weather, the government, you name it. It didn't matter. It was never him, always somebody or something else."

"You're nothing like that, and neither is Mary Beth."

Anita Louise

"Thanks. I'd like to think so. I always looked at being a mother as a total blessing, and I also saw it as an important responsibility. I used to have a poster on my refrigerator of that poem *Children Learn What They Live*. Do you remember that?"

"I sure do. My Mom had that same poem on *our* refrigerator growing up."

"That's probably one of the reasons I always loved coming over to your house. Your family always treated me so nice. Plus you kids were even nice to *each other*."

"Mom and Dad were pretty adamant about treating each other like we wanted to be treated. You know, the Golden Rule in action. Guess it worked." Brooke smiled.

"I think I used your family as a model for what I wanted mine to be like. Anyway, I just did my best to keep that poem in mind as Mary Beth was growing up. It helped me to be patient when it would have been easier to lose my temper. If something happened at school and she got in trouble, of course we'd talk about whatever it was. But I always made sure she knew it was what she *did* that was wrong, and there was nothing wrong with *her*."

"You're a great mom, Shell. I hope I can do as good a job someday when I have kids of my own."

"You will. Look at how you treat your students. Mary Beth isn't the only kid who loves having you for a teacher. Whether you know it or not, you're very popular among the students at Summit."

"Thanks, Shelly. I do my best." She smiled at her friend. "Well, I guess it's official. The Mutual Admiration Society has two new members."

"I'm in. Sign me up."

Bad Case of Lovin' You

"Hey, do you want to go shopping after dinner? Maybe we can get you that new outfit to make you feel like a million bucks at the party on Saturday."

"Sounds like a plan. What about you? What are you wearing?"

"Are you kidding me? Do you think I'm going shopping with you and not coming back with something new for myself? No way, Jose."

"All righteee," Shelly said with a grin. "This is going to be *fun!*"

Nathan Silvers drove slowly past the house on 18th Street for the fifth time in two days. Ever since he'd seen the cop on this street, he hadn't felt comfortable stopping, even if it was a couple of houses down. He'd driven by late Sunday morning before the bars were open. He thought maybe he'd see Shelly coming back from church. She used to go out every Sunday morning. She *said* she was going to church, but for all he knew she could've been meetin' up with some guy she was shackin' up with.

Wouldn't put it past her. Damn bitch. Always actin' like she was so high and mighty. Thought she was better 'n me.

Today he was cruising slowly by on his way home from work. It had become pretty much a habit, even though it was a little bit out of his way. He didn't really care. Somehow just driving by the house where his lousy wife was hiding out made him feel a tiny bit better.

Of course, he didn't *always* go straight home from work. Sometimes it was nice to go out with a couple of the guys for a few drinks instead of being home all by himself.

Anita Louise

One of the advantages to drinking at home was he didn't have some dumb ass bartender cutting him off.

Asshole thinks he knows better than me how much liquor I can handle. Stupid shit. Who does he think he is tellin' me I can't have another drink if I want one?

As he was coming around the block for the third time his persistence finally paid off. The garage door slowly lifted. *Son of a bitch.* It was Shelly's dark blue Volvo station wagon backing out.

Well, well, well, little Miss Goodie Two Shoes, where ya headin' this fine afternoon? I think I'll just find out for myself.

He hoped like hell Shelly hadn't seen his truck so he sped up and drove around the corner. Half way down the block he pulled into a driveway like he owned the place and waited. When he saw the Volvo pass through the intersection, he quickly backed out of the drive. By the time he got to the corner the Volvo was already a couple of blocks away.

Keeping far enough away so she wouldn't notice him without losing track of her car was the tricky part. He felt a sense of exhilaration. The adrenaline kicked in and his heart started pumping double time. It was looking like she was headed to Flatiron Crossing, the big mall off the Denver Boulder Turnpike. Even though it'd be a risk, he was going to have to keep a little tighter tail on her once she got nearer to the mall. Now that he was *this close* to meeting up with Shelly, he didn't want to lose her in the gigantic parking lot.

He could hardly wait to see the look on her face. Wasn't the little lady going to be surprised when he just *happened* to bump into her?

Bad Case of Lovin' You

Man, I wish I'd thought to bring a pint with me. A little slug of vodka would taste pretty damn good right now.

Just as he expected, the Volvo took the Interlocken Loop/Northwest Parkway exit. He sped up. Two vehicles were between him and his wife's car, and one was a delivery van.

Perfect. Maybe I shoulda been a cop. I'm pretty damn good at this stuff.

He did his best to keep far enough away so Shelly wouldn't notice him in her rearview mirror. At the same time he needed to make sure he didn't lose her. He licked his lips. He was definitely going to need a drink after this was over.

Finally, she pulled into a spot between Nordstrom and Macy's. He stayed in his truck and watched as Shelly stepped out of her car. Another woman with long dark hair got out of the passenger side.

That must be the bitch who's lettin' my wife hide out at her place. Wonder who the hell she is? No matter. She's gonna have ta pay for all the goddamn aggravation this whole thing's causin' me too.

Once he was sure the two women were headed into Macy's he quickly parked his truck in the closest available spot. Normally he would've found a location where there wouldn't be even a remote possibility of someone opening a door into his vehicle. Not this time. He was too close to let anything get in his way now.

He sprinted across the parking lot to the door he'd seen his wife and the other broad go through. Once inside he scanned the aisles and spotted the two women standing in front of the directory near the escalators. As he watched, the two laughed and smiled before giving each other a hug.

Anita Louise

Shit maybe those two broads are gettin' it on. Wouldn't surprise me if that stupid ass wife of mine was a closet lesbo. Well, let's see how the two dykes like it when a real man interrupts them.

He walked swiftly to where the two stood.

"Shelly. Honey? Oh, sweetheart, it's so good to see you. I've been missing you so, so much."

He pulled his wife into his arms. Even though he put every bit of sincerity he could muster into the embrace, he could still feel his wife stiffen.

Her arms remained limp at her side, and she stepped back as soon as he released her.

Some things just never change. She's as frigid as ever. Can't even show her own husband a little affection.

"Hello, Nathan." Shelly's response was cold. "What are you doing here?"

Plastering a jovial smile on his face, he answered, "Doing a little shopping. How 'bout you, Babe?" After a moment of standing there in silence, he looked at the woman standing next to him and asked, "Who's your friend, Shelly?" Still, neither of the women said a word, so he stuck out his hand. "Hi. I'm Nathan Silvers, Shelly's husband. Nice to meet you ... uh?"

He'd figured the broad would be too up tight to ignore him and he was right.

"Hello, Nathan. You probably don't remember me, but we went to high school together."

"We did? No way. I'd absolutely remember a girl as pretty as you. What did you say your name was?"

"I didn't, but my name is Brooke."

"Brooke? Hmm. Let me think." He crossed his arms over his chest, tipped his arm up and tapped his chin. "Brooke. Brooke. Wait a minute! Are you Brooke Adler? Don't you come from a family of like a million kids or something?"

Nate could see the woman was trying hard not to be amused, but it looked to him like she was succumbing to his irresistible charm.

"Yes, I do come from a rather large family, nine children."

"Oh, yeah. Now I remember. Me and Shell ..." He put his arm around his wife, but she shrugged him off and moved away quickly. He smiled congenially, and cocked his head as if questioning her behavior. "Anyway, a bunch of us used to hang out at your house every once in a while."

Shelly interrupted. "Nate. Stop it. I know what you're trying to do, and it's not going to work. Mary Beth and I are not coming back."

Nate managed to put on his best look of hurt. "Aw c'mon, Shell. I know I messed up, but we can work it out. You know I've always loved you."

"Then you sure have a strange way of showing it." Shelly looked at Brooke and said, "Come on. Let's go. This conversation is over." Hiking her purse up on her shoulder, she turned her back on Nate.

Instinctively he grabbed her arm. "Shelly. Honey."

She shook him off vigorously. If looks could kill, he knew he'd have been a dead man. "Get your hands off me, Nate. You will *never* lay a hand on me or my child again. *Never.*"

With that the two women turned and stepped onto the escalator.

Shelly was visibly shaking by the time she and Brooke got to the top of the escalator. Brooke put her arm around her friend's shoulders.

"You okay, Shelly?"

Shelly closed her eyes and took a deep breath. "I will be. I think I'm more mad than anything."

"You were pretty awesome, you know."

"I can't believe he thinks he can turn on the charm, and everything's going to go back to the way it was. He must really think I'm stupid."

"He's the one who's not too bright if he thinks you're going to buy into his Mr. Nice Guy act."

"That's the thing, Brooke. I always did before." Shelly shook her head. "I don't know what I was thinking. He's never going to change." She sighed deeply again. "Do you mind if we don't do this right now? Somehow I'm not really in the mood for shopping anymore."

"Me neither. Do you want to go someplace ... sit and talk?"

"Can we just go home? Any bar that's close by, we're liable to run into Nathan. I don't think I could handle him again so soon."

"Sure. I've got a nice bottle of Chablis all chilled in the fridge. How's that sound?"

"Sounds perfect. Thanks, Brooke."

"No thanks needed. Let's get home and put on our comfy clothes and relax. If you want to talk, fine. If you don't, that's fine too."

Bad Case of Lovin' You

"Okay." Shelly sniffed and swiped at her eyes with her knuckles. Then she straightened her shoulders, managed a feeble grin and said, "Take me home, Country Road."

Chapter Seventeen

Zack Carter arranged his shift so he was off on Saturday night. He didn't have to go back to the hospital until Monday. Of course, he was hoping Brooke would spend the night with him after the party on Saturday. But he knew there was a strong possibility it wouldn't happen, and he'd end up sleeping alone. He was almost positive she wasn't a virgin, but there was no doubt in his mind that the number of sexual encounters she'd had was very limited.

For some strange reason he'd yet to figure out, he wanted something more than just sex from Brooke Adler. Sure, she was beautiful, and even though she didn't seem to know it, sexy as hell. He'd lost count of how many times he'd replayed their encounter on his living room sofa the previous weekend. Recalling the fullness of her breast in his hand and her innately sensual response when he'd brushed his thumb back and forth over her taut nipple, left him struggling to control his own arousal.

Bad Case of Lovin' You

All of her inhibitions had somehow disappeared that evening. It would've been easy to take advantage of her vulnerability. Yet there was an innocence about her, and he was unable to ignore it. Even though they'd stopped drinking earlier, maybe she'd had a little more wine than she could handle. Maybe the alcohol was still affecting her. He wasn't really sure why, but he'd felt an almost instinctive need to protect her from her own seemingly uncontrollable desires. Had he not, he was quite certain whatever future might otherwise develop, could've been ruined before it even had a chance to begin.

It was still a couple of days before he'd see her again, and he was torn. He wanted to call her. He just wanted to hear her voice ... to talk about his day, but he didn't know whether or not he should. On one hand he didn't want to come across too needy, and he also didn't want to appear too aggressive.

He was finally home after a grueling day at the hospital, and really needed to vent. He'd learned through both experience and his upbringing that it helped to discuss whatever was bothering him. Better to talk it out than to lock his feelings away and try to ignore them. Instinctively he felt Brooke Adler would be a good listener and sounding board.

There'd been a big accident on the turnpike. Almost a dozen people were brought into the emergency room all at once. Fortunately, most of the injuries were not life threatening. However, the most serious one involved a six-year-old boy and his father. It'd hit Zack a little harder than any of the others.

The little guy had been misbehaving in the back seat of the car. The father had taken his eyes off the road for a moment to discipline the child. It was just then that the normally fast moving traffic came to a stop in front of them. By the time the man turned back around, he was too close. His car crashed into the back of a fully loaded delivery truck at almost fifty miles an hour. The good news was both the driver and passenger survived. The bad news was the impact had crushed the father's legs. It was too soon to tell whether or not the man would end up in a wheelchair for the rest of his life. The worst news was the six-year-old boy evidently blamed himself for the whole thing. The child kept screaming, "I'm sorry, Daddy."

A part of Zack kept remembering a fateful day in his own life. He was only five when an accident had cost Zack's father his life. *Thank God the man will live. Wheelchair or not, at least he'll be around. His wife still has a husband, and the boy still has his father.*

He'd been raised to believe there was always something positive hidden in even the most difficult circumstance. Yet he was having a hard time finding the silver lining in this case. Zack was sitting in one of his favorite spots ... a comfortable chair facing the view of the mountains. When his cell phone rang, he hoped it was Brooke. Quickly, he pulled his cell from his pocket. It wasn't Brooke, but he smiled when he saw it was his mother.

"Hi, Mom. I'm really glad you called."

"That's always good to hear. What's up?"

"Nothing really. Just had kind of a rough day at work." He told her about the accident involving the little boy and his father.

"Oh, honey. Something told me I ought to give you a call. You were so young when it happened. I was never sure if you had any recollection of that day we lost your dad. Sounds like this incident might have reminded you of it. Am I right?"

"Yeah. Of course I felt bad for the dad, but I felt just awful for the kid."

His mother repeated a quote from the Dali Lama. "When we meet real tragedy in life, we can react two ways ... either by losing hope and falling into self-destructive habits, or by using the challenge to find our inner strength."

Zack knew the phrase had helped sustain Nancy Carter through various trying circumstances she'd faced over the years. "I know you're right, Mom, but sometimes it's just so *hard.*"

"All we can do is pray the man and his son will both find their own inner strength."

"I have been."

"I will too." She paused. "How're things going with Brooke? How was your date?"

"It was great. I had a fabulous time. I'm pretty sure she did too. Saturday night I'm going with her to her brother and future sister-in-law's engagement party."

"Wonderful! Have you asked her about coming over here for dinner on Sunday? Dylan and Kaylee will be here."

"You'll be happy to know the answer to your question is 'yes.' I asked her while we were on our date this past Saturday. She was a little hesitant at first, but it didn't take much to convince her. She's really looking forward to meeting you, Mom."

"And *I'm* looking forward to meeting *her.* She sounds like a lovely girl, Zack."

"She is. You're really going to like her."

"I'm sure I will. Come on by around six. We'll have a few appetizers and chat before we have dinner. Is there anything special she likes, or anything she can't or doesn't eat?"

"I don't think so, Mom. She's pretty down to earth."

"I'm liking her better all the time. Have fun on Saturday, and tell Brooke I'm looking forward to meeting her on Sunday."

"Okay, Mom, I will. Thanks for calling. See you Sunday."

"I'm glad I listened to that little voice. It's always good to talk with you, Son. I love you, Zack. Bye for now."

"Love you too, Mom. Bye."

Zack sighed and stretched. Talking to his mother always made him feel better somehow. She was the one woman he knew he could always count on.

What about you, Brooke Adler? Are you the kind of woman I could always count on?

In spite of his earlier reluctance, he gave into the urge to call the woman who'd been on his mind so much of the time.

Brooke picked up almost immediately. "Hello?"

"Hi, Brooke. It's Zack."

"Oh, hi, Zack. I was in the middle of something. I just grabbed my phone without looking to see who it was. How are you?"

"I'm good, but if this is a bad time, we can talk later."

"No. Not at all. I needed a break anyway. What's going on?"

"Just got off the phone with my mother. She's really looking forward to meeting you on Sunday."

201

Bad Case of Lovin' You

"I'm looking forward to meeting her too, and your brother and sister-in-law. What time?"

"Mom said around six. We can talk about it more on Saturday." After a moment's hesitation he continued. "So how was your day?"

"Oh, you know, pretty typical day in the life of a middle school teacher. The kids seemed to be a little restless. Every once in a while we're getting these hints of spring. The end of the school year can get kind of crazy. The students are ready for vacation by then, and so are the teachers."

"I remember. As much as I liked school, I always looked forward to summer vacation."

"Me too." She paused. "So how was your day?"

"Quite honestly, it was rough. Did you hear about that big accident on the turnpike?"

"Yeah. It was on the radio on my way home. So you got slammed, huh?"

"Just like things get crazy at the end of the year for you, it can be pretty chaotic when there's a ton of people being brought in all at the same time."

"You okay?"

"I'm fine, but there was this little boy...."

"Oh no! Is he going to be all right?"

"Actually, he was in a proper car seat in the back, so he wasn't too bad. His dad wasn't so lucky. He needed surgery and was still in intensive care when I left."

Zack continued to tell her about the boy blaming himself, and how the incident brought back memories of the loss of his own father. Brooke's compassion was evident. Talking to her was like a soothing balm on his aching spirit.

Anita Louise

Their conversation went from serious to funny. She told him about a seventh grade boy who was standing outside waiting to get on the bus. The lad did something totally gross to try to get the attention of a group of girls.

"So what'd he do?"

"He rolled part of a brownie up to look like a piece of dog poop. After he dropped it on the ground near the girls, he pointed it out and yelled, "EW! Dog poop!" Then he picked it up and took a bite."

"That is totally *sickening!*"

She chuckled. "I *know.* Why in the world he thought that would be a good move is totally beyond me."

They shared tidbits about their childhood. Laughed about siblings and crazy family vacations. They discussed their values and beliefs ... dreams and goals, both met and still being sought after. It seemed as if they could talk forever.

Reminiscing about their initial reaction to one another when they saw each other for the first time in the hospital cafeteria, he felt the now familiar surge of desire.

"I couldn't take my eyes off you, Brooke. Even though Jane was waving her arms like crazy, it was almost as if no one else existed."

There was no way to know for sure, but he was almost positive that if they'd been on Skype, he'd have seen a lovely blush creep across Brooke's face.

"You had me pretty mesmerized too. I'm not usually a sucker for a guy in a lab coat, but there was just *something* about you. I was absolutely thrilled when it turned out Jane and you knew one another."

Bad Case of Lovin' You

"Even if I hadn't known Jane, I'd have figured out some way to meet you. But fate stepped in, and now it's up to us to see where this leads."

Zack wasn't used to the riot of emotions moving through him. There'd been plenty of women who aroused his lust, but none of them had caused these other, much more unfamiliar feelings. He wanted to be Brooke's protector, her confidante. Yes, he wanted her body, but for once, he wanted so much more.

Close to an hour later, Brooke finally said, "Zack, as much as I'm enjoying the heck out of this, I really should get off the phone."

"Me too." After a moment he went on. "Thanks, Brooke. I was feeling kind of down when I got home today. I don't feel that way anymore."

"I'm glad, Zack. I've really enjoyed our conversation too."

"Okay then. I'll see you on Saturday."

"You sure will."

Brooke was smiling when Shelly walked in the room.

"Well, don't you look like the cat who just ate the canary?" Shelly said. "What's going on?"

"I just got off the phone with Zack. We talked for almost an *hour*. I don't think I've *ever* talked to a guy for that long."

"Sounds like things are going pretty well for you and Dr. McDreamy."

"Seems like it. He'll be meeting Gabby for the first time on Saturday."

"So?"

"I don't know. You know how Gabriella is. She's so vivacious and everything."

"What the heck are you talking about? You and Gabriella are *twins.*"

"That's the point. We *look* alike, but we're so different in every other way. I'm quiet. She's outgoing. I'm conservative. She's way out there ... willing to try anything."

"But she's not *you*, Brooke. I've known Gabby just as long as I have you, and I like her ... a lot. She's a great person, but you have qualities she doesn't. There's a quiet strength about you. No one would *dare* mess with someone you care about. You're one of the most compassionate and caring people I've ever known. Look what you've done for me and Mary Beth. You took us in on a moment's notice. You're letting us stay here and not asking for a *thing* in return. There's no way we'll ever be able to thank you enough."

"Well, you have to admit under the circumstances, you're a little bit prejudiced in my favor. Gabby probably would've done the same thing."

"Maybe she would. Maybe she wouldn't. The thing is, you're not her, and she's not you. And I think Dr. Zack Carter is smart enough to tell the difference."

"We'll see. Like I said, Zack and Gabby will meet at the party on Saturday night. I've developed a pretty darn good radar when it comes to guys and my sister. If he's attracted to her ... I don't know. I know it'll hurt, but I'd rather find out now." *Before I totally fall in love with him.* Brooke didn't want to talk about her concerns regarding Zack and Gabriella anymore, so she changed the subject. "Speaking of the party, we never did get something to wear. How about the two of us go out to dinner? Then we can shop for a couple of gorgeous outfits."

"What are we waiting for?" Shelly asked. "Let's grab our coats."

The two friends hurried off to the mall. This time Brooke drove, and she decided to use the entrance near Dillard's. She didn't want to stir up any bad memories from their last visit to Flatiron Crossing.

Once inside the mall, they were having a hard time deciding between Mexican and Italian food. The aroma of the pasta sauce and spices emanating from Villa Fresh Italian Kitchen finally won them over. Their delicious dinner of salad and chicken parmesan was also filled with the laughter of close friends. The more time they spent together, the more Brooke felt that her friendship with Shelly had grown to an unbreakable bond.

After trying on at least ten dresses each, Brooke and Shelly stood outside the dressing room staring at each other. Brooke was wearing an elegant navy blue sheath dress covered with lustrous lace and enhanced with a short, flared peplum waist. The above-the-knee length showed off her long legs.

Shelly grinned broadly. "Gosh, Brooke, you look *fabulous* in that dress. You're going to drive that man crazy."

"Thanks, Shell. I really like how it's just lace on the sleeves and the top of the bodice. It makes me *feel* good wearing it."

"I'm sure it's going to make Dr. McDreamy feel good just to look at you." Shelly giggled.

"I hope so."

"I *know* so."

"I probably shouldn't say this, but the way you look in your dress is going to make Luke go ga-ga. You know he's always had a crush on you."

Shelly had chosen a black knee length cocktail dress with a sleek matte jersey bodice and a pleated taffeta skirt. The scoop neckline and taffeta sash at the waist accentuated her curves. Shelly looked down and smoothed her hands across the skirt. A blush crept across her face. "That was just a kid thing."

"Maybe." Knowing there was too much going on in her friend's life already, Brooke let the subject drop. "I think our work here is done. What do you say we go home and treat ourselves to that yummy looking low calorie dessert you made? What did you say it was?"

"It's a frozen dessert ... Cherry-Merlot Granita. Take sweet, dark cherries, some orange rind and orange juice, water, sugar, and merlot, put them in a blender, freeze and voila." Shelly waved her hand with a flourish. "I replaced the sugar with your stevia so the calorie count is super low, practically nonexistent."

"Sounds good to me. Besides, you know what they say ... a little red wine is good for you. Lots of antioxidants."

"Yeah. Want to hear my new motto?" Shelly asked.

"Sure. What is it?"

"I love to cook with wine. Sometimes I even put it in the food."

Laughing together, the women changed back into their street clothes. Their newly purchased dresses were hanging in the back seat of the car as they drove home.

Bad Case of Lovin' You

When Nate Silvers saw his wife and the woman he now knew was Brooke Adler, headed back to Flatiron Crossing, he knew he'd never get away with "accidentally" bumping into them again.

Might as well go get a drink. After all, it's Friday night.

He decided to go back to the little dive he'd found the previous Sunday. It was fairly close to his house. If he happened to have just a tad too much to drink, he could take back roads to get home.

*Damn cops are everywhere these days. Any more than two or three f***n' drinks and they act like you're drunk. Shit, I can down a six pack, and it doesn't affect me a bit. What do those assholes know, anyway?*

When he walked into the joint this time, it was filled with people and loud voices. The sound of pool balls clacking against one another filled the air along with music from the old jukebox in the corner. A group of guys stood around the pool table in the back of the room. He'd get to that later.

He found an open seat at the end of the bar near the door. It gave him a view where he could see pretty much everything going on in the place. The bar was filled with mostly men, but there were a few women in the room.

It was a different bartender than the one who'd been there on Sunday.

"What's your pleasure?" the barkeep asked.

"Shot and a beer. House whiskey and a PBR."

"You got it."

He saw a table of women sitting near the pool table. There was a redhead with big tits spilling out of her low cut top. He looked at her and smiled.

Man. I could sure use a piece of ass. I bet she'd love to have my dick between those knockers.

The bartender delivered his drinks. Nate downed the whiskey in one gulp. Sipping on his beer, he kept his eye on the chick with the big boobs. She looked his way and they made eye contact.

Lifting his drink in a mock salute, he waited to see what she'd do. After a slight hesitation, she lifted her drink too. Then she wrapped her lips around the straw and sucked, keeping her eyes locked with his the whole time.

He felt his dick twitch. *That broad's hot to trot. Damn. I'm gonna get me some pussy tonight.*

He flagged down the bartender.

"What can I do you for?"

"Send the little lady over there a drink on me. The redhead with the rack."

"Sure. Anything for you?"

"You can give me another shot."

Nate watched as the drink was delivered to her table. Once she understood who it was from, she got up and walked toward him. Her clothes were tight all over with a little too much skin hanging out of the top of her leggings. She had on red platform heels, big red plastic bangle bracelets and hoop earrings. He could smell her cheap perfume from ten feet away. She was *perfect.*

"Thanks for the drink, handsome. My name's Crystal. What's yours?"

"I'm Nate, and you're welcome, Crystal. Hard to resist a pretty little thing like you."

Bad Case of Lovin' You

When she squeezed into the narrow space between the barstools her tits rubbed up against him. He put his arm around her shoulder and nuzzled her neck.

"You smell almost as good as you look, Crystal."

"Why, thank you, Nate. You're not so bad yourself."

Motioning to an empty table in the front corner of the bar he said, "How about you and me sittin' down over there. We can get to know each other a little better."

"I'd *love* to get to know you better, Nate," she purred. She put her arm through his, and pressed up close as they walked across the room.

They sat side by side, as close as the chairs would allow. He put his hand on her thigh under the table. As they talked he moved his hand farther up her leg, closer to the vee where her thighs met. He was getting hard, and he knew she must be wet and ready.

"Why don't we get out of here?" he asked.

"Where do you want to go?" she inquired innocently.

"You want to follow me over to my place?"

"I would, but I don't have a car. I came with my friends."

"Well, tell your friends you got another ride home. Let's get the hell outta here. You got me so hot I can hardly stand it."

"Okay, sugar. Just a minute."

He focused on the sway of her hips as she walked back to her table, ignoring the jiggling fat. Nate walked back up to the bar and paid his tab.

"Have fun," the bartender said slyly.

"I plan to." Nate replied.

Anita Louise

Crystal snuggled close to him in the car and wasted no time. She started rubbing her hands over the front of his pants as soon as the doors were closed.

"Oooo. That's nice," she crooned.

He'd barely gotten out of the parking lot when she unzipped his pants. Pushing his jeans and underwear down, she released his throbbing cock.

"Ummm," she murmured just before she leaned down and took him into her mouth.

"Oh God, Crystal. That feels so f⸱⸱⸱n' good. If you don't slow down, I'm gonna come in your mouth."

"And I want you to, sugar. I want you to come in my mouth, but first I want to feel your big cock inside of me." She leaned over again and licked the pre-come off the tip. "Ummm."

He drove home as fast as he could, thinking, *If the cops pull me over they're gonna be in for a big surprise.* She continued to lick and stroke his rigid dick during the entire drive.

His house was a mess and his bed hadn't been made since Shelly left, but Crystal didn't seem to mind. They were both naked within minutes of entering the house. And shortly after they walked through the door, she rolled a condom over his length just before he entered her. He pumped wildly while she moaned with pleasure.

In only a few minutes he was totally spent. Crystal seemed content. Nate laid his head on the pillow with the buxom redhead tucked under his arm and quickly fell asleep.

When he woke up, Crystal was gone and so was all the money in his wallet.

Chapter Eighteen

"**S**on of a *bitch!*" Nate Silvers cursed loudly as he looked at his empty wallet. Not only was it empty of cash, his driver's license, credit cards, medical and social security cards were missing as well. Also gone was the spare check he'd always kept in his wallet "just in case."

That little cock suckin' broad is gonna pay for this. When I get ahold of her, I'm gonna wring her skinny little neck.

By the time he'd woken up, it was past four o'clock on Saturday morning, and the bars had been closed for hours. He'd have to wait till the next day. Then he'd go back to the bar where he'd met Crystal and raise some hell.

He wasn't too worried about the credit cards and other things missing from his wallet. With the big tits on that broad, there was no way she'd ever pass for a guy. Besides that, he didn't have more than a few bucks left before he hit his credit card limits anyway. He'd just go to the ATM later in the morning and get some more cash to get him through the rest of the weekend.

He chuckled to himself. *My credit's so f***n' bad, she can have it, if she wants it.*

Since the bar didn't open until eleven in the morning, there was nothing else he could do until then.

F*** it. I'm goin' back to sleep.

He threw the empty wallet across the room, climbed back into the rumpled bed and passed out.

It was finally Saturday morning, and Brooke was practically giddy with excitement. Not only was she looking forward to Aaron and Jane's engagement party, she could hardly wait to see Zack again.

Brooke was in the kitchen, and Shelly was still sleeping. This was the first morning Brooke was up before her house guest. While mixing the batter for banana walnut pancakes, Brooke hummed a song and sipped on her second cup of coffee. It didn't matter that the melody was slightly off key, the words to the old Robert Palmer tune, *Bad Case of Lovin' You,* totally captured her growing feelings toward Dr. Zackary Carter.

"Sounds like someone's feeling good this morning," Shelly said as she walked into the room.

"I *am.* I'm feeling absolutely *excellent* this morning. How about you, Shelly?"

"I'll let you know after I have a cup of coffee," she mumbled. Shelly poured the hot brew into her cup and sat down at the table. "I recognize that tune. Something about a doctor ... and *love,* isn't it?"

Brooke grinned. "Too soon to tell, but you never know."

"So what's the plan for tonight?"

"I forgot to ask you. Would you mind driving to the party? I figured we should be there no later than seven just to make sure everything's the way we want it."

"Sure. I'm happy to drive. Just a teensy little question." She paused. "Why?"

Brooke could feel the color move up her neck and across her face. "Zack. He ... uh."

Shelly finished the sentence. "He wants you to go home with him. Right?"

"Yes. Maybe I shouldn't. What do you think? Do you think I should?"

"I think you ought to do what you feel is right. There are no 'shoulds' when it comes to love." Shelly looked at Brooke seriously. "You've got it *bad*, don't you?"

Brooke brought her coffee over to the table and sat down next to her friend. "Yes. I do, and it scares the heck out of me. Any advice?"

"You're asking me for advice? A woman who's about to get a divorce? I'm probably not the best source of information on lasting love and a good marriage. Quite frankly, my track record sucks."

Brooke patted her friend's hand. "You were young, Shelly. Maybe things didn't work out with Nathan, but you've got Mary Beth."

"That's true. And I wouldn't trade her for the world."

"Quite honestly, Shell, I almost envy you."

Shelly looked at her friend in disbelief. "Why in the world would you say *that*?"

"You've got an amazing daughter. You're still young. Everything you've gone through has helped you to grow and become a stronger person."

"I never thought about it that way before. Thanks, Brooke." She reached over and squeezed the hand of the woman who had become her closest friend. "And you ... well, even though we're almost the same age, you're my role model. All the positive things I see happening in my life from here forward will, in large part, be due to your positive influence and your help."

"If you mean letting you stay here, it's not really a big deal. In fact, when the time comes for you and Mary Beth to get back out on your own, it's going to be kind of difficult for me. Remember, I grew up in a house with eleven family members. I'm used to having people around. I was a little lonely before you got here. Right now, I've been missing Mary Beth and am looking forward to her coming back."

Shelly smiled sincerely. "Here's my prediction. It won't be long before you'll start filling up this house with your own family."

"I hope you're right, Shell. I truly hope you're right.

The rest of the day seemed to fly by. Brooke spent part of her time finishing up the school work she'd brought home for the weekend. Since Shelly was studying to be a middle school teacher, she helped a great deal and was more than happy to assist Brooke. It was a win-win for both of them, giving Shelly intern-like training while lightening Brooke's work load.

Once that task was completed, the two women worked together to give the house its weekly cleaning. They finished in record time. Seeing the sparkling sinks and spotless floors gave Brooke a sense of satisfaction, and she was sure her friend felt the same.

Shelly stretched and yawned. "I think I'm going to give Mary Beth a call. Then I'm going to take a little nap."

"Thanks for all your help, Shelly. Say 'hi' to Mary Beth for me," Brooke replied. "I think I'll opt for a nice warm bath." She'd taken a shower and washed her hair earlier. The bath was meant for relaxing both her body and mind.

As soon as Brooke got into her bedroom, she stripped and tossed her sweats into the laundry basket. Then she walked leisurely into her master bath. Lighting a couple of scented candles and putting on some soothing background music made it a serene setting. The tub was squeaky clean from its recent scrubbing. As the water began to pour in, she added several drops of bath oil. The light fragrance matched the perfume she'd be wearing for the evening. Tying her hair up in a messy bun, she stepped in and slowly lowered herself into the water.

She sighed as the warm water and soft floral scent surrounded her. On the rim of the Jacuzzi, her tub pillow provided a comfortable spot for her head. Her mind drifted to the handsome doctor who would escort her later in the evening. Picking up the bar of soap, she closed her eyes and began moving the lather slowly across her breasts. Her heartbeat quickened as she pictured Zack's hands in place of her own. The tingling she felt between her legs caused her to moan softly.

Placing the soap back on the side of the tub, she took her breasts into her hands. Gently she rolled her nipples between thumb and forefinger, teasing them to hard peaks. Allowing herself to relax even more, her hands continued to

Anita Louise

move slowly across her body. A handsome face and brown eyes flecked with green appeared in her mind. She could feel the silky wetness caused by her arousal. Her breath quickened as she remembered how it felt to be held in his strong arms. One hand remained on her breast while the other moved lower ... across her stomach to the soft patch of curls between her thighs. As her fingers swirled in the most intimate of ways, her fantasies consumed her.

"Zack." She whispered her imaginary lover's name as a delicious orgasm caused her inner muscles to clench. Moments later she released a long, satisfied sigh as a languid calm flowed through her body. After several minutes had passed, she realized the water had cooled, and it was time to return from her delightful daydream. Perhaps tonight would be the night her fantasies would become reality.

Brooke's bath left her completely refreshed. Shelly's energy also appeared to be revived. Now it was time to indulge in the final extravagance leading up to the party. They'd discussed their desire to look their best, and decided to splurge and get their hair done for this special night.

The salon was only a few miles from Brooke's house. Smiles and smooth jazz playing quietly in the background greeted them upon their arrival. Shortly after entering, the receptionist at the high end salon offered them the choice of cappuccino or champagne. Deciding to skip anything alcoholic, the girls sipped on small cups of brewed coffee mixed with the perfect amount of cream. The pampering they received was similar to what might be given to a highly paid movie star.

Bad Case of Lovin' You

By the time they were ready to walk out of the salon, it had cost Brooke nearly a week's pay. Shelly said she just didn't want to think about how much she'd spent. But they agreed it was totally worth it. They both looked spectacular.

The long, dark hair tumbling around Brooke's shoulders looked silkier than ever. It was done in what the stylist called a "half up, rumpled bedroom hair" look. Both she and Shelly also had French manicures on their fingers and toenails. When a makeup artist offered her expert services, neither of the women were able to resist.

Looking into the mirror afterward, the difference was apparent. Brooke was pleased. Her brown eyes looked even darker than usual with an added sultry appearance. Her cheekbones were accented with an understated blush. A deep burgundy stain had been applied to her full lips, and was enhanced with the perfect amount of gloss.

"Oh, my gosh, Brooke," Shelly gasped, "you look ... I don't even know what to say. Stunning. Amazing." Finally she settled on, "Wow!"

"It's not too much?" Brooke asked hesitantly.

"Are you kidding? No way!"

"You're looking pretty awesome yourself, Shelly."

And it was true. Shelly's long blonde hair had been trimmed to collarbone length. Glamourous waves framed her face. The shadows and liner the makeup artist applied gave her blue eyes a subtle, smoky look. Red accents had been used on her lips to compliment the pink undertones of her fair skin. It was difficult to tell if the faint blush on her cheeks had been placed there, or was simply a natural result of the excitement showing on her face.

"Women always leave here looking great," said the young woman who'd greeted them when they'd first arrived, "but you two look exceptionally gorgeous. Whoever your dates are tonight better *watch out.* Would you mind if I took your pictures? We may want to use you on our website.*"

Shelly and Brooke looked at one another. This was certainly an affirmation of what Brooke already thought. Discussion about whether or not to have their pictures taken wasn't needed. They both agreed and signed the necessary waiver. The only caveat was they asked that copies of the photos be sent to them.

They walked out of the salon feeling and looking good. The grins on their faces spread from ear to ear.

"Hey, pretty lady, you hungry?" Shelly queried.

"Well, now that you ask, hot mama, I am a little. Besides, we really should eat something. There's just way too much time between now and when we leave for the party."

"That's what I thought too. I don't know about you, but the idea of going home and messing up the kitchen isn't sounding too appealing. I'm not sure what we have in the house to eat anyway."

Brooke nodded in agreement. "I'm thinking maybe half a sandwich and a small salad? How about we stop at Panera real quick? We can eat right there ... no fuss, no muss."

"Sounds like a plan to me," Shelly replied.

When the two women entered the popular chain restaurant, practically every set of male eyes were focused on them. A tall man who looked to be in his late thirties to early forties stood behind them in line. He was good looking and well built, clad in blue jeans and a CU-Boulder sweatshirt.

"Kind of late for lunch, isn't it?" he asked casually.

Shelly looked at him and smiled. "Yes, it is, but we've been so busy today, this is the first chance we've had to grab a bite."

"Well, I must say whatever you've been doing, it must've been something good. I hope you don't mind my saying so, but you're both very beautiful women."

A blush crossed Shelly's face. She turned to Brooke who responded, "Thank you for the compliment. We very much appreciate it, but right now, we're in a bit of a hurry."

"I understand," the man said politely. "You can't blame a guy for trying, right?" He smiled pleasantly. "Maybe I'll be fortunate enough to see the two of you in here again one of these days."

"Perhaps," Brooke said with a small smile.

He reached out his hand. "My name's Robert. So next time we meet we won't be strangers."

When Brooke hesitated, Shelly shook his hand. "Nice to meet you, Robert. I'm Shelly and this is Brooke."

"Nice to meet you both." He nodded as he backed away.

Shelly looked at her friend. "I'm sorry, Brooke. I just wanted to be polite."

"It's okay. I didn't mean to be rude. I guess I'm just not used to being approached by strangers like that."

"Me neither, but I think I could learn to live with it," Shelly said with a twinkle in her eye.

The women placed their order. While they were waiting for it to be filled, another man approached. This one was a little younger and quite a bit more forward.

"Hi. I'm Gus," he said with his hand extended.

When Shelly took his hand and said, "Hello," he held it a little longer than necessary.

"Are you an interior decorator?" he asked.

"Uh, no. Why do you ask?" Shelly responded.

"Because when I saw you, the entire room became beautiful." He lifted her hand, placing a kiss on her knuckles.

Shelly looked at Brooke questioningly. The teacher simply rolled her eyes and shrugged, leaving her friend to contend with this one on her own. Before Shelly could come up with a response, Gus released her hand and patted his pockets. "I seem to have lost my number. Can I have yours?" He grinned impishly.

The buzzer indicated their food order was ready, and the noise seemed to help Shelly regain her composure. "Gus, you seem like a real nice guy, and I appreciate the compliment. But my friend and I are just here for a quick lunch, and we really need to get going."

The irrepressible Gus was undaunted. After reaching into his pocket, he handed Shelly a business card. "This is me. I'd be happy to buy you a cup of coffee or something sometime. Just give me a call." With that he gave them a wink and a small salute before walking away.

Shelly and Brooke found a booth toward the back of the restaurant in the most private area they could find. When they placed their trays on the table, they looked at each other and burst out laughing.

"OMG! What was *that?*" Brooke asked.

Bad Case of Lovin' You

Shelly giggled. "I don't know, but I'm guessing we must be looking pretty darn good. Either that or we just hit the mother lode of desperate men."

"Actually, both of those guys were very nice looking. They didn't look like the desperate type in the least," Brooke replied.

After looking around the room surreptitiously, Shelly leaned forward and whispered, "I think I saw other guys looking at us too. Only they didn't approach us like those fellows did."

Brooke sighed. "You might be right, but for me the only guy I'm interested in attracting tonight is one super good looking doctor."

"If the men in this place are any indication, you're not going to have any trouble with that at all. One look at you and Dr. Zackary Carter doesn't stand a chance."

"Thanks, Shelly. I hope you're right," Brooke said wistfully. "I sincerely hope you're right."

Chapter Nineteen

When Zack Carter stepped into the private banquet area at Tom's Tavern/SALT, it was buzzing with activity. The room was decorated beautifully. Helium filled balloons in varying shades of grey and coral floated in the air. The bartender was making sure everything was ready for the guests. A banner floated above his head.

"Eat! Drink! Aaron & Jane are Soon to be Married!"

A large bowl filled with Jenga blocks sat on a table near the entrance. Felt tip pens were placed nearby. Guests were encouraged to "Help Build Memories for Jane and Aaron" by signing the Jenga pieces. Mason jars sat on the center of each table. Overlapping burlap hearts of coral and grey were attached to the outside of the glass, and small candles floated in each one.

As wonderful as the room looked, Zack's attention was captured by the dark-haired woman who stood with her back to him. She was talking animatedly with someone from the wait staff. The navy blue dress she wore was covered in lace and ended just above her knees, which allowed him a perfect view of her shapely calves and ankles. The fabric hugged her curves, and he couldn't help but notice the long, lean lines of her body. She'd done something different with her hair. Part of it was gathered near the top of her head in what appeared to be a careless grouping of curls. The rest of her ebony locks hung in long, silky waves ending just above her beautifully shaped bottom.

She must've sensed his stare. When she turned, their eyes met, and it was as if someone flipped a switch. It felt to him as if sunshine filled the room. The warmth in her eyes drew him to her like a magnet. Turning back briefly to complete her conversation, she quickly wrapped it up and began to move toward him. Everything about her was captivating and alluring. When they met in the middle of the room, it was difficult for him to resist the temptation to taste her luscious looking lips.

"Zack. You're early," Brooke commented as she looked at the clock on the wall, "but it's awfully good to see you."

She opened her arms, and he pulled her gently into his embrace. He would've preferred to place his lips on hers, but instead opted for the more appropriate kiss on the cheek. Her skin was soft and velvety smooth. He breathed in her scent as they stood for a moment enfolded in each other's arms. She smelled delicious, a light floral fragrance with a hint of vanilla. He allowed his eyes to survey her as he stepped back.

"You look absolutely beautiful, Brooke," he said sincerely.

"Thank you, kind sir." She dipped in a mock curtsy. "You're looking quite handsome yourself. Do you want something to drink? I think the bar's open."

"I didn't come early to drink. I offered to help. Remember? What do you need me to do?"

"Honestly, Zack, there's really nothing. Everything's good to go. All there is to do now is wait for Aaron, Jane and the guests to arrive so we can get this party started."

He noticed a DJ in the far corner next to a small dance floor. Soft dinner music was already playing.

"Save me a dance for later?" Zack asked while nodding toward the dance floor.

"I'd love to." She paused. "So how's your week been? No more massive car accidents or other traumas to deal with, I hope."

"Nope. Nothing major. I must say though, Brooke, talking with you the other night was really nice." He took her hand and gave it a soft squeeze. "It helped a lot. Thanks."

Brooke smiled sweetly. "I didn't really do anything. But it was nice for me too. I'm glad you told me about what happened and how you were feeling."

"You're a good listener, Brooke. And that's only one of the many qualities I'm growing to appreciate about you. The more I get to know you, the better I like you."

He thought he detected a slight blush, but it was hard to tell in the dimly lit room. Just then Brooke's friend walked over.

"Hi, Dr. Carter," Shelly said. "Nice to see you under much more pleasant circumstances." "None of this doctor stuff tonight, Shelly. Please, just call me Zack. Okay?"

"Of course ... Zack." Shelly then turned to Brooke and said, "Sorry, but he needs to talk to you about something." She motioned toward the catering manager who was standing near the door to the kitchen.

Brooke murmured, "Excuse me." She pressed her hand to his arm before moving away. His gaze followed her.

"She looks great tonight, doesn't she?" Shelly commented innocently.

"She sure does," Zack replied. Somehow he managed to shift his gaze from the mesmerizing sway of slender hips clad in navy lace. Almost as if realizing she was there for the first time, he looked at Shelly. "You look very nice too."

Shelly grinned. "Thanks for noticing, Doc."

"I'm sorry. I didn't mean to slight you."

"Not at all. I'm glad to see that you and Brooke are getting along so well."

Not wanting to share his feelings with someone he barely knew, Zack changed the subject. "How's Mary Beth doing? Will she be here tonight?"

"No, she won't be here, but she's doing fine. She's visiting her grandparents in Arizona for a little while. I think she needed to get away, and get some of that pampering her grandmother loves to pour on her."

"That's good. I'm sure her being there is a treat for both of them."

Other guests began to join the party, and Shelly excused herself. Zack found a seat at a table on the far side of the room, positioning himself so his back was to the wall. From that vantage point, he was able to check out everyone as they entered.

Anita Louise

A few minutes later an older couple came in. Zack watched as Brooke practically sprinted across the room. No doubt the very attractive duo was her parents. The three exchanged loving hugs. Once Brooke's father released his daughter from his embrace, he held Brooke's shoulders and stepped back. The man was beaming like only a proud parent could.

Brooke took the hand of the distinguished gentleman, and the threesome moved toward him. Zack stood in anticipation. The man's hair was mostly white with hints of silver. He stood well over six feet, and was, apparently, the source of Brooke's long and lean stature. The smile on Brooke's face was filled with what looked to Zack like love and admiration as she brought her parents to meet him.

"Mom ... Dad, this is Dr. Zackary Carter, my date for this evening." Her beautiful face turned slightly pink. "Zack, I'd like you to meet my parents, John and Juliette Adler."

The two men shook hands cordially.

"Nice to meet you, Dr. Carter," the head of the Adler clan said formally.

"Nice to meet you too, sir. I hope you'll call me Zack."

"Of course. And please call me John." Without hesitation, he put his arm around his wife. "And this is the love of my life, my wife Juliette."

Mrs. Adler extended her hand. "It's a pleasure to meet you, Zackary. Not only has Brooke told us nice things about you, but I understand you were somewhat instrumental in this evening's celebration."

Zack chuckled as he took the striking woman's hand. "Oh, I don't know about that. Somehow I think Jane and Aaron would've found each other one way or another."

Cocking her head to one side, Juliette looked at him questioningly. "So do you believe in fate, Dr. Carter?"

He took a moment to consider his response. "I'm not sure, but I do believe there are people who complement each other so well, it would be a shame if they weren't together."

"Interesting," she replied. "Would you mind if we joined you, Zackary? I think I'd enjoy getting to know you better."

"It would be my honor," Zack said sincerely.

Brooke had placed her small purse next to him on the table. Her parents took the chairs on the other side of their daughter.

A moment later, Brooke excused herself once more, returning to greet the guests as they entered the room. Zack watched as she engaged with each person. Smiles, handshakes and hugs were in abundant supply. As he observed her poise and charm, Zack's respect for his date grew even more.

Several other people had entered the room while Zack was speaking with Brooke's parents. Each one of them made their way to the table where he was seated and acknowledged the parents of the groom-to-be. After introductions were made, Zack sat quietly and observed more of the Adler family dynamics.

A more youthful version of John Adler entered the room. Zack noted the remarkable resemblance immediately. A hint of silver at the temples of the younger man's dark hair foreshadowed the look his father wore with panache. The man came directly to his parents' table and was introduced as Michael Adler. He seated himself next to his father, and made no attempt to reserve the chair on his opposite side. Evidently, the eldest of the now adult Adler children had come without an escort. Judging by the eldest Adler's looks, bringing a date would've been as simple as offering an invitation to any eligible woman.

Father and son engaged in a discussion about work. John Adler took a moment to explain to Zack that Michael was the lead architect for the building and development company the senior Adler had founded.

Zack didn't want to eavesdrop on the Adler men's business conversation. So he excused himself from the table when he noticed Luke Adler walk into the room. Zack and Luke didn't know each other all that well. But Zack's positive opinion of the officer had grown recently. When Shelly and her daughter had come to the hospital emergency room, Luke handled the situation both professionally and with compassion.

"Hi, Luke. It's good to see you again," Zack said.

"Oh, hi, Doc. Good to see you too." Luke was cordial, but appeared to be distracted. His gaze scanned the room.

Zack had a feeling he knew who his new friend was searching out. "You looking for someone?" he asked innocently.

"Uh ... me? No one in particular." Luke shrugged, but continued to scan the guests. It was obvious when he found the person he was looking for. Luke's frown turned upside down when he spotted Shelly Silvers. "Hey, Doc, would you excuse me a minute?" Without waiting for Zack's reply, Luke moved toward the pretty blonde in the black cocktail dress.

Looks like Shelly has herself a suitor. Zack chuckled to himself. Even though he wasn't much of a drinker, he didn't want to rush back to the table. Taking his time, he wandered over to the bar.

"What can I get for you?" the bartender asked.

"I see you have a couple of wines from Bookcliff Vineyards. I'll have a glass of the cabernet sauvignon."

Zack looked around the room while waiting for his drink. Brooke was busy chatting with guests and fulfilling her role as an excellent hostess. She looked perfectly at ease mixing and mingling with friends and family from old to young.

The room was quickly filling with people. Applause broke out when Aaron and Jane appeared at the entrance. The couple's arms were linked when they walked in. Soon the sound of silverware clinking on glasses filled the air. Aaron and Jane looked lovingly at each other. Putting his arm around his fiancée, Aaron swept her back dramatically. The couple then gave each other the kiss the guests had demanded. They were both beaming afterward.

"You did a fine job putting those two together." Brooke had made her way to his side. "They make a great couple, don't they?"

"Yes, they do." Zack smiled at her, raised his glass, and asked, "Would you like something to drink?"

"Sure. I'll have what you're having."

Zack nodded to the bartender. "Another glass of the cabernet, please," and his request was quickly fulfilled. He handed the glass to Brooke and raised his in a toast. "May we have the good fortune to win a true heart, and the merit to keep it."

"I believe I've heard that somewhere before, Dr. Carter. It seems even more appropriate now than it was the first time." She took a sip. "Umm. Excellent. I wasn't familiar with this winery, but the sommelier highly recommended it. I liked the idea of using someone local."

"They've earned quite a bit of recognition. Bookcliff Vineyards has become one of the premier wineries in Colorado."

"I just love success stories," said Brooke, "especially when they're right here in our own backyard." She clinked her glass to Zack's once more.

Aaron and Jane were moving toward them. The couple being honored stopped to chat with several people along the way. When Jane finally stood next to Brooke, she gave her friend a warm hug. Then the bride-to-be opened her arms to Zack. "Come here, you." Jane grinned. "You know, if it wasn't for you, this party might not be happening tonight."

Zack gave her the hug of a friend. "You're giving me way too much credit, Jane. As I was saying to your soon-to-be mother-in-law a little while ago, 'there are some people who are just *meant* to be together.' You and Aaron are two of those people."

Looking into the eyes of her fiancé, Jane echoed Zack's sentiment. "I believe you're right, Zack. Some things are just meant to be." She and Aaron sealed her statement with another kiss.

Moments later, Aaron pulled himself somewhat reluctantly away from Jane. The groom-to-be hugged his sister and then extended his hand to Zack. Their handshake was followed by a bro hug.

"I'm glad you're here, Zack. And you couldn't have chosen a better person to be with. Not only is she one of my favorite sisters, Brooke's also done an amazing job putting all this together."

Brooke spoke up. "Hold on a minute, brother dear. Your lovely fiancée has been totally involved in making tonight a huge success. Let's give credit where credit is due."

"Absolutely, Brooke," Aaron replied. "I couldn't agree with you more. You've kept Jane involved in practically every detail. But you must admit, you did an awful lot of the legwork."

Jane interjected, "And we appreciate everything you've done so very much, Brooke."

"We sure do, Sis. Besides, I've been keeping Jane awfully busy." Aaron smiled warmly at Jane and pulled her snugly to his side. "She's got her job at the university, her counseling practice, and she's also been helping me edit my latest book. Her input has been invaluable."

Just then a member of the wait staff walked up to the group. "I'm sorry Miss Adler, but Chef has a quick question for you."

Brooke looked at the other three apologetically and shrugged. "Duty calls."

Aaron and Jane also excused themselves to mingle with the other party goers. Zack was left alone once more. His attention was soon drawn to the room's entrance where there was a slight commotion. A tall woman with long straight black hair and dark eyes walked in. She was wearing a curve hugging animal print dress. Zack was certain that *this* was Gabriella, the identical twin Brooke had told him about.

Practically everyone in the room turned to look at the stunning brunette. Already one of the tallest individuals in the place, she wore platform heels with the same animal print as her dress. The shoes added another six inches to her height. It was obvious that she was *not* afraid to stand out in a crowd.

The man Brooke's twin was with was almost as tall as she. He was built like a runner, slender with long limbs. He appeared totally enamored with his date. The pair walked across the room. When they reached the table where the Adler parents were seated, John, Juliette and Michael all rose. One by one they each gave Gabriella a hug. Zack watched as Brooke's twin introduced her date, after which handshakes were exchanged.

There was no doubt Gabriella Adler was a beautiful, confident woman. But even from a distance Zack could sense a distinct difference between her and Brooke. First of all, he knew Brooke would be totally uncomfortable wearing an outfit like the one worn by her twin. Gabriella seemed to thrive on having as many people as possible staring at her. *His* twin was more apt to stay in the background and work to help others without even thinking of herself.

My twin? *Where did that come from?* He pushed the thought to the background for further examination at a later time.

When he noticed Brooke step back into the room a moment later, Zack couldn't help but smile. There was a quiet strength about her that was undeniable. She'd put so much time and effort into this party, yet she made sure Jane was given credit. He thought of how much she cared for others. *Look at the way she took in Shelly and Mary Beth without hesitation. They needed help, and Brooke was more than happy to give it. She's probably not looking for anything in return either.*

He watched as she walked toward him. An emotion he hadn't experienced in a very long time tried to grab his attention. *Love? Could it be?*

Without question, he appreciated the way her curves filled out the lacy sheath she wore. But there was so much more to Brooke Adler than what was displayed for the world to see. Brooke was sensitive to the needs of others. She was also willing to use her energy and assets to see to it those needs were met.

On the outside, Brooke's twin was equally lovely in appearance. Gabriella was certainly vivacious. And it looked as if she had an easy ability to charm anyone and everyone. She was smiling and laughing, and so were those in the circle around her. There was no doubt Gabby enjoyed being the center of attention. Yes, Gabriella Adler was lovely, but to Zack, Brooke's star outshone that of every other woman in the room in so many ways.

When Brooke reached his side, he put his arms lightly around her waist. She didn't stiffen, but seemed a bit surprised at the gesture.

"What's up, handsome?" She joked.

"Just wondered if I might steal a kiss from the prettiest girl in the room."

"You don't have to steal what's given freely," Brooke replied with a smile. After placing her arms around his neck, she moved her hand up into the nape of his hair. "Did I ever tell you how much I love your hair?"

"Not until just now. I have the feeling there are lots of things we haven't told each other yet. But we've got lots of time." Pulling her closer he tilted his head. It was as if no one else in the room existed as his mouth moved toward hers.

Her eyes closed and her lips parted slightly. When their lips met he felt her muscles relax and his did too. Something magical happened in that moment. Wrapped in each other's arms in a crowded room, he felt as if they were an island of complete contentment.

Only a short while later they broke the kiss. Standing with their arms around each other, they looked silently into one another's eyes. Brooke laid her head on his chest.

"Ummm, that was nice," she whispered.

"Very," was all he could say.

Gabriella and her date suddenly appeared next to them. "Am I interrupting something?" she asked. Her question was followed with a genuinely happy smile. "Brooke, you've done it again! I don't know how you do it, but I'm sure glad you do. I swear you could make a picnic on a rainy day turn out magnificently."

"Thanks, Gabby, but remember Jane was involved every step of the way."

"I know. I know, but we both know you were the mastermind behind all this."

Brooke shrugged, and Gabriella pulled her twin into her arms. The love between the two sisters was apparent.

"Gabby, I want you to meet Zack, *Doctor* Zackary Carter." Brooke stepped back to allow the two to clasp each other's hands.

"Hello, Dr. Carter. So nice to meet you. And this is my friend Devin Stockwell." The men exchanged handshakes as did Brooke and her sister's date. "We're sitting at Mom and Dad's table too, so we'll be able to chat more later," Gabriella said. "I just wanted to come over and say 'hi' and let our fellas meet one another."

Bad Case of Lovin' You

"I'm really glad you did, Gabby," Brooke replied. "We'll get over there in a little bit. Most everybody's here, and they have things under control in the kitchen. I just want to make the rounds. You know, say 'hello' to a few more folks before everyone gets stuck in one place."

"K," and with that Gabriella and Devin turned to walk away. Looking back over her shoulder, the attractive girl in the animal print dress wiggled her fingers. "Toodles," she said with a charming grin.

Chapter Twenty

Nathan Silvers' day was not starting out well. Luckily he had a spare ATM card tucked away. It was back in the corner of his top dresser drawer. There were also a couple of credit cards Shelly was trying to pay off. She'd "forbidden" him to use them.

*F*** her! If I wanna use my own goddamn credit cards, I will. Who the hell does she think she is anyway, tellin' me how to spend my own f***in' money?*

But when he went to the ATM to withdraw fifty bucks, the stupid machine denied his request. By the time he'd gotten out of bed, it was already way past the time the banks closed. They wouldn't open again until Monday morning.

What a pain in the ass. Guess I'll just have to use credit cards until Monday.

He chuckled to himself when he thought of how pissed his wife would be when she found out the cards were maxed out again.

Serves her right for runnin' out on me like she did.

Luckily Nate's credit was passable ... just barely. Hell, the only reason it was even semi decent was because he'd always allowed Shelly to pay the bills. She was good at making sure things got paid on time. The only time anything was past due was when he'd 'accidentally' spent a little too much on partying and booze.

So what if I spent part of it on other women? What that bitch don't know won't hurt her. Besides, if she wasn't so goddamn frigid, I wouldn't have needed other women.

Not paying a couple of bills on time wasn't that big a deal anyway, and it sure as hell wasn't *his* fault. He was the one who went to that f***n' job every day and worked his ass off. Didn't a man have the right to spend *his* money any way he damn well pleased? If that dumb bitch of a wife wasn't always buying something they probably didn't even need, there'd be plenty of money.

*Seems to me like that damn little mini-bitch was always asking for and spending <u>my</u> money on something too. 'I need this for school. My clothes are getting too small. I gotta buy my lunch.' Wha, wha, wha ... always whinin' about somethin'. Shit. She oughta pack her own goddamn lunch! Stupid kids these days expect everything to be handed to them on a f***in' silver platter. No wonder I lose my temper with the little bitch sometimes. She's just like her a-hole mother. Good riddance to both of their sorry asses.*

Brooke had watched the interaction between her twin and her date carefully. She hadn't noticed or *felt* even a twinge of a spark between the two. But still she had to ask, "So what'd you think of Gabby?"

"She seems very nice," Zack responded. "The two of you really look quite a bit alike. But, I see lots of differences too."

"Really? In what ways?" Brooke's stomach did a little flip-flop. She had to hold herself back from grilling him with questions.

"Hmmm, seems to me that might be something we can discuss in detail a little later. Like when you come over to my place after the festivities are over. What do you think?"

Brooke was more than a little curious to discern Zack's reaction, or more to the point, *attraction* to her flamboyant sister. But she knew he was right. This was not the time or place. It was better left till later.

She only hesitated a moment before replying, "That sounds like a good idea, Dr. Carter. Depending on how late it is when we get to your house, it may be a discussion that will have to wait until morning." She watched his face as he took in her somewhat subtle hint, and saw his eyebrows raise in question. Without a word he seemed to ask, *Did you just say what I think you said*? His demeanor remained calm, but he did take her hand and give it a gentle squeeze.

"I'm inclined to agree with you, Miss Adler. Guess we'll just wait and see how it goes." Brooke's only answer was the twinkle in her eye. She pulled him behind her into the now crowded room.

"Come on, I want you to meet the rest of my family."

"And I want to meet them too," Zack replied with sincerity.

"Now let me think. We just chatted with Gabby, and you met my folks and Michael at the table. You know Luke,

Bad Case of Lovin' You

Aaron and Jane already. So that leaves Rachel and Phil, Olivia, Whitney and Connor."

"Is that all?" he quipped.

"I can't help it if you only have one brother." She chuckled as she led him toward a group of her siblings standing nearby. "Hi, guys. I want you all to meet my date. This is Zack. Dr. Zackary Carter."

Phillip was the second oldest and was the first one to break the ice. "Hi. I'm Phil. This is my wife Rachel." The two men shook hands amiably. All of Brooke's siblings were good looking, but she thought the sun rose and set on this particular brother. He was a tall man with sun-streaked sandy brown hair, and standing next to him was his very pretty and very pregnant wife.

Rachel kept one hand on the top of her stomach as she and Zack clasped hands. "Nice to meet you, Dr. Carter. I'm glad there's a doctor in the house ... just in case." She joked.

"Child birth's not my specialty," Zack replied, "but I'm sure I could handle it if need be. When are you due?"

"Any day now. Phil and I missed the last little family get together at Mom and Dad's house. There's just no way to get up or down that winding road to their place quickly. My doctor tells me it could be quite a few hours from the time my labor starts till the baby actually comes. But she also doesn't want me or Phil panicking when we're on our way to the hospital. After Jane's accident, I think we're all a little more cautious on that road. From here it's less than three miles to the hospital, so the probability of it being necessary for you to go into obstetrician mode is pretty slim."

"Do you know if you're having a boy or a girl?" Zack asked.

Before Rachel had a chance to answer, a petite blonde spoke up. "It's a boy, and as far as I know, they haven't settled on a name yet. Hi. I'm Olivia. Nice to meet you, Zack."

Brooke watched Zack practically wince after he took the petite blonde's hand. It was almost a family joke. Olivia liked to prove she was a force to be reckoned with by using a much stronger grip than necessary ... especially when she was introduced to a man. No one expected such strength from the tiny beauty with the pixie's haircut. "It's a pleasure to meet you, Olivia," he replied.

"Do you want me to massage your knuckles for you?" Brooke joked. "Olivia's nickname is Tinker Bell. She may be tiny, but she's power packed. Most people find it hard to believe that she and Luke are fraternal twins."

Olivia grinned. "I know I don't have quite the same look as the rest of this bunch ... especially when it comes to my height. Mom says I'm the spitting image of my Grandmother, but we have to take Mom's word for it since Grandma was gone before any of us were born."

"Are you a gymnast, by any chance?" Zack asked.

"Good guess, but no." Olivia laughed. "Actually, I did quite a bit of gymnastics when I was younger. I had no desire to try to make it to the Olympics, so I went a different route."

Brooke chuckled as Whitney, another of her absolutely gorgeous sisters, stepped into the conversation with Zack. "Yes, Olivia took up martial arts. Now even though she's the smallest of all of us kids, she could even take on Luke and most likely win the battle."

Bad Case of Lovin' You

There was a look of confusion on Zack's face. "Do I know you?" he asked as he smiled up at the stunning woman with the reed thin and beautifully elongated body. Without answering, she tilted her head back and allowed her thick blonde hair to cascade down her swanlike neck in the classic pose of a model. Zack hit himself on the forehead with the palm of his hand. "Of course! You're Whitney Adler. I've seen your picture dozens of times. It's a pleasure to meet you."

Whitney Adler's face and figure had graced the covers of *Sports Illustrated, Vanity Fair* as well as dozens of other well-known magazines. Plus she'd been identified with brands like Dior, Versace, and companies equally as famous across the globe. "Nice to meet you too, Zack. Brooke could have been a model if she'd wanted to, but she was much more interested in teaching. Me?" She shrugged. "I haven't opened a book since I left high school."

Olivia spoke up again, "Humph. Didn't I hear you were going to start taking college classes, Whitney?"

"I've been thinking about it," the model said without conviction. She then looked wistfully across the room at Phillip and Rachel. "Who knows? Maybe someday I might even want to settle down and have a family."

Connor, the youngest of the Adler children, was nowhere to be seen. So Brooke excused herself and her date from her siblings. "I thought you might need a break from my family," she said feigning sympathy.

"There sure are a lot of them, but you're the only one I'm interested in right now," he said.

As they walked back toward their table, Zack put his arm around her waist and whispered in her ear. "How about that dance you promised me?" When she pointed out that there wasn't a soul on the dance floor, he nuzzled her neck and crooned, "Maybe we'll start a trend." They stepped onto the smooth surface, and he wrapped his arm securely around her waist. Her right hand locked with his. The music playing was slow and romantic. He hummed and sang the title of the song softly, "Hmm, hmmmm, hmm, hmm, hmm. I only have eyes for you."

Their bodies were pressed lightly together. As she heard and felt the sincerity in his voice, Brooke felt the pull of desire increase. She laid her head on his shoulder, and they swayed in time to the music. Following his skillful lead, they moved slowly across the dance floor. The words of the song and the rhythm of the music seemed to ignite a passion in her. It was unlike anything she'd ever experienced before.

He moved his hand slightly lower on her back. Their hips pressed even closer together. Her eyes were closed, but she heard the sound of other dancers joining them on the floor. Feeling less in the spotlight made her bolder. She pressed a soft kiss to his neck.

"*Brooke.*" Her name sounded like a sigh on his lips.

The song was over too soon. They stood together in the corner of the dance floor silently looking into each other's eyes. The DJ changed to a current up-tempo tune, and many of the other couples started moving to the beat. Brooke and Zack continued to stare at each other. Finally, as if by some unspoken agreement they moved apart. He took her hand as they made their way back to their table.

Before she even sat down, Brooke excused herself. Thank goodness she was the only one in the restroom. She looked at her reflection in the mirror. The woman staring back at her was indeed lovely ... dress, hair, face all perfect for the occasion. But there was something different in her eyes. Before she could analyze it further, the door opened and Shelly walked in.

Standing next to Brooke, Shelly smiled and said softly, "You and Zack looked really good together out there on the dance floor."

"Did we?" Brooke answered with a question. The women made eye contact in the mirror.

"I don't know what it was exactly, but it just *felt* good watching you two," Shelly responded. Brooke didn't reply, but smiled dreamily. Almost shyly, Shelly said, "I danced with Luke."

Brooke turned and looked directly in her friend's eyes. Taking Shelly's hands in her own she said, "You know he's always had a thing for you."

"I know, but right now, with everything so up in the air with me and Mary Beth ..." She hesitated. "And, of course, there's Nathan."

"Luke knows that, Shell. I've known my brother for a very long time. One of the things I know for sure is, that man's got *patience*. He'll never push you. He's just not made that way."

"I know. He's not been pushy at all. Just nice, and so sweet. He asked about Mary Beth and seemed ... I don't know, I guess he seemed genuinely *interested* in how she was doing."

"I'm sure he *is* genuinely interested. He's tough when he needs to be, but he's really a softy underneath it all."

"Yeah. I can see that," Shelly responded.

Brooke looked at her friend seriously. "In case you didn't know it, I might as well tell you. Luke's also one of the most *determined* people I've ever known. Once he sets his mind to something there's almost no stopping him."

"That's good to know." There was a smile on her face when Shelly opened her small handbag and carefully applied fresh lipstick.

When Brooke went back into the banquet room, the party was in full swing.

A few new guests had arrived. Jane called Brooke over and introduced her to Millie Worthton. Millie was Aaron and Jane's next door neighbor. Brooke recalled Jane saying that Millie shared some sage advice that proved to be very helpful at a crucial time in Jane and Aaron's relationship. The neighbor was probably in her sixties, but appeared to be a Baby Boomer who took good care of herself. Just then, a younger woman Brooke didn't recognize came up and stood next to Mrs. Worthton.

"Oh, this is my niece Analese Martin." Millie Worthton beamed with pride.

"So nice to meet you, Analese," said Brooke.

"I'm glad you could join us," Jane responded.

"I didn't want to intrude," said Analese. "But, for some reason, Aunt Millie really wanted me to come with her."

"Of course, I wanted you to come with me," Millie said. "You know, you've always been like a daughter to me." Millie patted her niece's hand and looked from Brooke to Jane. "I never had children of my own, and Analese was my sister's only child. She's always been special to me, and even more so after we lost Grace, Analese's mother." Millie saw her niece as one of those people who had the ability to light up a room when she entered. The poise and grace her niece exuded always reminded Millie of her sister.

Bad Case of Lovin' You

The stylish, yet older woman excused herself, and took Analese to the table where Michael Adler sat with his parents. Nodding toward Michael she said, "Analese, this is the architect I was telling you about. Remember? He's the one who designed that lovely home next to mine, the one where Jane and Aaron live. You said you wanted to have a custom home built. I think this is just the man for you. Mr. Adler, this is my niece, Analese Martin." Millie's eyes were twinkling mischievously.

Analese smiled. "Oh, yes, I remember, Aunt Millie."

Millie watched carefully as Michael and her niece made contact for the first time. The stunning auburn-haired woman with the startling blue eyes extended her hand. Analese and Michael's eyes met and their palms touched. Just as Millie Worthton had hoped, it looked as if the two were somehow momentarily mesmerized before dropping hands as one would a hot potato.

Millie chuckled to herself as she listened to her usually unflappable niece practically stutter when she said, "N-nice to meet you, Mr. Adler."

"Please. Call me Michael."

"Of course, Michael. I'm Analese. Analese Martin." Once again she seemed to lose her normal composure. "I ... I don't know why I said that. Aunt Millie already told you my name." She blushed prettily.

"It would be a pleasure to discuss what you're looking for in a home, Analese. Here's my card," he said as he pressed his business card into her hand.

"Oh. Thank you. I'll ... I'll call you."

"Please do," he said capturing her hand once more. "I very much look forward to hearing from you."

Having accomplished her mission, Millie Worthton spoke up. "Analese, I think we should find our seats now. I'd like to sit down." She smiled knowingly at the eldest Adler son. "See you soon, Michael."

Brooke and Zack were seated at the table with the guests of honor and her parents, when Brooke heard a commotion at the banquet room entrance. Connor, the youngest of the Adler children, had just arrived. He was almost an hour late.

So what else is new? she thought.

Connor's lack of respect for the clock was notorious in the Adler family. The standing joke was that Connor had been late starting with the day he was born. Juliette Adler had been well into the third week past her due date when her last child, her "baby," finally decided to make his way into the world. Ever since then, it seemed like the family was always waiting for Connor.

Connor had also been a contributing factor in bringing Aaron and Jane together. The young man had gotten into some trouble, and the court had assigned him to Jane for counseling. Somehow, he'd managed to convince her to drive him to his parent's anniversary party when his car was in the shop. When she left the party, Jane's little car had slid off the treacherous road coming down from the Adler's mountain top home.

"Hi, everyone," Connor said as he approached the table. "Sorry I'm late."

"It's okay, little brother," Aaron replied with a smile. "If it wasn't for you bringing Jane to Mom and Dad's that night, we might not all be sitting here right now." Aaron began to recount the fateful event. "On my way home from the party I noticed headlights shooting out from a strange angle on the wrong side of the road, so I called for help. Once I realized the occupant of the vehicle was Jane, I did what I thought was right and followed the ambulance to the hospital. Dr. Carter somehow got the idea Jane and I were a couple, and she ended up coming to my house to recuperate."

Zack chuckled as he added his two cents. "Excuse me, but anyone would have made the same assumption. You never left her side after she was brought in. I've seen couples who've been together for *years* who didn't seem anywhere near as concerned about the person in the hospital bed as you were about Jane."

Juliette Adler smiled at both Aaron and Zack when she spoke up. "Some accidents aren't really accidents at all. Fate has a way of stepping in when people are just *meant* to be together."

Looking at the happy couple, everyone in the group smiled, nodded and murmured some form of agreement.

The party was a huge success, and for Brooke, the rest of the evening seemed to fly by in a blur. The food was delicious, and the wait staff was solicitous without being intrusive. Jane and Aaron kissed so many times due to the guests tapping on their glasses with their silverware, the couple of honor barely had time to enjoy their meal. Apparently, they embodied the phrase "living on love." The happy smiles on their faces showed their kisses were more important to them than food.

John and Juliette Adler's toast to their son and future daughter-in-law was simple yet beautiful. After asking the guests to raise their glasses, they stood with arms around each other's waist. John Adler's baritone voice filled the room.

"When your children find true love, parents find true joy. Aaron and Jane, may you bring to each other as much joy and happiness as your mother and I have always shared."

Since Brooke knew Zack enjoyed sharing a toast on special occasions, she'd set it up with Jane to request a toast from the man who'd had a hand in bringing Jane and Aaron together. Even though Zack hadn't been told in advance he would be asked to give a toast, Brooke wasn't surprised when he stood confidently and raised his glass.

"To Aaron and Jane, two very special people who have been blessed with the good fortune of finding each other. May you share a lifetime filled with exquisite happiness and joys as bright as the morning sun."

Once all the toasts had been given, everyone had the opportunity to indulge in a scrumptious dessert. The evening then culminated with Aaron and Jane on the dance floor. While the pair swayed in each other's arms, the DJ played *Just the Way You Are,* the tune the couple had adopted as "their song." After a few bars, the dance floor filled with other happy couples, laughing and enjoying the special celebration.

The closer it got to the end of the party, the more nervous Brooke became. She watched as people went up to Jane and Aaron to wish them congratulations once more before leaving.

Zack must have sensed her agitation. He put his arm around her waist and whispered in her ear, "It's okay, Brooke. If you just want me to take you home, I will."

Bad Case of Lovin' You

How'd I get so lucky to have a guy like this? she thought. Instead of expressing what was in her mind, she simply shook her head from side to side and whispered, "I *want* to go home with you, Zack. I really do," and she meant it.

Chapter Twenty-One

It was after one o'clock in the morning before the last of the guests left. Zack had been waiting patiently and had watched in admiration as Brooke fulfilled her role as hostess.

She truly is extraordinary. Always putting the needs of others before her own.

Tonight he wanted to focus on *her* needs for once, and in doing so he was certain his own would be more than met.

Even though she wore a smile, he could sense her fatigue as she walked toward him.

"Great party, Brooke. You did a magnificent job." He patted the seat beside him. "Do you want to sit for a minute before we go?"

"I do, but I'm afraid if I sit down I won't want to get back up again." She sighed, but there was a look of satisfaction on her face. "It was good, wasn't it?"

"Indeed. You should be very proud of yourself. Aaron and Jane couldn't have asked for a better engagement party." He stood and wrapped his arms around her in what was meant to be a congratulatory hug. However, when her arms went around his waist, and she laid her head on his shoulder, his pulse kicked into high gear. The stirring in his loins was unmistakable.

"Thanks, Zack," she whispered.

When she tipped her head up, their eyes met. She ran her tongue over her full bottom lip, and there was no way for him to hide the effect she was having on him. He lowered his mouth to hers.

Her response was immediate. She moaned softly. "Take me home, Zack. Please."

He quickly retrieved their coats and held her hand as they waited for his car. For the first time since he'd purchased his little Jeep Wrangler, he thought perhaps it might be time to get a less sporty vehicle. It wasn't the smoothest of rides, and the seats were a bit stiff. He realized her comfort was important to him. *She* was important to him.

After driving in silence for a while, Brooke commented, "You're a good dancer, Zack. I'm sorry I was preoccupied so much of the evening. It would've been nice to have a couple more spins around the floor with you."

"I would've liked that too, Brooke." He paused. "Can I let you in on a little secret?"

"What's that?"

"The truth is, the only reason I'm a halfway decent dancer is because of my mom. I didn't want to, but she made me take dance lessons when I was thirteen. I only agreed because she told me it'd help with girls." He chuckled. "Looks like she was right, huh?"

"Yep. Your mom's a pretty smart cookie. I'm not the world's best dancer, but like all girls, I want to have fun, and dancing is just that ... fun." She smiled. Then she was thoughtful for a moment. "You could've danced with some other people if you'd wanted. I really wouldn't have minded."

"Brooke," he said seriously, "if I'd *wanted* to dance with anyone else, I would have." He reached for her hand and covered it with his own. "*You.* You're the only one I wanted to dance with. You're the one I want to *be* with."

"Not even Gabby?" she asked shyly.

"Honestly, Brooke, I don't understand why or how you could ask me that. Like you, your sister is a beautiful woman. And, as identical twins, the two of you obviously share many of the same physical characteristics, but she's not *you*." He paused to let his words sink in. "Gabriella was there having a great time, just like all the other guests. But *you* ... you were the one making sure everything and everyone else was being taken care of. Don't you see, Brooke? It's time for you to take care of *you.* And I'd like to help. I'd like you to experience what it's like to have your own needs met instead of always putting others first."

"I think I'd like that too," she whispered.

When they got to his house, he could tell she was a little uneasy. He brushed his hands softly down her arms as he helped her take off her coat. As she stood with her back to him he whispered into her ear, "Did I tell you how beautiful you look tonight, Miss Adler?"

"I believe you did, Dr. Carter," she said as she turned to him demurely.

He put his hands on her shoulders and took in a deep breath as he leaned toward her. "I love the way you smell."

"*Zack ... I ...*"

"And I love the way you say my name. I love the sound of your voice." He felt her tremble as he caressed her cheek and then allowed his knuckles to slowly brush the side of her neck. "Your skin is so soft." Her eyes locked with his, and he traced her collarbone with his finger. Finally, he gently ran his palm over the length of her arm and locked his fingers with hers. "Come on," he said softly as he led her to the couch in the living room.

When she sat down, he sat next to her and moved so that her back faced him. Placing his hands on her shoulders, he used his thumbs to massage the muscles near the base of her neck. He could feel her tension begin to fade as she relaxed into his hands.

"Ahhh," she sighed. "That feels incredible."

"*You* feel incredible," he whispered. Brushing her hair aside, he pressed his lips to her neck. "You're so beautiful." Softly he nipped the tender flesh where her neck and shoulder met.

When she turned to face him, her lips were parted, her eyes heavy lidded. She placed her hands on his face and brought his mouth to hers. He pulled her onto his lap, and she wrapped her arms around him, weaving her fingers into his hair. She wiggled her bottom against his already raging hard on, making him feel like he was going to explode way too soon.

He pressed his mouth to hers, then traced her lips with his tongue. When she moaned, his tongue entered her mouth, tasting her. Delicious ... slightly salty with the faintest hint of wine.

Anita Louise

It'd been a while since he'd had sex. Making sure the woman he was with enjoyed herself as much or more than he did, had always been a priority to him. Therefore, he'd practiced and become accomplished at the art of how to turn a woman on ... how to satisfy her. But Brooke's response, her apparent need for him, and his for her, was unlike any of his prior encounters. What he felt for Brooke was somehow different. He'd fallen for her practically at first glance, and now being with her in an intimate way stirred stronger and deeper feelings than he'd ever felt before.

She shivered slightly as he began exploring her body with his hands. Moving from her back down to her hips, he could feel the firmness of her muscles beneath the texture of the lace. The hem of her dress had hiked up and as he moved his hand down her leg he felt it. *Skin.* She was wearing stockings held up by the thin straps of a garter belt. The skin of her thighs was even softer than the silk of her stockings.

He needed to touch her, to feel more of her flesh in his hands. With his other hand he found the top of the zipper at the back of her dress. As he lowered it, his hand brushed down her spine. Pulling his mouth away from hers, he groaned and said, "I need to see you, Brooke. All of you. Please."

She didn't say a word, but took his face in her hands and kissed him deeply. Then she stood before him and peeled the lacy dress from her body. When she stepped out of it, she was clad only in a delicate low cut bra with a matching garter belt and thong.

"Oh, God, Brooke. You're so damn beautiful." He was hit with a surge of desire unlike anything he'd ever experienced before. His erection was straining for release. He wanted nothing more than to bury himself into her–hard and fast. Yet somewhere a part of him knew he must allow her to be in control. He watched. He waited.

Taking a deep shaking breath she straddled him, and then rubbed her sex against him. Up and down she rocked. Silently she began to unbutton his shirt. As she opened each button, she followed with her teeth and tongue, licking and nipping softly.

"I'm not going to stop you this time, Brooke. I can't. I want you too badly."

She silenced him by placing her mouth on his. Rubbing her chest against him, she pushed the shirt off his shoulders. Her eyes watched his reaction as she rolled his nipples between her thumbs and forefinger.

He groaned. Reaching up he inched the thin straps of her bra off her shoulders, releasing the fullness of her soft globes. "I love your breasts ... they're perfect." *You're perfect.* He took them in his hands, and knew he had to have them in his mouth. He had to find out if they tasted as wonderful as they looked. *Ah, yes.* He laved his tongue over her, suckling and teasing her nipples.

His hard on throbbed behind his zipper, and once again he moved to cover her mouth with his. This time their kiss was different. His desperation for her had grown to a new level. She continued to rub her pelvis against him and press her chest to his. "Your breasts feel so good against me. I want to feel all of you next to me, Brooke. I need to."

She whimpered as he again filled his hands with her full, soft globes. Her nipples puckered as he tweaked them with his thumbs. A moment later his mouth replaced his hands again. First he swirled his tongue over her swollen peaks, and then lightly scraped his teeth over her aroused flesh. As he sucked her nipple into his mouth, he slid his hand up her inner thigh. Her panties were damp with her arousal.

She was so sensual, so responsive. Maybe it should have surprised him, but it didn't. Somehow he knew that's how she would be. He slid his finger along her panty line and then under the thin material. She gasped as his finger slid into the slick warmth between her legs.

"You're so wet. So hot and so wet for *me*. I have to taste you." He felt her stiffen slightly. He looked into her eyes as he put his finger into his mouth. "Ummmm. Delicious," he said as he tasted her juices. He watched as her eyes grew even darker with passion. "*More*. I want more," he said. Then he hooked his fingers into the sides of the tiny slip of lace on her hips, pulling her panties down and then off. She started to close her legs. "No," he said as he placed his hand against her thigh. "Open. Open for me, Brooke." His eyes were locked with hers as he lowered his mouth to enjoy the sweetness between her legs.

Brooke had never felt this out of control ... or this good before. Her legs were shaking, and his name fell from her lips as shock waves of pleasure moved through her body. Her hands gripped the cushions below her and then moved to his shoulders. She looked down her nearly naked body. Their eyes met and his were filled with such desire ... such passion. She gasped as he inserted two of his long, tapered fingers deep inside her.

Bad Case of Lovin' You

"My God, Brooke. You're so wet–so tight." He moved his tongue in a circular motion around her most sensitive spot as his fingers moved in and out. "Come for me, Brooke. I want to watch you explode. I want to feel your muscles grip me as you do."

"Not yet," she protested. "First I want to touch you— taste you. I want you inside me. Please."

He acquiesced wordlessly, pushing his fingers in and out of her once more before removing them. Then he slid up her body, pressing his erection to where his hand had been. Slowly he lowered his head to hers, parted her lips and slipped his tongue into her mouth. She tasted her own juices for the first time. Because they were on his tongue, the pleasure was unexpectedly delightful.

Moving her hand to his waist, she tugged on his belt. "Please," she begged.

He got up and stood before her, much like she had stood in front of him earlier. Her hands fumbled as she moved to undo his belt and his trousers as quickly as possible. Finally she was able to unzip his slacks and push them down over his slim hips. As soon as his erection was released, she took it in her hand, feeling the smoothness of his skin over his rock-hard shaft.

"Brooke," he groaned as she greedily took him into her mouth. With one hand she continued to stroke his shaft. With the other she grabbed his hip as if to take him in even deeper. His buttock was firm and round in her hand, yet the muscles in his legs were shaking. "I ... I have to sit down," he managed to say before dropping onto the coffee table in front of the couch. She continued her ministrations, and he brushed her hair back from her face. "Oh my God, Brooke,

you have no idea what you're doing to me." He gently lifted her head. Leaning into her, he smiled and once more pressed his lips to hers. "Come on," he said as he slipped his feet and legs out from his shoes and the pants crumpled beneath him. Taking her hand, he stood, pulling her up from the couch with him. "Bed," he said.

"Yes," she replied softly. "Bed."

The next thing she knew, he had swept her into his arms and they were walking across the room. When they moved through the doorway she could see there was another sliding glass door to the deck in his bedroom. Light from the moon streamed in.

Standing next to the bed with her in his arms he asked, "Will you flip the blankets down please, sweetheart?" Releasing one of her arms from his neck, she did as he requested. He laid her gently down on the soft sheets. "Here," he murmured, "let's get you out of these." With that he began to release her hose from their fastenings. Every spot he touched was followed with a soft kiss to her thigh. Then he pushed her stockings down and off her feet. "You might need to help me with this," he said, indicating her garter belt. Rolling over slightly, she undid it and dropped the strip of lace to the floor. When she started to undo the clasp between her breasts, he stopped her. "Let me," he whispered. Before reaching for the fastener, he engulfed her fullness in his hands once more, kneading and stroking her hardening peaks. He followed with his mouth, licking her nipples with his tongue before suckling. "Ummm," he murmured as he continued to suck. Finally he removed the last garment she wore.

Bad Case of Lovin' You

Once she was completely naked, he laid down beside her. Pulling her close, once again he covered her mouth with his. The kiss was slow and sweet, the most sensual and seductive kiss of her life. It felt as if he poured every ounce of his desire into it, and she drank it in like nectar from the gods. Looking back later, she would recognize this moment as the one where she knew she wanted more than just his body. She wanted his heart.

Her own passion had ratcheted up to an even higher level. For once she wanted to let go completely ... to hold nothing back. She wasn't *trying* to be seductive, nor was she trying to be anyone other than herself. She was simply a woman giving herself completely, allowing her desires to overcome any and every reservation. Her hands caressed his body, exploring every inch. She loved the way the soft skin of his shaft moved with each stroke of her hand up and down. Her body seemed to move of its own accord. Without even knowing how it happened, she found herself straddled across one of his thighs. She pressed her sex against the strong, firm muscles of his leg. Finally, she moved again and rubbed her wetness up and down his rigid member. She didn't even realize she was making little whimpering sounds of need.

He reached over and pulled a condom from his bedside table. Taking it from him she said, "Let me." His gaze burned into her as he watched her tear the foil package with her teeth. She felt him throb and heard him groan as she rolled the soft latex over his length.

When he moved on top of her, she spread her legs to allow him to position himself between her thighs. As much as she wanted ... needed him inside her, she also needed to

Anita Louise

kiss him again. Her arms went around his neck, and she pulled his mouth to hers. There was so much passion in their kiss, she could think of nothing else except the feel of his lips on hers, his body crushed against her own.

She arched upward when she finally felt the head of his shaft touch the slick opening between her thighs. "Yes. *Yes,*" she whispered urgently. He slid into her slowly, and she relished every inch. "Oh, God. *Zack.*" He pulled back until he was almost out of her completely and then pushed back in all the way. She had never felt so filled or so fulfilled before. She moved in rhythm with him, a dance as old as time. With every thrust she came closer and closer to her peak.

At last, it was as if fireworks exploded, and she gave into complete and total pleasure. There was an intense sense of gratification as her inner muscles contracted around him. She heard him groan in ecstasy as they went over the edge together.

Chapter Twenty-Two

It was morning. Brooke was half asleep, and for some reason, she was feeling the best she could ever remember. As she started to stretch, she felt the strong male arm encircling her. Immediately she remembered where she was, and why she felt so fantastically wonderful. Not only was Zack's arm around her, but his naked body was pressed, spoon-like, against her own nudity.

I could get used to this, she thought languidly.

The memory of their previous evening of lovemaking flashed vividly into her mind. Along with it came a surge of desire. She could feel the solid muscles of the front of his thighs against the back of her own. In an attempt to remove every bit of space between them, she snuggled toward him. Her movement caused him to stir. She smiled when his hand moved slowly from her tummy to her breast, leaving a trail of shiver bumps in its wake. At the same time she felt his erection begin to grow against the small of her back.

"Good morning, beautiful," Zack whispered. Then he began to plant soft kisses along her shoulder.

Anita Louise

"Ummm. This *is* a good morning," she murmured. Moving slightly away from him, she reached behind her back to take him into her hand. She loved the contrast between the softness of his skin over the hardness of his shaft. Rolling from her side to her back, she adjusted her grip and began to stroke him slowly ... up and down, up and down.

She felt the rumble in his chest as he released a low groan of pleasure. He continued to kiss, lick and nip his way up her neck to her jawline. "I love the way you taste," he said softly. The sensation of being savored like some fine delicacy had her shivering with the sheer enjoyment of it. As his lips, tongue and teeth worked their way up, his hands continued to massage her breasts and tease her nipples to hard peaks.

When he reached her face, he planted soft kisses all over her cheeks, chin, eyes and forehead. Finally he worked his way to her mouth and covered it with his own. At first he gently kissed the corners of her mouth, her cupid's bow. Then he began nibbling on her full lower lip. Next he ran his tongue over the seam of her lips. When her lips parted, he thrust his tongue into her mouth, and it tangled with hers. She delighted as their tongues played inside each other's mouth ... licking, thrusting, tasting.

Their foreplay had completely turned her on, and just kissing was no longer enough. She needed more of him. She needed to taste more than just his mouth. Disengaging their tongues, she did just the opposite of what he'd so recently done to her. She nibbled his lower lip softly. Then sweet kisses were planted on the corners of his mouth, as well as each peak of his cupid's bow. Little velvety pecks were then placed on his eyes, forehead, cheeks, and chin. While continuing to stroke his manhood, she then nipped, licked and kissed her way across his jawline and down his neck. She could see and feel his pulse beating rapidly in his throat.

His well-defined chest was next. Continuing the same delicate torture, she discovered the delight of watching his nipples grow erect. Next she worked her way around his pecs. Sucking on the tiny peaks, she flicked their hardness with her tongue. As she moved her own breasts deliberately across his body, she knew his guttural response was an expression of his enjoyment.

Her mouth continued its exquisite torture as she moved down his abdomen. While she gave attention to his hipbones with her mouth, one hand continued to stroke his shaft. Her other hand was used to gently caress the sacs between his legs.

"Brooke. Oh, my God. That feels so good."

She smiled and hummed a delighted response. Continuing to caress his genitals, her mouth at last reached its destination. First placing her lips gently around the tip of his erection, she then traced her tongue across the top. She delighted in giving extra attention to its center, before circling around the circumference. Zack groaned again and arched up into her warm and welcoming mouth.

"Ummmm," she hummed again as she took his shaft deep into her throat.

After enjoying her ministrations for several minutes, he gently brushed her cheek. Whispering softly, he said, "My turn, darling. Move your hips up here so I can touch you." When she did as he asked, he slid a finger along the slick length between her thighs. "Lord, Brooke. You drive me crazy. I love how wet you get for me ... how good it feels." He pushed his fingers inside her. Their eyes locked. She watched as he pulled his fingers from between her legs and put them into his mouth ... savoring her juices. "God, I love the taste of you." Then he watched her take his length deep into her mouth and throat. "I want more," he said. "I need you to move your hips over my face. I want to taste you while you're tasting me."

Trembling, she positioned herself as he wanted. When she did, he gripped her hips and lifted his head to her sensitive core. Using his lips, tongue, and teeth he took her higher and higher. She'd never done anything like this before and found it totally exciting ... totally thrilling.

As he took her to even greater heights, she felt his erection grow larger ... harder in her mouth. She heard herself moaning, and her hips seemed to move of their own accord as he licked her most intimate of places.

"Umm, umm, umm," she whimpered. She moved her hand up and down his shaft while sucking as much of his length into her mouth as she could.

"*Brooke. I'm going to come,*" he cried. He pushed his fingers inside her as he buried his face between her legs. She felt her inner muscles clamp down on him at the same time he experienced his own release. As orgasms rocked them both, they cried out their pleasure.

Brooke didn't realize she'd fallen into a satisfied sleep after their morning lovemaking, until she woke up. She was in Zack's bed. Somehow he'd put a pillow under her head and covered her with a blanket without waking her. She inhaled deeply and smiled with satisfaction. All the bed linens smelled of him and of very fulfilling sex. She'd never considered herself a particularly sexy or sensual woman before, but being with Zack was revealing, even to her, a whole new aspect of herself.

Stretching her arms, she realized she was alone in bed. At first she was disappointed. But her disappointment vanished when she heard the sound of movement and detected the aroma of sizzling bacon coming from the kitchen.

Food. Her stomach growled. *As much fun as it might be to try, I guess I can't just live on love.* She chuckled to herself.

Sitting up in bed, she looked around the room for the dress she'd worn the night before. It was hanging neatly on a hook on the back of the bedroom door. Lying on the end of the bed was a University of Washington t-shirt. *Did he put that there for me? He's so considerate. It's no wonder I've fallen in love with him.*

The realization stopped her in her tracks. It'd been years since the last time she'd allowed herself to love a man. And that first experience had ended in heartbreak. Was she ready to put her heart at risk again?

By the time Nathan Silvers went back to work, he'd run the credit back up to the limit on the cards his wife had been trying to pay off. He'd been out partying most of the weekend. After his experience with Crystal, he'd decided to stay away from women for a while. So he'd been hanging out with a few of his buddies, shootin' the shit, playing pool and downing plenty of shots and beers. He'd used up the last of his available credit when he restocked his supply of booze at home.

*No big deal. There's plenty more where that came from. Now that I don't have to worry about Big Bitch and Little Bitch spending my paycheck for me, I'll have more than enough to do whatever the hell I want to do. It's about damn time Nate Silvers took care of **himself** for a change.*

He'd overslept again. If he didn't get his ass into work, his friggin' boss would be all over him for the millionth time. He got busy as soon as he walked in. A big job had come in so they were slammed. There wasn't even time for his usual break. It was after noon by the time he had a chance to call the bank.

Listening to one damn 'menu' after another was just about driving him crazy.

*What the hell is this? Ya can't even talk to a live goddamn person anymore. 'Press one for this. Press two for that.' F*** that shit. I just want to talk to a friggin' human being for christsake!*

When he finally got to a Customer Care Representative, he found out they didn't 'care' one little bit. He was put on hold before he hardly got a word out of his mouth. Then the asshole broad he was talking to said she couldn't help him, and she transferred him to another department. His entire break had been wasted sitting on hold and ultimately accomplishing nothing.

"Hey, Silvers." Nate heard the voice of his boss. "You better get your ass back to work if you want to keep your job. Make your personal calls on your own time. You ain't gettin' no free lunch here. If you want a paycheck, you're gonna have to work for it."

That son-of-a-bitch. Since I'm not part of his little goddam group of ass kissers, he's on my butt every time I turn around. How the hell am I gonna get this shit straightened out? The only time these mother f···in' places are open is when I'm at work!

Nate hung up and jammed his phone back into his pocket angrily.

Looks like I'm gonna have to take a sick day or somethin' to take care of this crap. What a pain in the ass. If I ever see that goddamn Crystal again I'm gonna wring her f···in' neck!

As far as Zack was concerned, he'd never seen anything better. When Brooke padded quietly into his kitchen in her bare feet and his old t-shirt, he felt an unfamiliar stirring deep inside. The smile on his face came from an unexpected, but very real happiness brought on simply by her presence.

"Hey, sleepyhead." He joked. "Hungry?"

"I didn't know I was, 'til I smelled that bacon ... which smells delicious, by the way." Walking over to where he stood in front of the stove, she wrapped her arms around him from behind. He felt her sigh as she laid her cheek against his back.

Turning off the flame underneath the sizzling meat, he rotated to face her. Wrapping his own arms around her, he asked, "Everything okay?"

"Yes," she whispered. "Everything's more than okay. Everything's wonderful."

When she tipped her head up and their eyes met, he couldn't help but gently place his lips on hers for a sweet, sweet kiss. "I could get used to this," he murmured.

"Me too," she responded softly.

They stood contentedly in each other's arms in front of the stove for several minutes, each lost in their own thoughts. Finally, he stepped back slightly. "I'm really glad you're here, Brooke. I had a great time last night ... *and* this morning." He hesitated a moment. "I don't know if I should tell you this or not, but no one's ever spent the night here before. You're the first."

She seemed to be thinking about her response before speaking. "I'm glad you told me, and I'm even *more* glad I'm the first. And I ..." She stopped in mid-sentence.

"What were you going to say, Brooke?"

Shaking her head and looking down, she said, "Nothing really."

She started to move out of his arms, but he held her in place. Gently, he tipped her face up to his. "If you were going to say, you hope you're the last, I hope so too." Wasn't it unusual for a couple with a relationship as new as theirs to understand one another so well? He felt *something*. Did he see that same *something* shimmering in her eyes? Even if he did, he just wasn't sure either one of them was ready to name it.

Brooke grinned and gave him a quick kiss before changing the subject. "When's breakfast going to be ready? I'm starved." With that she went to the coffee maker, poured herself a cup, took it to the kitchen table, and sat down.

"Just a few more minutes." He turned back to the stove. "How do you like your eggs?"

The rest of the morning passed in comfortable conversation. Their banter was filled with light-hearted teasing and jokes sprinkled with sexual innuendo. After breakfast, they worked together amiably to clean up the kitchen. Once the counters were sparkling, Brooke looked down at her attire and grinned.

"This outfit is totally comfy, and I absolutely love the dress I wore to the party last night. But I don't think either one's appropriate to wear to your mother's house for dinner."

Zack licked his lips and looked at her lasciviously. "You look fantastic now and you did last night too, but I have to agree. It's probably not the best look for meeting Mom for the first time. I guess we're going to have to do something about that." A moment later he said, "I could give you a pair of my sweats to go with the t-shirt, but you'd still be stuck with high heels. What do you think?"

"Thanks for the offer of the sweats, but I think I'll just put my dress back on."

"Do you want some help changing?" Zack wiggled his eyebrows and grinned.

Brooke shook her finger at him knowingly. "Oh, no you don't. You know as well as I do, Dr. Carter, if I let you go back in that bedroom with me, we might not *ever* get out of here." She walked over and gave him a quick peck on the cheek. "Just give me a few minutes, and then you can take me home."

Watching the sway of her hips and her shapely legs as she walked out of the room, he knew she was right. But the temptation to follow her and "help" her anyway was almost too hard to resist. Somehow, instead of following her alluring figure back down the hall into the bedroom, he forced himself to sit on the couch and slip his feet into his shoes.

When she came back into the living room, he was struck by how much natural beauty she possessed. She hadn't yet put on her heels, swinging them in her hand as she strolled into the room in stocking clad feet. Still, she practically took his breath away. Even without the perfect makeup and hairdo of the previous evening, she looked stunning.

Brooke must have noticed his stare, because she looked down at herself questioningly. Seeming a little self-conscious, she smoothed her hands over her skirt and then her hair. "What is it? Did I forget something?"

He stood and shook his head as he walked toward her. "Not a thing. Everything about you is just the way it should be." *Perfect. Absolutely perfect.* He took her into his arms. "Not only are you beautiful, you're also a pretty smart cookie, Brooke Adler. If I'd have given into the urge to follow you into that bedroom again, we'd never make it to my mom's house for dinner."

"I told you so," she whispered just before their lips met. When he started to deepen the kiss, she pulled back breathlessly. "Zack, please. As much as I'd love to spend the entire day in bed with you, it's super important to me to make a good impression on your family. If I'm going to do that, I really have to go."

"You're right," he said reluctantly before kissing her again softly. "You can bet I'm going to be taking you up on the 'entire day in bed' suggestion. But for right now I'll get your coat."

Chapter Twenty-Three

"Oooo, tell me everything," Shelly said when Brooke walked in the door.

Brooke sighed and smiled dreamily. "It was wonderful. *He's* wonderful." She spun around in a happy pirouette. "Let me get out of these clothes and I'll give you as many of the delicious details as I can. Some things are just too private to share." Giving her friend a significant wink, Brooke practically floated up the stairs to her bedroom.

Standing in the shower, Brooke's imagination went on a delightful journey. Instead of being alone under the fine spray, a handsome doctor stood next to her in all his naked glory. Humming, she soaped up her body and washed her hair. Her breasts throbbed when the spray hit her chest. She moved the soap slowly across her breasts and her heartbeat quickened as she pictured Zack's hands caressing and massaging the swollen tips. Desire raced through her. *Why didn't I take a shower at Zack's when I had the chance?* She was tempted to move her hand down to the clump of soft curls at the apex of her thighs and release the sexual tension. But then a delightfully wicked idea crossed her mind.

Rinsing off quickly, she stepped out of the shower. Then she picked up her cell phone and dialed Zack's number. He answered after the second ring.

"You miss me already, huh?" he said in a teasing tone.

She could hear the pleasure in his voice.

"Do I ever," she said breathlessly. "Are you home yet?"

"Just walked in the door. What's up? Did you forget something?"

"Yes, I did." She used her free hand to tease the nipples of her breasts.

Zack sounded a little suspicious. "What are you doing, Brooke Adler?"

"I just stepped out of the shower, and I'm standing here naked. I'm wishing we'd showered together before I left."

"Why didn't I think of that?" He groaned, and his breath became erratic. "What do you think we should do about it?" he asked.

"I'm already playing with my nipples. Want to have phone sex, Dr. Carter? I'll tell you what I want you to do, and you tell me what you want me to do. How's that sound?"

"Sounds delightfully wicked, Ms. Adler. I love picturing you playing with your nipples. Are they getting nice and hard?"

"Oh, yes. They're standing up like pencil erasers. I'm squeezing and twisting them, and it's really turning me on.

Are you naked yet? If not, I need you to strip down. Right now."

"Your wish is my command," he said. "I just stepped out of my sweatpants."

"Are you nice and erect?"

"Yes."

"Ummm. I love that. I want you to stroke it for me, Zack." She listened as his breath became more ragged. "How's that feel? Make sure you're sliding your hand all the way to the top and then back down. Do it nice and slow."

"Oh, my God, Brooke. It feels really good. I need to sit down."

"Okay. I want you to go into the bedroom and I want you to lay down on the bed ... completely naked. Keep stroking yourself while you walk, and tell me when you're in the bedroom."

There was silence for a few moments before Zack spoke again. "I'm in the bedroom. I just put the phone on speaker so I can get out of the rest of these clothes. Are you in your bedroom too, Brooke?"

"Yes."

"Are you wet?"

"Oh yes. Very wet."

"Good. Because I want you to taste yourself. I want you to lie down on the bed, and spread your legs nice and wide for me."

She did as she was told. "Okay. I'm lying down on the top of my bed. Are you?" Desire raced through her. She closed her eyes and allowed herself to relax while she pictured his naked body, and his hand moving up and down his rock-hard erection.

"Yes, I am, and I'm still stroking myself just like you told me to. How about you? Is your hand between your legs? Are you nice and slick?"

As her hands moved down her stomach, then lower to the clump of soft curls between her thighs, a moan escaped her lips at the exceedingly pleasurable sensations that coursed through her. "Oh, Zack. I can't believe how wet I am." In her mind's eye she saw the gorgeous face and hazel eyes of the man on the other end of the phone. The silky wetness caused by her arousal made her breath quicken.

"Now put your fingers in your mouth, Brooke."

"But ..."

"No arguments. You taste so good. If I was there with you, my mouth would be on you and my tongue would be in you. I'd be lapping up as much of those delicious juices as I could. Taste yourself and tell me."

She pushed her fingers inside herself once ... twice, then did as he asked and tentatively touched her tongue to her fingers. The slick juices were salty. She then engulfed her fingers in her mouth. "Umm. Salty, but good."

"Oh, Brooke. You've got me so turned on! How I wish you were here. I'm so hard, and it would feel so good to be inside you."

"I'd love to have you inside me too," she whispered. She swirled her fingers around her most sensitive spot. "Zack, I'm going to come. Are you close?"

He was panting. "Uh, uh, uh. Yes, Brooke, yes. I'm coming. Come with me, Brooke. Come with me."

"Oh, Oh, Zack. Yes, yes." She felt her muscles spasm, and her body exploded in a delicious orgasm. Moments later she released a long sigh as she felt the languid calm that flowed through her now satisfied body. "Wow," she whispered softly into the phone.

"Yeah. Wow. That was pretty amazing," he replied.

"It was." Suddenly, her boldness disappeared, and she felt like a shy, bookish school teacher again. "You don't think I'm ..."

"I think you're wonderful, Brooke Adler. You're wonderful, amazing, sexy, beautiful and a zillion other things that my brain isn't able to think of right now. I can't wait to see you again tonight, and I'm excited for you to meet my family. They're going to love you." She heard him hesitate. "I'll pick you up about six. Is that okay?"

"Perfect. I'll be ready. See you then, Zack."

"Yeah, I'll see you at six." There was that hesitation again.

It sounded to Brooke as if he wanted to say something more. "Is everything all right?" she asked.

"Everything's fine. I'll see you later."

"Okay then. Bye, Zack."

"Bye, Brooke, I ... uh, bye."

I love you, Brooke Adler. The realization hit Zack like a Mack truck. He'd almost told her. He'd *wanted* to tell her, but how would she feel about it? He couldn't really understand it himself. How was it possible for a man to fall head over heels in love in such a short period of time?

He'd always wanted what his parents had ... a relationship in which two people loved each other, unconditionally ... forever. Could he have that with Brooke? Only time would tell if the love he felt for her would be worth risking his heart once more.

Anita Louise

When Brooke finally emerged from her bedroom, Shelly had lunch ready. It was a delicious looking salad with chunks of baked chicken, crumbled bacon and chopped tomato in some sort of a light mayonnaise dressing over a bed of lettuce and spinach. Brooke's stomach growled.

"Wow! That looks great, Shelly."

"Good. I'm glad you're hungry because I've been waiting for *hours* to talk about that absolutely fabulous party last night. You did an amazing job putting everything together, Brooke. Everyone had a magnificent time."

"It really did turn out well, didn't it? I'm so happy for Aaron and Jane. They're just the perfect couple."

"You and Zack looked pretty darn perfect together last night too. He's a good dancer. I loved watching you two out there on the dance floor."

"It was all him, that's for sure. I've always enjoyed dancing, but never considered myself to be all that good at it. He told me his mother tricked him into dance lessons when he was thirteen by telling him it would help him with the girls." Brooke giggled. "She was right too. I can't wait to meet her. She sounds like an amazing woman."

"That's right! I almost forgot to tell you. I made some banana bread today. I thought it'd be a nice little treat for Mary Beth's homecoming tomorrow. Anyway, I made some extra you can take with you to Zack's mom's house tonight if you want to." Shelly hesitated, seeming to second guess herself. "I hope that's okay?"

"Of course it's okay! In fact, it's great. I wish I would've thought of it myself." The smile on Brooke's face was a combination of gratitude, excitement and apprehension. "Zack's brother and wife are going to be there too."

"What's going on in that pretty little head of yours, Brooke Adler? You *are* happy about meeting his mom and brother, aren't you?" Shelly asked suspiciously.

Brooke hesitated before speaking. "What if they don't like me?"

Shelly burst out laughing. "Bwahaha! You've *got* to be kidding me. Not *like* you? It's more likely they're going to *love* you and want you to be part of their family whether Zack likes it or not."

"Do you really think so?" Brooke asked tentatively.

"I *know* so. Honestly, Brooke. I really don't understand how you could even *ask* that kind of a question. You're one of the sweetest, kindest, most *likeable* people I've ever known in my entire life. And you've *always* been that way. Even in high school, you were the one who was nice to the kids other people would make fun of and not want anything to do with. You were the one who stood up to the bullies—not for yourself but for others. You're like the *poster child* for likeability."

Shelly's response was so emphatic and sincere it practically had Brooke in tears.

"Gosh, Shell, thanks. And thanks for making the banana bread too. You're so good to me. I don't know what to say," Brooke said as she dabbed at her eyes.

Shelly gave her friend a warm hug. "You don't have to say a word. There's no way Mary Beth and I can ever repay you for what you've done for us. Besides, everything I said is the gospel truth, Brooke. You're the best friend I've ever had, and I love you to pieces."

"I love you too, Shelly. Mary Beth too." The two women embraced while they laughed and cried tears of appreciation for one another. When they drew apart, Brooke continued. "Speaking of Mary Beth, I'm glad that girl's coming home tomorrow. I miss her."

"Me too! I'm picking her up at the airport in the afternoon. I can't wait to see her." Shelly's smile was genuine. "Hopefully, she'll be looking good and feeling good. She's going back to school on Monday, ready or not."

"She'll be ready. Kids that age are very attached to their friends. She's probably been texting and connecting with her besties the whole time she's been in Arizona," Brooke commented knowingly.

"You're right. Mary Beth's probably more anxious to see her friends than she is to see her own mother." Shelly sighed resignedly. "I was probably the same way when I was a teen. Guess you don't really appreciate your parents until you're older." She shrugged. "All that's well and good, but even more importantly ... what are you going to *wear* tonight?"

Brooke grinned ear to ear. "Not sure yet, but it'd be great if you'd help me decide."

Arm in arm the two women mounted the stairs to Brooke's bedroom.

Having the contents of his wallet stolen was proving to be a bigger deal than Nathan Silvers ever anticipated. When he was finally able to speak to someone at the bank about cancelling his credit card, he learned his bank card had been maxed out.

"Well, it wasn't me. I didn't even *have* that card on me all weekend," he explained as calmly as possible.

"I'm sorry, Mr. Silvers. We will put a stop on the card you have with our bank, but you're going to have to contact all your other credit card issuers. You'd be wise to also place a fraud alert with one of the three credit reporting agencies. We have some forms we're going to need you to fill out for us. Then we'll do what we can."

"Whadda' ya' mean, 'you'll do what you can?' I got no money 'cause my wallet was stolen. How the hell am I supposed to get by 'til payday?"

The person at the bank sounded as if this was something that happened on a regular basis. "We have a comprehensive booklet from the Federal Trade Commission. It's specifically designed for our clients who become victims of identity theft. It walks you through all the steps you're going to need to take to resolve this. It'll also help you if you experience any other issues due to the loss of your wallet. Would you like to pick the booklet up, or would you like me to mail it to you?"

Nate's patience was wearing thin. "I don't want no goddamn booklet. I want some *money*. I *need* my money. It's my own goddamn money for christsake!"

"I'm sorry, Mr. Silvers, but we do have our policies and procedures. Have you filed a police report? We're going to need a copy of that as well."

"No! I haven't filed a f***in' police report." He exploded.

"Well, you're going to want to do that as soon as possible, Mr. Silvers. It's my understanding the police report will need to be included with the Identity Theft Affidavit you'll need to file with the FTC."

"What the f***? I got no time for all this shit! I got a job. I gotta go to work."

The bank clerk continued unfazed. "You'll also want to order your free credit reports from all three credit repositories to see if any new lines of credit have been opened in your name that you might not be aware of. Everything you need to do is listed step-by-step in the FTC booklet."

"Okay. I'll pick up this friggin' booklet. How long is it anyway?"

"Oh, it's only a little over a hundred pages," the clerk replied calmly.

"A hundred pages! You gotta be *kiddin'* me. I got no time to go through a hundred friggin' pages of instructions."

"I'm sorry, Mr. Silvers. Just stop by the bank and ask for the FTC booklet for victims of identity theft. Anyone can help you." Before hanging up the clerk said in a sing-songy voice, "Good luuuck."

Chapter Twenty-Four

Zack arrived at Brooke's house a few minutes early. He was surprised by how anxious he was about taking her to meet his mother, brother and sister-in-law. Shelly Silvers opened the door and ushered him in after his first ring of the doorbell.

"Hi, Zack," Shelly said casually. "Brooke'll be down in a minute. Can I get you anything?"

"No thanks, Shelly. I'm good." Looking around the room and not seeing any evidence of her teenaged daughter he asked, "How's Mary Beth doing?"

"As far as I know, she's doing just fine. I've talked to her every day, but I haven't seen her in about a week. She's been staying with her grandparents in Arizona for a little while. I'll be picking her up at the airport tomorrow afternoon."

"I bet you'll be glad to have her back here."

Shelly beamed. "You betcha! She's a teen, and sometimes she can be a real handful, but she's still my baby girl." Tilting her head to one side she said thoughtfully, "I guess our kids are our kids no matter how old they get."

Zack smiled and nodded his head. "Yep. Sometimes I think my mother forgets I'm all grown up now."

Just then Brooke walked down the stairs. Once again he was struck by her beauty. She was wearing burgundy slacks in a muted plaid that she'd paired with a black cowl neck sweater. He suspected the black flats she wore were intended to minimize her height. Her hair hung long, straight and silky, just the way he loved it.

"You look great, Brooke," he said sincerely.

"Thanks." She smiled and twirled around. "So you think I'll pass inspection?"

"Well, you're *not* being inspected, but I know for sure Mom, Dylan and Kaylee are all very much looking forward to meeting you. I expect you're going to make a great impression on everyone."

"I'm really looking forward to meeting them too, but I must admit ... I'm a little nervous."

He walked over to where she was standing and squeezed her shoulders reassuringly. "There's no need for you to be nervous, Brooke. They're all going to love you. Just like ... uh, well, we should probably get going. We don't want to be late." He gulped. *What in the world is wrong with me? I can't just blurt out the "L" word like it's no big deal. "Oh, by the way, Brooke, did I forget to mention, I just recently realized I've fallen in love with you?" That would go over like a lead balloon.*

Brooke looked at him curiously, but made no comment.

Shelly grinned, and saved the day by asking casually, "Do you want your leather jacket, Brooke?"

"Yes. Thanks, Shelly."

Shelly handed Brooke's coat to Zack who helped his date slip it on. Just before the couple walked out the door, Brooke gathered up a small package adorned with a small bow.

"What's that?" Zack inquired.

"Banana bread for your mom. Shelly just made it today."

"That's very thoughtful of both of you." Looking at Shelly he smiled and said a polite, "Thank you," before the couple walked out the door.

Once they were settled in the car and on their way, Brooke inquired, "So where does your mother live?"

"Mom still lives in the same house we grew up in. It's more than she needs, but she loves it."

"Seems like it would be hard to give up the home where you raised your children. My parents are still in the house where my brothers, sisters, and I grew up too. Dad built it." Zack was sure he detected a note of respect for her father and his work in Brooke's voice. "Aaron was a newborn and Gabby and I were barely walking when we moved there. The younger kids were all there from birth."

"Your folks' house is probably paid off like Mom's. Her gardens are her pride and joy, and she swims in the pool almost every day in the summer. I think both of those things are part of what keeps her looking and feeling young."

"How old is she, if you don't mind my asking?" Brooke queried.

"I don't mind telling you, but I'm not sure how Mom would feel about it. I *will* tell you I'm thirty-four and she was twenty-five when I was born. Let's just say she's coming up on a pretty significant birthday next year." He winked to emphasize his point.

"She's very close to my parent's age. My dad turned sixty-one last year, but he's in great shape. He's always been an avid snow skier, and he loves golf. Of course, he still works full time in his building business too."

"Sounds like he's got plenty to keep him busy. What about your mom?"

"She's three years younger than Dad. As you can imagine, with nine children she never worked outside the house while we were growing up. All us kids kept her pretty busy. She helped Dad with some of the office work during a lot of those years when we were young. But with her background in nursing, she wasn't really the secretarial type." Brooke shrugged. "She did what she could. Once most of us were out of the house, Mom went into real estate. Now *that* was a good fit with Dad's business."

"I can well imagine. So your mom still works too?"

"She's an independent agent, so she works as little or as much as she wants. Mom and Dad are pretty well set financially. But she enjoys helping people, and she likes to keep busy. It gives her something to do while Dad's still working. My guess is once she's got a bunch of grandchildren her real estate career may come to a screeching halt." Brooke grinned and looked a bit wistful. "I think Mom misses being a mom. Now that her kids are grown, she doesn't have all the things that keep mothers busy seven days a week like she did when we were younger."

"I know what you mean. My mother's been dropping subtle and not so subtle hints about missing the 'patter of little feet' around the house lately."

Brooke rolled her eyes and chuckled. "Sounds familiar. My mom even made a big speech at her and Dad's fortieth anniversary party last month. She said it was about time for us kids to get married and start giving her grandchildren. As you know, Phillip and Rachel are having their first soon. Hopefully, that will calm her down for a while."

Zack did his best to sound casual and unconcerned when he asked, "What about you, Brooke? How do you feel about the whole traditional love and marriage thing? Do you want children? A family?"

"Absolutely!" she said without hesitation. "A big part of the reason I bought my house is because it's a great neighborhood for families. I loved growing up with brothers and sisters. I guess I always figured I'd fall in love, get married and have a family of my own someday." She paused thoughtfully. "It seems like ever since I can remember I wanted to be a teacher and a mom. I figured if I was teaching, once my kids started school our schedules would coordinate. I think being an educator is the best possible occupation for a working mother." Turning toward Zack, she asked, "How about you?"

"I'll be honest with you, Brooke. For quite a long time now, I'd pretty much given up on the whole idea of falling in love and having a family." He looked and saw what he thought was disappointment on his passenger's face. "But

I've been thinking about it differently lately." Carefully he watched Brooke's reaction.

She asked, "Why, Zack? Why had you given up the idea, and what's made you rethink it?"

"I was engaged once ... to my high school sweetheart. She was living with me when I started medical school. When things didn't work out with her, I just threw myself completely into school and then work. I love what I do, but the hours can sometimes be brutal. I don't know. I guess I just put my career first ... until recently."

"What happened recently?" she asked.

He thought he heard a note of cautious optimism in her voice. "Honestly?"

"Of course, I want you to be honest," she replied adamantly.

"I know we've only known each other for a short time, and we've only gone out on a few dates, but it's *you*, Brooke. It's because of *you.*"

She turned toward him as much as her seat belt would allow. "Can *I* be honest with *you*, Zack?"

"Why, of course you can, Brooke. I hope we'll always be honest with each other," he replied sincerely.

"Well, I was involved in a disappointing relationship in college too. I think now that you've met Gabriella, you can see how different she and I are, even though we're twins. She's flamboyant and outgoing. I'm more the quiet, shy type. Ever since we were teens, the boys all seemed to prefer Gabby. Marcus, the guy I fell for in college, he *swore* to me he had no interest in Gabriella at all, but it turns out it was a big, fat lie. Anyway, after that I was super cautious with men ... dating ... the whole thing."

Bad Case of Lovin' You

"I figured it had to be something like that," Zack replied gently. "What about now? How about me?"

"Like you said, we've only known each other a fairly short time. And you've only met Gabby the one time at Aaron and Jane's party, but ... I don't know. I guess I just *feel* like I'm safe with you. Like you really *do* prefer me ... my style ... my personality, to Gabby's." Brooke's voice trailed off.

Zack put every bit of sincerity he possibly could into his words. "You're right, Brooke. I *do,* and you *are* safe with me. I prefer everything about you. And not just over your sister, but over every other girl I've ever met."

When she turned to him and put her hand on his, he thought he saw the glimmer of a tear in her eye.

Brooke said, "I wish you weren't driving right now, because I'd like to give you a big hug and a kiss."

"Can I have a rain check on that?" He grinned as he squeezed her hand.

"You sure can. Are we almost there?"

"Only a few more minutes."

The couple held hands and smiled happily until they reached their destination.

Brooke was lost in thought during the rest of the drive to Nancy Carter's house. She was particularly focused on something Zack said earlier ... before they'd even left her house. After she'd mentioned being a little nervous about meeting his family, she remembered him saying, "They're all going to *love* you. Just like ..."

He hadn't finished his sentence. Was it possible he was about to say "... just like *I* do"? She'd already admitted to herself she was falling in love with Zack. If he was feeling the same way about her ... well. Not wanting to get too far ahead of herself too soon, she put the thought on the back burner for further consideration at a later time.

It was only a few more minutes before Zack pulled into the driveway of a well maintained ranch style home. It was in a neighborhood northeast of the city of Boulder proper. Heatherwood was part of a community known as Gunbarrel. The area contained privately owned agricultural land along with publicly owned open spaces. A large park including two reservoirs, jogging trails and lots of green areas made it a desirable community for a wide variety of people. Everything from young families with children to retirees lived in the area.

Nancy Carter's love of gardening was immediately apparent. Her flowerbeds were obviously well cared for. March was an unpredictable month known for dramatic swings in temperatures. The most ambitious Colorado gardeners used that time of year to get some tidying up done. Brooke could see the soil in the gardens had been carefully worked, and spring bulbs were starting to pop their heads out of the ground.

When Zack came around to Brooke's side of the car, he held out his hand to help her out of the vehicle. As they stood next to the open door he said, "May I collect on that rain check now, Miss Adler?"

"Of course you may, Dr. Carter," Brooke replied with a grin.

The space between them disappeared as their arms went around each other. Their kiss began gently. It was amazing to Brooke how a sweet little kiss could also be filled with passion and desire. When his tongue ran over the seam of her lips, demanding entry, she quickly complied. But, rather than deepening the kiss, Zack seemed to take into consideration where they were. He seemed to understand the importance of meeting his mother for the first time. Only a few moments later he ended their kiss with a delightful, but much less erotic pressing of his lips to hers.

"If it's okay with you, we'll resume that a little later ... in a more private setting," Zack said as he gradually pulled away.

"Yes. That would be perfect," Brooke responded. *How did I get so lucky?* Everything about this man was proving to be as much or more than she could've ever hoped for. He seemed to understand and show concern for her feelings even before she expressed them.

Brooke reached back into the car and carried her little gift in one hand. Her other hand was held securely by Zack as they walked to the front of his mother's home. Without knocking he opened the door and went in.

"Maahhm," he called out, "we're here."

Brooke heard footsteps coming quickly into the foyer of the comfortable home. A petite woman with blonde, chin length hair came around the corner. Nancy Carter wore her hair in a tousled, layered look that made her look ten years younger than her age. The woman's smile was genuinely warm and welcoming. It was obvious to Brooke that Zack inherited his hazel eyes flecked generously with green from his pretty mother. Watching the parent and son share a loving embrace not only brought a smile to Brooke's face, but also warmed her heart.

"Zack, sweetie, I'm so glad you're here." Stepping away from her son, Nancy opened her arms to Brooke. "And

Anita Louise

you must be Brooke! Zack's told me so many wonderful things about you." Drawing Brooke into a friendly hug, she continued. "It's such a pleasure to meet you."

"It's a pleasure to meet you too, Mrs. Carter."

"None of that, now. Please call me Nancy," the woman said with a twinkle in her eye.

"Of course ... Nancy," Brooke replied. Holding out the gift she'd brought, Brooke said, "Here's a little something for you, Mrs. ... I mean, Nancy."

"How thoughtful!" Zack's mother exclaimed. "What have we here?" Before Brooke had a chance to answer, the older woman turned to her son and said, "Zack, please take care of Brooke's coat for me."

"Banana bread. Homemade," Brooke answered belatedly.

"You made banana bread for me? How sweet. I'll bet it's delicious." The little blonde took Brooke's hand and led her into the living room.

"Actually, I didn't make it. I have a friend who's staying with me for a while. She's the one who made it," Brooke explained.

"No matter." Nancy shrugged it off as if who made the bread was completely inconsequential. "You brought me a nice little treat and I very much appreciate it regardless of who made it."

They were standing in the center of a large room with a vaulted, wood paneled ceiling. The dining area was adjacent to the main living space. The table looked casually elegant with place settings for five already in front of the chairs.

"Would you like a tour of the house, Brooke? Or would you prefer to just sit for a while until Dylan and Kaylee get here?"

"Your home is lovely, Nancy. I'd very much enjoy seeing the rest of it, if it's not too inconvenient," Brooke answered. "I bought my first home not too long ago, and I love to show it off when people come to visit."

Nancy Carter's delighted smile was firmly in place when she responded, "Well, then, I guess I'll just have to come over so you can show me around your place. In the meantime, just follow me." Heading toward the hallway, she began telling Brooke about her beloved residence. "My home was built in 1972. My husband and I were the second owners. It was such a blessing to have it paid off when we lost him. The boys were so young, and it was such a shocking blow. If we'd have had to move on top of everything else, I'm not sure how I'd have survived it all. Thank God, Frank was the kind of person who was always prepared." She appeared to be reminiscing and chuckled softly. "He always used to say, 'I'm an optimist, but I'm an optimist who carries an umbrella.'"

"Sounds like he was a wonderful husband," Brooke said sincerely. "I'm so sorry for your loss. I can't imagine raising two boys on my own like you did. And it's obvious you did a marvelous job. Zack's a fine man."

"Thank you, Brooke. You're very kind. It was a long time ago, but sometimes I still miss him. I'm so glad I had the boys. I think I needed Dylan and Zack as much as they needed me." Nancy sighed and then seemed to quickly shake off her melancholy. "Enough of that. We're here to have a good time."

"Absolutely," Brooke agreed, "and I'm enjoying myself already. I've been looking forward to getting to know you, Nancy. Zack can't say enough nice things about you."

Zack's mother continued to escort Brooke on a tour of the Carter family home. The rooms her two sons had occupied were pointed out. One was now a guest bedroom, and the other had been converted to an in-home office. The master suite was tastefully decorated in a muted pattern combining pale ice blue, taupe, and steel blue. Soft silver gray draperies emphasized the twelve-foot ceilings and accented the French doors leading to the deck. Taupe silk velvet covered the upholstered headboard, and the same fabric used in the drapes was repeated in the bed skirt. The room felt luxurious, serene and sophisticated.

As the two women re-entered the main living area, Brooke commented, "You have a great eye for decorating, Nancy. Your house is as beautiful as a model home, yet it feels comfortable and lived in."

The smile on Nancy Carter's face showed her pride and pleasure from the compliment. "Thank you, Brooke."

Zack was standing on the other side of the island that separated the kitchen from the rest of the living area. "What can I get you two lovely ladies to drink?" he asked.

"Nothing for me just yet," Brooke replied.

"I think I'll wait until Dylan and Kaylee get here. Then we can open a nice bottle of wine for all of us." Turning to Brooke, Nancy said, "We're having chicken so there's a Savignon Blanc breathing in the kitchen if that's all right with you."

"Sounds perfect. Thank you, Nancy," Brooke replied.

Bad Case of Lovin' You

Moments later the doorbell sounded, and Nancy Carter jumped to her feet.

"That must be Dylan and Kaylee. I'll be right back."

Chapter Twenty-Five

As far as Zack was concerned, the dinner at his mother's had been a rousing success. As usual, his mother was the perfect hostess. And, to his delight, Brooke had also been the perfect guest. She'd dressed appropriately, and Mom had loved the little gift of homemade banana bread Brooke surprised her with. He'd watched and listened as his date carried on fun and interesting conversations with all the dinner guests. Brooke was adept at asking questions to get the other person talking. She then showed a sincere interest in listening to their response.

Zack wasn't really surprised when Brooke offered to help clear the table and tidy up the kitchen. He *was* surprised when his mother accepted her offer. He and Dylan sat on the couch watching one of the NCAA March Madness games while the three women worked companionably in the other room. Although he couldn't hear the exact words of their conversation, their comradery was apparent from the laughter he heard coming from the trio.

Bad Case of Lovin' You

Brooke and Kaylee hit it off as if they'd known each other for years instead of just meeting. Zack overheard his sister-in-law say to Brooke, "You're like the sister I *wish* I'd had."

While the two men were sitting in front of the television, Dylan had given Zack some sage brotherly advice. "Oh, my gosh, Zack, do you hear how much fun those women are having in there? I'm telling you, this girl is a *keeper.* I don't know how you got so lucky. Not only is Brooke beautiful, she also seems very kind and considerate. On top of that, she's got a good head on her shoulders. Mom loves her. Kaylee loves her. Even I can't see a thing wrong with her, and you know how I am about women."

"I've got to agree. She *is* pretty special. Just between you and me, bro, I think I've fallen for her ... big time."

Dylan had taken on a serious tone. "Then don't mess this up, man. Don't make the same mistake I did. I almost lost Kaylee because I was afraid to admit I'd fallen in love with her. I think I *knew* the first time I met her that she was the one for me, but I was doing my best to deny my feelings for her. When I found out she'd married some other guy, I was *devastated.* If that jerk Kaylee tied the knot with hadn't been so stupid, she and I might never have had the chance to be together."

Zack listened and took his brother's advice to heart. "You're right, Dylan. It seemed like everyone but you could see that you and Kaylee were made for each other. I'm sure glad it worked out for you two in the end."

"If you think *you're* glad, just imagine how I feel. I've never been happier in my life than since Kaylee and I have been together," Dylan replied. His voice dropped to a whisper. "Kaylee didn't want me to say anything yet, so don't tell Mom, but we might be pregnant."

Zack could see the excitement in his brother's eyes and hear it in his voice. "Really? Congratulations, man! That's totally cool."

"Yeah, thanks. I think so too. Can you imagine? Me? A dad?" Dylan sighed.

"Let me know when you and Kaylee decide to let the cat out of the bag. I want to see the look on Mom's face when you tell her. She's going to be ecstatic."

"I know. It's been almost impossible for me to keep my mouth shut about it, but I have to respect Kaylee's wishes. Probably another couple of weeks. By then, she'll be bouncing off the walls wanting to tell anyone and everyone herself." Dylan was grinning from ear to ear. "Anyway, back to you and Brooke. My advice is, tell her how you feel. If the feeling's not mutual, it's probably best to find out early anyway ... before you get your heart broken. One way or another, you can't lose by being honest."

Zack thought back to a conversation he'd had earlier with Brooke about always being honest with each other. "You know, I guess I was a little worried about how Brooke would react if I told her I was falling for her this early in our relationship. I know for sure there's a definite connection between us, but I'm just not sure how deep her feelings for me go. Maybe it's time to put myself out on that limb and see if it's going to hold up or not."

"You know what they say. 'The biggest risk is the one not taken.' Somehow I think this one is going to be totally worth it. Good luck, Bro."

Bad Case of Lovin' You

The two brothers had given each other a manly hug just before the women came out of the kitchen.

"I'm glad to see you boys are getting along so well," the mother of the two men had commented with a smile. "What brought about that little display of affection?"

"Nothing special, Mom," Dylan had replied while giving his brother a knowing wink.

Now Zack and Brooke were back in his vehicle leaving Nancy Carter's home.

"Did you have a good time?" Zack asked.

Brooke beamed. "Oh, yes! I had a *wonderful* time. Your mother is incredible, and I feel like I've found another sister in Kaylee."

"I thought so." Zack smiled happily and put his hand on his passenger's knee. Desire sizzled through him at the mere touch. "Do you want me to take you straight home, or would you like to come over to my place for a while?"

Brooke must've felt the same electricity. He sensed a hunger in her voice, a hunger the delicious dinner they'd just consumed had no way of fulfilling. "Your place. Please. Let's go to your place, Zack."

The sexual energy in the air was almost palpable. His hand remained on her knee as he drove as quickly as was safely possible to their destination.

An undeniable warmth flooded Brooke. Just the touch of his hand on her leg filled her with a flood of desire. Suddenly her breasts felt heavy and there was a telling throbbing between her legs. *Being with Zack seems to have turned me into a wanton woman*, she mused. If he hadn't suggested going back to his place, she may have had no choice but to suggest it herself.

Once inside his condo, she shed her inhibitions completely. As soon as her coat was off, she put her arms around his neck, threaded her fingers through his hair and drew his mouth to hers. She felt his hands move possessively up and down her back. Then he took her bottom into his capable hands and pulled their bodies together in a most intimate way. His erection fit perfectly between the vee of her legs. She widened her stance to allow him easier access.

As their tongues tangled and his scent filled her nostrils, she experienced such an overpowering craving, her knees threatened to buckle. "I think we've got way to many clothes on," she whispered seductively in his ear.

"Brooke." Her name on his lips was accompanied by a low growl. Within seconds he swept her up into his arms and carried her into his bedroom. After laying her down on the king-sized bed, he stood next to it for a moment staring at her hungrily.

"What do you want me to do, Zack? How can I please you?" she asked.

"You please me just by being you," he replied without hesitation, and he leaned over and pressed his lips to hers. His kiss was warm and potent. His hands moved to her breasts and kneaded the soft globes. Waves of carnal need rushed through her body. "You're right," he whispered, "way too many clothes. Got to get you out of these. Lift your arms for me."

She did as he requested, and he swiftly pulled her sweater up over her head. "Is that better?" she asked.

Bad Case of Lovin' You

"Yes, better." She was wearing one of her favorite bra and panty sets that made her feel sexy. Running his fingers between the lace and her skin, he found her nipple and massaged it to a tight little bud. "I like the way this lace looks and feels. I think we'll leave this on for a little while longer," he said as he changed his focus to the removal of her slacks. He quickly opened the clasp on the waistband, unzipped them, and slid the trousers down her legs. The thong panties she wore matched the lacy bra. "Much better," he said as he appraised her nearly nude figure. Now his fingers slid between the lace around her hips and down to the vee between her legs.

Brooke could feel the moisture begin to pool between her legs. When he slipped his fingers between her lower lips, they slid easily into her most private parts.

"Ummm, that feels so good," she said. Her hips began to move in a sensual rhythm. She reached over and found the hard length of him beneath his trousers. Moving her hand up and down, she felt his member grow even harder and thicker. "You're right," she said, "still too many clothes."

While he continued to massage her most sensitive bud, she undid his belt and opened his trousers which then fell to the floor. She pushed the waistband of his boxers down on his hips, releasing his throbbing erection. He continued to alternately dip his fingers into her and then use his slicked digits to massage the tiny, secret node. Adjusting herself on the bed, she moved her head to where he stood and took him into her mouth.

"Oh, my God. Brooke," he moaned.

"Ummm," she hummed as she moved her hand down his shaft and took more of his length into her mouth. When she got back to the tip, she ran her tongue around the head before taking him between her warm, receptive lips once again.

"I need to be inside you, Brooke," he said and reached for the condom on the bedside table.

"Let me," she replied and took the foil packet from his hand. He continued to slide his fingers in and out of her as she ripped open the foil. Smoothing the thin rubber over his length, she continued to stroke it up and down.

"Time to get rid of these." He removed her panties, stepped out of the clothing pooled at his feet, and climbed onto the bed. Kneeling between her legs, he used his erection to massage up and down between her moist lips.

Brooke was arching her back and moving in rhythm with his delightful torture. "Please, Zack. I need you inside me ... now."

Granting her request he plunged smoothly into her super wet opening. "Ahhh," he moaned as they began to move together in perfect synch. He'd pushed the lace of her bra down and rolled her nipples between his thumbs and forefingers as he pumped rhythmically in and out.

Needing to be as close as possible, Brooke wrapped her legs around his waist, taking him into her fully. Together they moved their hips until she felt her inner muscles begin to tighten. "Oh, Oh, Oh," she cried. "Oh, Zack, *yes!*"

Zack groaned loudly and ground his hips forcefully into hers as the two of them went over the edge together.

Bad Case of Lovin' You

Things were going from bad to worse for Nathan Silvers.

"Do you know how long I've been on *hold?*" he screamed at the person on the other end of the phone. "Seems like I've made ten *zillion* phone calls, filled out twenty million forms, and written letters to everybody but the friggin' President about all this crap!"

"I'm sorry, sir, but you're going to have to calm down, and speak to me civilly if you want my assistance with this," said the anonymous voice at the other end of the phone.

He was in the process of disputing the fraudulent charges on his existing credit card and bank accounts. When he'd finally gotten his free credit reports, he found out several new accounts had been opened in his name. The available credit on each one had been pushed to the max within twenty-four hours of approval.

Instead of getting the tax refund he'd expected, he got a letter from the Internal Revenue Service telling him they'd already sent out his refund. Now it was up to *him* to prove that it wasn't him, but someone else who'd received the money.

When he started getting medical bills from doctors, hospitals, labs and pharmacies across the country, he almost lost it.

"I keep *tellin'* ya. I still *got* my appendix! And I ain't never *been* to Wisconsin! It ain't me!"

Once he'd convinced them he hadn't had the surgery, they announced that the records were sealed due to the privacy rights of the real patient who'd claimed to be him.

"Then how in the hell am I supposed to get this mess straightened out?" he roared.

Anita Louise

"Well, sir, sounds like you might need the help of an attorney."

"Ok, fine. I'll get a friggin' lawyer."

But he didn't know who to call, and found out different lawyers specialized in different areas of law. He'd need an attorney who practiced law in Wisconsin to help him out in that state and another who practiced Colorado law.

"This is a f***in' *nightmare!*"

Chapter Twenty-Six

When Zack woke up it was after midnight, and Brooke was snuggled up to him spoon-like. The sound of her relaxed breathing told him she was fast asleep. As much as he didn't want to wake her, he knew how important it was for her to be fresh for her students the next day.

I love you, Brooke Adler, he thought whispered before kissing her neck. He continued to press his lips softly over her supple skin until she began to arouse. "It's after midnight, sweetheart. As much as I'd love for you to stay, you probably want to get home so you'll be fresh for school in the morning."

Brooke relaxed languidly in his arms and tilted her head to allow him greater access to the tender skin below her chin. "What a lovely way to be woken up," she murmured as she turned in his arms. Their kiss was sweet and tender. "I could get used to this."

"So could I, Brooke. So could I." He smoothed his hand up and down her back. *Should I tell her?* he wondered.

Anita Louise

Nervous anticipation came over him and his heart rhythm sped up.

Brooke must've sensed something. He heard concern in her voice when she said, "Is everything all right, Zack?"

"Uh, well, um ..."

"What is it, Zack? You can tell me. Please?" She was running her fingers through the back of his hair tenderly.

"Oh, Brooke, I want to tell you something, but I just don't know if I should. Everything's so great with us right now, and I don't want to mess this up."

She continued to stroke his head softly and whispered, "Remember, we said we'd always be honest with one another? I don't want us to keep secrets from each other either. Honest and open, right from the beginning. Okay?"

"You're right." He took a deep breath and positioned himself so he could look directly into her eyes. "Here goes ... Brooke Adler, I've fallen completely, irrevocably, unconditionally in love with you." *There, I said it,* he thought as he waited for her response.

She gulped. "I ... I ..."

Zack felt his heart plummet. "It's okay, Brooke. I'm sorry. I figured it was too soon. Please, don't be scared. We can take it slow. I'll give you as much time as you need." She propped herself up on her elbow, and he saw tears falling gently from her eyes. Wiping away the tears he said, "It's okay. I *knew* it was too soon. Please, don't cry."

"But Zack, you don't understand. It's *not* too soon, and these are tears of *joy.* Oh, Zack, don't you see? I love you too," she said with a smile. "I've fallen completely, irrevocably, and unconditionally in love with you too."

Bad Case of Lovin' You

"You *have?*" The love he felt almost overwhelmed him. "Oh Brooke, that's like the best, most awesome thing I've ever heard in my entire life!" Pulling her into his arms, he crushed her mouth to his. He could feel her lips curl into a smile, and she moved her hands to his face. Once their lips were apart, he brushed her hair softly away from her cheek. "I love you so much," he whispered again. "I want to wake up with you in my arms every day. I want to go to sleep with you in my bed every night. Brooke Adler, will you marry me?"

"Really?" She sounded incredulous. "You're asking me to *marry* you?"

"Did I blow it? Should I have waited? Maybe I should have had it written on a billboard, or hired a flash mob to dance and sing to Bruno Mars's tune 'Marry You.' I could have made arrangements to have a waiter bring you an engagement ring for dessert, or ...?"

She put her finger to his lips, "Hush, silly man. None of that's necessary. Of course I'll marry you. I love you, Zackary Carter." When she pulled his mouth to hers, he felt as if one of the final pieces of the jigsaw puzzle that was his life had been put into place.

The lovemaking that followed was slow and gentle and oh so sweet.

Brooke was so excited about Zack's profession of his love and subsequent proposal, she had to resist the temptation to wake Shelly up when she finally got home. Instead, she tiptoed up the stairs and slipped quietly into her room. When she finally fell asleep, her dreams were filled with hazel eyed children playing with their handsome father on the front lawn of the home they shared.

Even though she'd had little sleep, she woke the next morning feeling aglow with love. During her shower and while she dressed for school, she found herself humming the tune *Chapel of Love,* an oldie about a girl on her way to the wedding chapel to get married. Brooke was smiling and still humming the song when she walked into the kitchen where Shelly and Mary Beth sat.

"Mary Beth, you're home!" Brooke exclaimed excitedly when she saw the teen. The young girl stood and the two embraced warmly. Stepping back, Brooke looked carefully at what remained of the bruises on the child's face. "You look really good, sweetie. With that tan and the little bit of makeup you're wearing, I don't think anyone will even notice." Brooke hesitated. "You ready to go back to school?"

The girl nodded affirmatively. "I sure am. As great as my grandparents are, it'll be good to be back around kids my own age again." Mary Beth grinned happily.

"There's scrambled eggs and bacon on the stove for you, Brooke," Shelly said.

"Thanks, Shelly. You're so good to me." Brooke gave her friend a quick peck on the cheek, and then resumed humming the tune that had been running through her mind all morning.

Shelly looked at her friend curiously. "You seem awfully chipper this morning. What's up?"

"Hmm?" Brooke replied.

"Okay. Something's up. What is it?" Shelly demanded.

Brooke twirled around with the plate of food in her hand and smiled broadly. "Love," she sighed. "I'm in love." Bringing her food to the table, she plopped down into a chair.

"Oh, my gosh, Brooke," Shelly said excitedly, "what happened? Tell me, tell me, tell me."

Brooke took her friend's hand in one of hers and clasped Mary Beth's with the other. "It's Zack. He ... He and I ... well ..."

"Spit it out, girl! Don't leave us hanging like this!" Shelly said almost breathlessly.

"He asked me to marry him! We're going to get *married!*"

The three females jumped to their feet. Shouts of joy were mixed with half-formed questions, smiles, laughs and happy tears.

"Oh, my gosh, Miss Adler, that's so cool. I'm so happy for you. Dr. Carter seems real nice too." Mary Beth hugged the teacher who had become like a second mother.

"You haven't set a date yet, have you?" asked Shelly.

"No, not yet, but whenever it is I want both of you to be in the wedding party, bridesmaid and junior bridesmaid. Okay?"

"Of course!" the mother and daughter cried in unison.

Nathan Silvers' frustration with all the problems he was having since his wallet had been stolen was taking its toll. Finally, he decided to forget about it as much as possible and go to the bar and have a couple of drinks with the guys. He was looking forward to relaxing and was almost to his destination when he got pulled over.

"Just what I need," he grumbled to himself.

"Driver's license and registration," the officer said when Nate rolled down his window.

"What'd I do?" Nate asked as he gave the man the requested documents.

"Did you know that one of your brake lights is burned out?"

"No, I didn't. Must'a just happened."

"Ok. Just a minute." The officer went back to his patrol car while Nate waited impatiently. Expecting to be sent on his way after being issued a minor ticket, Nate was surprised when the officer said, "I need you to step out of the car, Mr. Silvers."

"What for? I ain't done nothin'. Why'da I need ta step outta the car?" When the policeman put his hand on his pistol, Nathan almost panicked. "Whoa, man. Whatcha doin'?"

"I need you to step out of the car," the officer repeated. "And keep your hands where I can see them."

"Okay, okay," Nathan replied nervously. Once Nate was out of his car, the officer spoke again.

"Turn toward your vehicle, and put your hands up on the roof," he instructed and then began to pat down Nate's clothing.

"I ain't carryin' nothin', man," Nate assured the policeman. "What's this all about? I ain't done nothin'. Whatcha doin' this for?"

"Are you aware there's a warrant out for your arrest in Arkansas, Mr. Silvers?"

"What? A warrant? In *Arkansas?* I ain't never even been to Arkansas. There's got to be some kinda mistake. It ain't me. I swear. It ain't me."

"That's what they all say," replied the patrolman as he snapped the cuffs onto Nathan Silvers' wrists.

Epilogue

Michael Adler could hardly believe it. Not just one, but *two* of his siblings had gotten engaged in the past few months. Sure, he liked his brother Aaron's fiancée, Jane Barloc and now his sister Brooke's new fiancé Zack Carter just fine, but *marriage*? Why? Michael wasn't the least bit interested in making that kind of commitment to any woman. In today's society, he figured marriage was simply an old, outdated institution.

Now, that didn't mean he wouldn't like to find an attractive, sexy woman to be with. In fact, he'd recently met someone he thought might be an excellent candidate. He had to admit, there was *something* about Analese Martin that had him totally intrigued. Her Aunt Millie had introduced them at Aaron and Jane's engagement party, and ever since they'd met, he couldn't seem to forget about her.

Chemistry seemed a paltry word for the electricity that flowed between them when their eyes had locked and their hands had touched. Luckily, the auburn-haired beauty was looking for an architect to design her dream home, and

Anita Louise

Michael Adler was the best in the business. If she was looking to build a house anything like the one Michael had designed and built for his brother Aaron, she must have some bucks. Of course, Millie Worthton, her aunt, lived right next door to his brother's custom home. Even though Mrs. Worthton's home was older and smaller home, it was still a very valuable piece of property.

It'd been over a week since the engagement party where he'd met Analese, and he'd yet to get a call from her. Perhaps it was time to take matters into his own hands. He wasn't accustomed to chasing after women. Normally, it was the other way around. He'd rejected more advances than he could count from clients and potential clients. It was even fairly common for him to rebuff the wives of some of his married customers.

Business was booming at Adler Building and Development. Michael had almost more projects than he could handle already, but he *wanted* this particular assignment more than he'd ever wanted anything else before. Working with Analese Martin to design and build the perfect home would take many months. Surely spending as much time together as the job would require would also result in her ending up in his bed, something he was very much looking forward to.

Picking up the phone in his office, he dialed his brother Aaron's cell phone. After only a couple of rings the line was answered.

"Hey, Mike, what's up?" Aaron asked cheerily.

"Same old, same old. How about with you?"

"Jane's in the thick of wedding plans. She and Brooke have become even closer now that they're both engaged.

There was some talk of a double wedding, but I'm not sure if that's still an option. I do my best to stay out of it as much as possible."

"Smart man." Michael wasn't much for small talk. He was more of a get to the point kind of guy. Besides that, in addition to being a super successful author, Aaron was a psychologist and had a tendency to start analyzing every little thing. Going through his nosy brother to get Analese's number was going to be a tricky proposition. "Quick question, bro."

"What's that, Mike?"

"Do you have your next door neighbor's phone number handy?"

"Millie Worthton? Why in the world would you want Millie's number?" Aaron asked.

Damn. Michael did his best to sound as casual as possible. "Seems Mrs. Worthton's niece is looking for an architect."

"You mean the hot looking woman with the long red hair? That niece?" Aaron sounded amused. "I thought you had more business than you could handle right now and weren't looking to take on any new clients."

Shit. "Come on, Aaron. Cut me some slack here, will you? Okay, so the niece is hot. She also needs an architect, and I just happen to be the best around. What happens from there ... well, you just never know."

"Wait a minute," Aaron said, "Didn't I see you give her your business card when you met her at the party?"

"Yes, dammit, I gave her my card, but she must've lost it." Michael's patience with his brother was wearing thin.

"You really think she lost it? Maybe she's found another architect. Did you think of that?" Aaron teased.

"Will you give me the friggin' phone number or do I have to go over there and knock on your neighbor's door?"

Evidently, Aaron had had enough fun at his elder brother's expense. A few minutes later Michael was dialing Millie Worthton's home phone.

Millie picked up after several rings, and she was a bit winded when she answered, "Hello?"

"Hello, Mrs. Worthton. This is Michael Adler, your neighbor, Aaron's brother ... the architect?"

"Oh, yes! Michael Adler. Of course. How nice to hear from you. Have you and Analese gotten together yet to talk about her new house?"

"That's why I'm calling, Mrs. Worthton."

"Oh, please, you must call me Millie. Or you can call me Aunt Millie like Analese does, if you prefer," she said sweetly.

"Fine, Millie. I haven't heard from your niece yet, so I ..."

"Oh dear, that will never do. Here, let me give you her number, and you can contact her directly. Just hold on a moment while I go get it for you."

That was even easier than I expected. He grinned to himself. *Hopefully, the lovely Ms. Analese Martin will come around just as easily. On the other hand, I've never been one to walk away from a challenge.*

When Millie Worthton came back to the phone, she seemed almost gleeful as she gave Michael the information he was seeking. "Now you make sure to call Analese right away. We wouldn't want her going out there and looking for another architect, now, would we?"

"Of course not, Mrs. Worthton."

"Millie. Just call me Millie. I'm *sure* we're going to be getting to know one another a lot better as time goes by. I'm so glad you called, Michael. Analese is going to be so happy to hear from you."

Analese Martin picked up the business card bearing the name Michael Adler, Adler Building and Development, for what must have been the fiftieth time in the last week and a half.

I don't know why I've even kept this thing for so long. I'm absolutely not going to call this man. She threw it into the trash can next to her desk with a finality she didn't really feel. Less than a minute later, she picked it out again. *What is wrong with me?*

"What're you doing, Mom?" Analese's son Trevor rolled his wheelchair into her home office.

"Hi, sweetie." She reached over and ruffled his hair. "At the moment I'm doing absolutely nothing. What's up?"

Trevor, who'd just turned ten, had been diagnosed with muscular dystrophy, a genetic disorder that weakens the muscles that help the body to move, just after his second birthday. In spite of his illness, he was one of the happiest and most optimistic people you could ever hope to meet.

It was believed that Trevor's father Eric had shared with his son the gene that prevented the boy's body from making the proteins needed for healthy muscles. However, taking responsibility for anything had never been Eric's strong suit. He'd deserted his wife and young son less than six months after the boy's diagnosis. The man paid minimal child support payments and sent his son a card and gift for his birthday and Christmas, but that was about all. He hadn't bothered to call or visit since the day he'd walked out on them.

"Can I go swimming?" her son asked plaintively.

"Oh, Trev, you know I'd love to take you to the pool every day if I could, but ..."

The boy sighed resignedly, "I know, it's so far away, and you've got so much to do." He sat quietly for a moment, and then a smile lit up his handsome little face. "When are we going to get our new house? You said we could have a pool when we get the new house. Then I can go swimming any time I want."

It wasn't luck, but hard work and a burning desire that made it possible for Analese Martin to be in a position to afford to hire Michael Adler. If not Adler Building and Development, she could engage just about any other architect she wanted to build the perfect home for her and Trevor. She was one of the highest paid people in the network marketing industry. She'd recently been listed as one of the Top 100 Direct Selling Lifetime Earners.

It was shortly after Eric left, and Analese was working as a cashier to make ends meet. A virtual stranger had come to her register and given her some helpful information. In the course of conversation, she'd complained about an insurance claim for Trevor that was being denied. The man told her about a service that could get her the assistance she needed at a price she could afford. He also told her she could make some extra money on a part-time basis by telling other people about the service. Since it helped her and her son a great deal, she'd made the small investment to get started in her own business. It started out as a way to get by until she could finish her degree and get a decent job to support herself and her son. But after a few years, it had turned into a multi-million dollar enterprise.

The beauty of her industry was that in the process of earning her fortune, she'd helped hundreds of people make substantial incomes and thousands more to earn good supplemental revenue in their spare time. Hers was still a field that many labeled as a scam or pyramid scheme, but she knew that without her home based business, both she and Trevor would be leading very different lives.

"Mom?" Trevor interrupted her thoughts. "How soon are we going to get our new house ... and the *pool?*" Her son had lots of wonderful characteristics, persistence being close to the top of the list.

"Funny you should ask. I was just thinking about that," she said as she looked once more at the business card she'd just pulled out of the trash. If she was honest with herself, she'd been thinking about the attractive architect way more than she wanted to admit. Actually, *attractive* didn't even come close to describing the tall, dark and incredibly handsome man who'd given her his card.

Analese had met plenty of good looking men since Eric left. She'd even dated a few, but Trevor was the most important male in her life. Usually, she didn't even bother to go out with a guy more than once or twice. She didn't want to introduce a parade of men to her son only to have them come and go from his life like his father had. Trevor rarely asked about his father anymore. As much as Analese

Anita Louise

wanted to protect her son, she wouldn't lie to him. His father had left and he wasn't coming back. It was that simple.

She'd been completely stunned by her reaction to Michael Adler. When his hand touched hers, she'd felt a pull so strong it'd been difficult to remove her hand from his. Analese Martin was an experienced and articulate speaker, yet she'd fumbled over her own name when they'd met. Engaging Michael Adler as her architect could be extremely hazardous to her health, both physically and mentally.

Analese regularly told people they needed to step outside of their comfort zone if they wanted to achieve their goals. Maybe it was time for her to follow her own advice.

~ THE END ~

Thank you for sharing your thoughts about Brooke & Zack's story with me, by writing your review on Amazon at http://hyperurl.co/fq90qo.

Look for the other books in the Adler Family Series – available now!

JUST THE WAY YOU ARE
Aaron & Jane

A HOUSE IS NOT A HOME
Michael & Analese

SHOULD I STAY OR SHOULD I GO
Connor & Gina

YOU LIGHT UP MY LIFE
Olivia & Tyler

Connect with Anita Louise:

Website & Blog:
http://www.anitalouiseromance.com

Amazon Author Page:
http://www.amazon.com/Anita-Louise/e/B018UGM56C/

Smashwords Interview:
https://www.smashwords.com/interview/CandlelitePublishing

Facebook:
https://www.facebook.com/AnitaLouiseRomance

Twitter:
https://twitter.com/anitaromance

Instagram:
htttp://www.instagram.com/anita.louise.romance

Google Plus:
https://plus.google.com/111029186791103969418

Pinterest:
https://www.pinterest.com/romanticanita/